'Shane Maloney is one of the funniest writers in the [...] and Whelan one of the great comic creations of Australian literature.' *Courier Mail*

'Brilliant…Maloney is on his own now as a highly original crime writer.' *Australian*

'Sucked me in right to the end. Maloney's writing is full of class and depicts the shenanigans with verve and wit. If only real politicians were as interesting.' *Bulletin*

'Shane Maloney is the master of a genre of his own making—apparatchik lit. Stories from the murky, lurky world of Australian politics (especially inside the Labor Party and union movement) have no better teller in contemporary Australian fiction.' *Age*

'Cinematic action…and deadpan wit.' *Herald Sun*

'Jokes…proliferate and, as always, depend on Maloney's wicked way with words…passages of Rabelaisian delight… Murray parades his multicultural knowledge with panache and I'm missing him already.' *Sydney Morning Herald*

'From the opening pages, the story gallops along, powered by Whelan's laconic observations and Maloney's rare ability to make the complexities of Labor Party machinations interesting and entertaining.' *Canberra Times*

sucked in

SHANE MALONEY

TEXT PUBLISHING MELBOURNE AUSTRALIA

The Text Publishing Company
Swann House
22 William St
Melbourne Victoria 3000
Australia
www.textpublishing.com.au

First published in Australia by The Text Publishing Company 2007
Reprinted 2007
This edition 2008

Typeset in Baskerville MT by J&M Typesetting
Printed and bound in Australia by Griffin Press

National Library of Australia Cataloguing-in-Publication data:

Maloney, Shane.
  Sucked in.
  ISBN 978-1-921351-44-0 (pbk.)
  Whelan, Murray (Fictitious character)--Fiction.
  Murder--Fiction.
  A823.4

Australia Council
for the Arts

The author gratefully acknowledges the support of the Ghirardelli Foundation, the Cape Liptrap Lodge for Demented Writers, the Patramani family of Episkopi, Crete and Señora Luisa Guzman of Cochabamba, Bolivia.

To my sister, who saved my life in Puno,
and my wife, who helped.

Prelude

On a cool and overcast April afternoon, a retrenched Repco salesman from Benalla named Geoff Lyons and his fishing mate, Craig Kitson, drove the forty-three kilometres to Lake Nillahcootie in Geoff's Toyota 4 Runner. When they got to the boat ramp, they sat for a minute, staring out the windscreen.

'Jeeze,' said Craig. 'That was quick.'

Geoff said, 'Told ya.'

The lake, an eight by three kilometre reservoir on the Broken River where it flows out of the High Country, was almost completely empty.

At the end of January, VicWater had commenced stabilisation work on the weir wall, a concrete dam constructed in the 1950s. They were sinking new reinforcement plugs, a project which involved opening the sluices and draining the lake. Since Craig and Geoff last saw it, the water level had dropped ninety percent. For the first time in forty years, the course of the original river bed was visible, its meandering progress marked by an intermittent line of truncated, long-dead trees.

The two men walked out onto the lakebed, testing the surface. The gradient was slight and the hot summer and long dry autumn had dried the clay pan to a firm crust. Craig said, 'Think it'll take the Toyota?'

'We get bogged,' Geoff warned, 'you're the one walks to town.'

Closer to the trees, the clay was covered with cracks like the stained fissures in an old teacup and the sharp edges of blackened stumps broke the surface of the ground. When the Toyota's traction started to slip, they got out and walked the last hundred metres, carrying their waders. Craig took a plastic bucket, just in case they found anything worth keeping.

They had fished Lake Nillahcootie many times over the years, although they preferred Eildon or, better still, Lake Mulwala. But Nillahcootie was handy, only half an hour out of town and too small to interest the watersport crowd. There was a camping ground near the weir and holiday houses scattered along the shoreline but some weekends they'd virtually have the place to themselves.

Mostly it was redfin and brown trout on live bait from Geoff's tinnie, but they'd also taken some nice rainbows on spinners from the shore, particularly in the shaded shallows where the trees ran right down to the water. The Murray cod that preferred the deep holes of the old river bed had eluded them, however, and cost them some top-shelf trolling lures on hidden snags.

So they'd come up with the idea of doing a bit of reconnaissance while the water level was down. A better idea of the lay of the lakebed might improve their chances when it was again hidden beneath opaque, red-brown water.

The old riverbed was now a chain of shallow pools linked by a feeble trickle of muddy water, its surface swarming with midges. All the useable timber had been cleared before the dam was flooded, leaving only dead or diseased trees. Their denuded trunks now jutted out of the sludge, bleached and sepulchral, surrounded by fallen, half-buried logs. The men followed the river's meandering course upstream, checking their location against the undulating paddocks and clumps of trees that marked the shoreline.

Oddments of litter were scattered across the lake floor, mainly old bottles and cans. They fossicked as they went and within half an hour they'd picked up some metal lures in pretty good nick, an assortment of wire traces and a slime covered Tarax lemonade bottle. By then, they'd given up the idea of discovering the hiding places of the fabled cod. No way were they going to start sloshing around in the murky black water that now filled the riverbed.

'Careful.' Geoff pointed to a sinuous grey shape draped over a fallen tree-trunk. 'Snake.'

'You reckon?'

Whatever it was, it wasn't moving. Craig waded through the ankle-deep water and took a closer look. 'A deadly nylon python,' he called. One end was buried in the mud, the other disappeared into dark water between two logs. 'Could be an anchor rope.'

He straddled the logs and hauled. The rope offered little resistance. It came up in a loose tangle, slimy and thick with a black mass of rotted vegetation. Trapped within its coils was a ball of fibrous mud, an oversized coconut.

'Hey, check this out,' he called back to Geoff.

'What is it?'

'Looks like a skull.'

Geoff came closer, primed for one of Craig's lame jokes.

Craig reached down gingerly, hooked his fingers through the eye holes and held it aloft for Geoff to see. 'Human, I reckon.'

The bone was stained tan, the bottom jaw was missing and the nasal socket was eaten away at the edges, but the shape of the cranium was unmistakable.

Geoff shaded his eyes with his hand and took a long hard look.

'Well I'll be fucked.'

I stood at the edge of the grave and sprinkled a handful of soil onto the lid of the coffin, adding it to the mound of clay and carnations. It was a classy box, rosewood with silver handles, befitting its distinguished occupant.

Charles Joseph Talbot, MHR. A cabinet minister in three successive Labor administrations, twice as Minister for Industrial Relations and, until the previous week, member for Coolaroo and manager of opposition business in the House of Representatives of the Commonwealth of Australia. A pillar of the community. An elder of the tribe.

At sixty-four, Charlie Talbot was as dead as a man can get. It was hard to believe he was gone, even though it had happened right in front of me.

'You're in good hands, mate,' I murmured. 'The Lord's a Labor man.'

Charlie and the Lord went way back. Back to when he

was a lay preacher, whatever that means, in the Methodist church. It was down that obscure tributary that Charlie had floated into the union movement, and thence into the Australian Labor Party. A world in which the Lord's name is not often invoked, except in vain.

I couldn't say if Charlie's faith survived the journey. It was not a subject we had ever discussed, although we'd talked of many things, often at great length, in the decades of our friendship. But whether he was now enrolled in the choir eternal or merely, as I suspected, compost, I knew I'd never forget him.

Ceding my place to the next mourner in line, I wandered a little further into the cemetery. It was an autumn afternoon, late in the twentieth century, and there was still enough lustre in the stainless-steel sky to have me squinting against the glare. I pulled a pair of sunglasses from my breast pocket, lit a pensive cigarette and took in the scene.

After the interminable eulogising of the funeral service, the graveside formalities had been brief. The crowd was drifting away, gravitating down the gravel pathway to the cars at the graveyard gate. The widow was escorted by the federal party leader, a stout man, if only in the physical sense. She was still a good looking woman, Margot, no diminution of assets there.

Charlie's three daughters kept their distance, husbands and children clustered around them as they accepted condolences. Although she'd been married to Charlie for almost ten years, Margot was still the Other Woman as far as his children were concerned. The Jezebel who'd snared their grieving father while the flowers were still fresh on their mother's grave.

She slept elsewhere, the sainted Shirley. She was taking

her eternal rest beside her mother and father at Fawkner cemetery, fifteen minutes up the road.

But even in death Charlie had civic obligations. And so it was here in Coburg cemetery, ceremonial burial site of the electorate he had represented for almost twenty years, that his mortal remains were interred. Here, cheek-by-jowl with the district's other deceased dignitaries, a hundred and fifty years of extinct aldermen and mouldering worthies. I suspected Charlie would find them dull company. Not that he was any too lively himself anymore.

Still, he had a pretty good view.

Melbourne is a city of many inclinations but very few hills. Its northern suburbs are almost unremittingly flat but the cemetery occupied the slope of a low ridge, screened from six lanes of traffic by a row of feathery old cypresses, so even the slight rise of the bone yard offered a rare vantage point. To the west stood the grim shell of Pentridge prison, a crane jutting from its innards. The old bluestone college was currently being made over into luxury apartments and B Division, home of the hardened, would soon be equipped for designer living. A gated community of the newer kind, vendor finance available.

The last two mourners were lingering at the graveside. Men of Charlie's vintage, dark-suited, they were conducting a hushed but animated conversation across the pit. I contemplated the bleached inscriptions and grievous angels for as long as it took to finish my cigarette, then crushed the butt with the toe of my shoe. At the sound, the pair turned and looked my way.

One of them cocked his head sideways, a summons. He was a compact, beetle-browed man with wavy black hair above an alert, self-assured face. His companion, a stoop-shouldered scarecrow of a man with thinning gingery-grey hair and a matching beard, opened his mouth as if to object, then closed it again. He pushed his thick-framed spectacles back up the bridge of his nose and watched me approach.

'Senator,' I said, dipping my head to the darker one.

Senator Barry Quinlan. The grey eminence of the Left faction of the Victorian branch of the Australian Labor Party. Punter, bon vivant, all-round philanthropist and currently the Shadow Minister for Telecommunications.

'Murray,' he nodded back. 'Sad occasion.'

As befitted a champion of the underdog, Quinlan took great care with his appearance. His tailored three-button suit and immaculate white shirt were set off with a Windsor-knotted black tie and expensive cufflinks. The morose beanpole beside him, by contrast, was so nondescript that he might almost have been invisible. But that, I reflected, was Colin Bishop's greatest talent.

'G'day, Col,' I said. 'Or is it Professor Col these days?'

When I'd last seen Colin Bishop, he was running the Trade Union Training Authority. Now he was Pro Vice-Chancellor of Maribyrnong University, a federally funded provider of post-secondary education in the fields of tourism, food technology and hospitality studies.

'Show some decorum, you cheeky bugger,' said Quinlan. 'A bit of respect for your elders and betters.'

Unholstering a silver hipflask, he toasted the coffin, took a shot and offered it around. I obliged, for form's sake, and passed the flask to Bishop. Col hesitated, then took a long slug.

'Lard-arse Charlie,' he intoned, peering downwards. 'Wonder how they got him in that box?'

'Levered him in with fence pickets,' Quinlan suggested.

There was no malice in the banter. Life goes on. Big boys don't get soppy. We were just four blokes, chewing the rag. Charlie was the quiet one in the rosewood overcoat.

'And you were there when it happened?' said the senator, suddenly serious again.

I nodded. 'Sitting at the same table in the dining room of the Mildura Grand Hotel.'

It was a story I was already sick of telling. But these two were entitled. They'd known Charlie even longer than I had.

'We'd just finished our back-to-the-bush roadshow. *Labor Listens*.'

Half a dozen of us trooping around the back-blocks in shiny new Akubras, listening to the yokels bitch about the axing of government services that everybody knew we had neither the present ability nor the future intention to restore. It had been a proper pain in the bum. A thousand kilometres in four days, preaching to the converted in community recreation facilities and civic halls.

'Charlie was in Mildura for some regional and rural gabfest in his capacity as Shadow Minister for Infrastructure. We all ended up at Stefano's for dinner.'

'As you would,' said Quinlan. Stefano's was the town's landmark eatery, five toques in the *Age Good Food Guide*. 'Did you try the saltbush lamb?'

Colin Bishop looked up from the coffin and sucked his cheeks impatiently.

'Let's just say we made a night of it,' I said. 'First thing next morning, the rest of the team took the early plane back to Melbourne. Charlie and I were booked on the noon flight, so we had time for a leisurely breakfast.'

Poor Charlie, under doctor's instructions to watch his weight, had settled for the fresh fruit compote. If only he'd known it was his last meal, he'd probably have ordered the lamb's fry and bacon.

'We were taking our time over coffee and newspapers when he started to make groaning noises. Not particularly loud so I didn't pay much attention. Just assumed he was muttering to himself as he read. Then, suddenly, the paper cascaded to the floor and he was clawing at his collar. He'd gone all pale and clammy and his eyes were bulging out of his head. Heart attack. Cardiogenic shock.'

Despite the repeated tellings, I still didn't quite believe it.

'What paper?' said Bishop, pushing his glasses up his nose, avid for detail.

'The *Herald Sun.*'

'Can have that effect,' nodded Quinlan. 'Although it's rarely fatal.'

Bishop eyed me keenly. 'Went quick, did he?'

'Here one minute, bang, gone the next. One of the hotel staff gave him CPR and the paramedics got there pretty fast but he was cactus by the time we reached the hospital.'

On the far side of the cemetery, a back-hoe started up. We were the only ones left now, three men in dark suits, perched on the lip of a grave. A trio of crows. Not a trio. What the hell was the collective noun for crows? A parliament? No, that was owls.

'Heart attack,' said Quinlan as we started towards the gate, hands in pockets. 'It's a caution. None of us are getting any younger.'

Bishop and Quinlan were well into their sixties, older than me by a generation. Quinlan seemed fit enough, buoyed by inexhaustible reserves of self-regard, but Bishop looked well past his use-by date, his skin loose and mottled.

'Let's hope he didn't suffer too much,' said Quinlan. 'I

hear you were with him in the ambulance.'

I nodded. It was a short trip, just long enough to make me feel completely fucking useless.

'Unconscious, was he?' said Bishop.

'In and out.'

'No famous last words?'

'More a case of unintelligible last mumbles,' I said.

'Like what?'

'Jesus, Col, you want me to do a fucking impression?'

'Just asking. No need to get shitty.'

We clomped down the slope a bit further. There was a hint of humidity in the air and my skin prickled under my shirt.

'You mean to keep in touch, but somehow you never find the time.' Col was trying to make amends. 'Then you wake up one day and it's too late. Must be donkey's years since I last saw Charlie.'

Quinlan nudged the subject sideways. 'Our young protégé Murray has done well for himself, hasn't he, Col?'

'Mail room to the state legislature,' agreed Bishop, falling back into step. 'Who'd've thunk it?'

'Always a bright one, our Murray,' said Quinlan. 'I saw his potential right from the start, flagged him to Charlie.'

That was news to me. Very late news indeed, two decades old. Colin and I had been working for Charlie well before Barry Quinlan came on the radar. But claiming credit was one of Quinlan's trademarks. He'd even been heard to maintain that he cut the deal that first got Charlie into federal parliament, all those years ago. If so, he hadn't got much out of it. Charlie was ever his own man.

'The transition will be smooth, I trust,' said Quinlan. 'No hugger-mugger from the locals?'

'How about we let Charlie get cold first?'

'Ah, Murray,' sighed the senator. 'Always the sentimentalist, God love you.'

Simultaneously we checked our watches, busy men, and stepped up the pace. The quick deserting the dead.

We made our brief goodbyes at the gate. As I headed for my car, I glanced back. Quinlan and Bishop had resumed their private conversation, leaning close and speaking intensely. Quinlan's finger was stabbing the air and Bishop kept screwing his neck back towards Charlie's grave. Maybe it was yawning a little too loud for comfort.

My electorate office was less than ten minutes away, a refurbished shopfront between Ali Baba's Hot Nuts and Vacuum Cleaner City in an arcade off Sydney Road. The mid-afternoon traffic was light, so I took the direct route along Bell Street through the heart of my electorate. Melbourne Upper, my seat in state parliament for the previous five years.

Those years had not been kind to the Australian Labor Party. The voters hadn't just shown us the door, they'd bolted it shut behind us. We barely held enough seats to play a hand of Scrabble, let alone influence the running of the state.

Fortunately for me, Melbourne Upper was one of the safest Labor seats in the state. Rusted-on blue-collar meets multicultural melting-pot, a stronghold in our besieged heartland. With 54 percent of the primary vote and an eight-year term in the Legislative Council, I was, at least, secure in my employment. Many a colleague had gone down, better men than me among them. Better women, too.

Now Charlie had also vanished from the political landscape. Not turfed by the electors of Coolaroo but felled by a fit of fatal dyspepsia while leafing through a Murdoch rag. Suddenly his seat was up for grabs.

Not that I had a dog in the fight. Charlie was federal, I was state. But the borders of our electorates overlapped and there were party branches and personalities in common. As a responsible member of the parliamentary team, I'd be expected to see they toed the line during the anointment of Charlie's successor. I knew this. I didn't need to be reminded of the fact by Barry Quinlan, the presumptuous prick.

As long as most people could remember, Quinlan had swung a very big dick in the Left faction of Labor's Victorian machine. Over a twenty-year period, he'd risen from union official to federal senator to a member of the federal cabinet. And even though our electoral battering had eroded his influence, he was still a major player. It was axiomatic that Barry Quinlan would have a finger in the Coolaroo succession pie. Which finger and exactly how deep remained to be seen. Nor would his be the only digit in this particular opening.

By long-established custom, the ALP is loath to pass up any opportunity to erupt into a full-fledged public brawl, particularly with a safe seat at stake. As the long years of opposition grew ever longer, however, the faction bosses had called a truce in the internal bloodletting. Rather than carrying on like a sackful of rabid badgers, we now tried to pretend we were one big happy family.

But old habits die hard. Top-level jostling continued behind closed doors and some of the rank-and-file persisted with their delusions of democracy. Hence Quinlan's grave-side remarks.

A block after Bell Street crossed Sydney Road, I turned left and drove into the carpark behind the shopping strip. At three-thirty on a Wednesday afternoon, the place was chockers. Italian senior citizens loading groceries into modest sedans. Somali women, swathed in turquoise and aqua-marine, waddling down the ramp from Safeway. Schoolkids on skateboards slaloming through the parked cars. I nabbed a spot vacated by a fat new Landcruiser and parked my taxpayer-funded Mitsubishi Magna next to the overflowing skips behind Vinnie Amato's Fruit and Veg Emporium.

I locked the car and entered the arcade. Exchanging familiar nods with the track-suited layabouts at their table outside the nut shop, I bought two takeaway coffees at Vida's Lunch'n'Munch, then pushed open a plate-glass door with my name on it.

Murray Whelan—Member of the Legislative Council—Province of Melbourne Upper.

My reception area contained six metal-frame chairs upholstered in fish-belly vinyl, a side-table strewn with infor-mation brochures, three framed prints from the Victorian Tourism Commission, an artificial fern, *Philodendron bogus*, and one modular reception desk, off-white.

A teenage girl in track pants, a Mooks sweatshirt and a hijab was leaning on the desk, a slumbering child in a cheap fold-up stroller parked beside her.

'Anyway,' she was saying. 'I reckon it sucks.'

Sitting behind the desk was my electorate officer, Ayisha Celik. 'Sucks big-time,' she said. 'But Supporting Mothers Benefits are a commonwealth matter. We're state. You've come to the wrong place, I'm afraid.' She clicked her tongue and gave an empathetic shrug.

Empathy was one of Ayisha's strong suits, along with a good memory for names, extensive networks, an inside knowledge of the bureaucracy and a well-tuned political antenna. The package made her indispensable to the smooth functioning of my retail operations. Parliamentary matters, the upstream side of the business, she left to me.

The girl in the hijab heaved a resigned sigh and angled the stroller towards the exit, another dissatisfied customer. I held the door open and gave her my most benign smile. She looked at me with a mixture of contempt and pity. The baby started to wail. A normal reaction all round. It came with the territory.

Ayisha reached across the desk and relieved me of one of the coffees. Done up in her funeral weeds, a navy pants suit and cream blouse, her jet black hair piled up in a mushroom, she could've passed for an SBS newsreader. Back when I first met her, the resident radical spunk at the Turkish Welfare League, she favoured skintight jeans and a *keffiyeh*. But that was before a career in public administration had dampened her activist zeal and two children had gone to her hips.

'So Charlie Talbot is laid to rest.' Ayisha raised her polystyrene cup.

I returned the salute. 'And now the games begin. I've just had Barry Quinlan pissing on my lamp-post.'

She cocked her head at the glass wall that separated the reception area from the inner office. Through the angled slats of half-closed slimline venetians, I could see a dark-suited figure sitting at the conference table.

'Speaking of which, Mike would like a word.'

I locked the front door, hung up the CLOSED sign and

followed Ayisha into the windowless heart of my political fiefdom. A laminex-topped conference table occupied most of the room. The rest was taken up by an Uluru-sized photo-copier-printer, a row of filing cabinets, a steel stationery cupboard and three colour-coded recycling bins. Office Beautiful.

Our visitor was a slim, good-looking man in his late thirties with close-shaved olive skin and the liquid eyes of an Orthodox icon. He, too, had come straight from the cemetery. Come, I assumed, to ventilate the pressing topic of the moment, Charlie Talbot's succession.

'*Yasou*,' I said.

Michelis Kyriakis had trodden the well-beaten path from immigrant childhood to university to local politics. He'd worked for Charlie Talbot for a while, keeping the home fires burning while Charlie was busy running the country. Now he was mayor of Broadmeadows, the *primus inter pares* of the coterie of Laborites who controlled the sprawling municipality at the centre of the seat of Coolaroo. Capable, energetic and well-motivated, he was going to waste in the small world of roads, rates and rubbish. This fact had not escaped his attention.

'Sorry if it looks pushy, mate, turning up like this straight after the funeral,' he said. 'But things are moving pretty fast.'

I sat down, facing him across the table. 'I've been a bit tied up, Mike, dealing with the undertakers and so forth, but I've heard murmurings about the FEA being convened ASAP.'

A conclave of local branch members and delegates appointed by the central machine, the Federal Electorate Assembly would select Charlie's successor.

'Saturday week,' said Mike. 'Ten days away. That must be a record.'

Ayisha perched herself on the desktop, legs dangling. 'The FEA's just a formality, you know that,' she said. 'There's a cross-factional agreement that the next federal vacancy in Victoria goes to the Left.'

'Yeah, but who in the Left?' said Mike. 'Charlie promised me that I'd get the seat when he retired. But now that he's gone, I've been sidelined. I'm out of the loop and it's obvious somebody else has been given the nod.'

I shrugged and showed him my empty palms. 'Your guess is as good as mine, Mike. Better, in fact. You are a member of the Left, after all.' I turned to Ayisha and raised an eyebrow. 'You heard anything?'

'Not a whisper,' she said. 'None of the usual suspects at state level have been mentioned, not that I've heard.'

'Maybe they're airlifting somebody in from Canberra,' I shrugged.

Mike made an acid face. 'Fucking typical,' he said. 'You put in the time, pay your dues, bust your gut, then some prick nobody knows gets handed a seat on a platter. Waltzes in, brushes you aside and you're expected to grin and bear it.'

'Welcome to the Labor Party,' I said. Or any party, for that matter. Mike knew the rules. You pays your money and you takes your chances.

'What would you say if I told you I'm thinking about throwing my hat into the ring?' he said.

I glanced sideways at Ayisha. She widened her eyes in mock horror. Mike had a lot of friends, us included, but he lacked clout in the places that counted.

'I'd say you'll be pushing shit uphill,' I said. 'It's obviously a done deal.'

'Even so,' he said. 'It's a matter of principle.'

Principle. The weeping scab of the Australian Labor Party.

'Climb aboard your saw-horse if you like, Mike. Point it at the windmill. Wave your lance around. But tell me, end of the day, what'll you get for your trouble?'

Mike straightened up and fixed me with the earnest expression he used for citizenship ceremonies. 'I feel very strongly about this, Murray. And I'd like your support. You've got a lot of sway in this part of the electorate.'

I ought to, I thought. I was paying the annual dues of half the branch members.

'You'd be an ornament to federal parliament, Mike,' I said. 'And I'm not the only one who thinks so. But you know the current party line. Heads down, bums up, noses to the grindstone. Strictly no muttering in the ranks. I'd need some pretty compelling reasons to buck company policy. Apart from my profound admiration for your personal qualities, of course.'

'Fuck you, too, comrade,' said Mike, letting out a little air. 'It's not like a bit of grass-roots democracy is going to damage our electoral prospects, since we currently have none. And by the time the next federal election rolls around, the punters will have forgotten all about it anyway.'

'Probably,' I agreed. 'But you've got to appreciate my situation.'

Mike nodded. 'I know I've got nothing to offer in return,' he said. 'I'm just trying to be straight with you, that's all. Your help would mean a lot to me.'

I leaned back in my chair, crossed my arms, pursed my lips and impersonated a man wrestling with his conscience.

'Tell you what,' I said at last. 'Why don't we sleep on it? Nominations don't close until next week. By then, we'll know the identity of the mystery candidate and meanwhile you can do your arithmetic, see how the numbers stack up. We'll talk again after the weekend.'

Mike knew it was the best he could expect for the moment. He stood and extended his hand. 'Fair enough.' We shook on our mutual good sense. 'See you at the wake, then. Broady town hall, right? Sundy arvo.'

Mike had taken upon himself to organise an informal send-off for Charlie, one for the constituents rather than the apparatchiks. Broadmeadows Town Hall was Mike's home turf. A good choice of venue for a man with his eye on the empty saddle.

Ayisha showed him to the door and came back grinning. 'Did that sound to you like a wheel squeaking?'

Mike Kyriakis hadn't come down in the last shower. He was well aware that he didn't stand a snowball's chance of elbowing his way into serious contention. But he also knew that by threatening to upset the apple cart with a grass-roots lunge, he might be offered an inducement to drop out. The promise of a seat, possibly, or even a paying job. At the very minimum, he'd be noticed—the essential requirement of political survival. Either way, it would cost him nothing to take a shot.

'He can squeak all he likes,' I said. 'But I don't think it'll get him any grease.'

Ayisha fished a blank sheet of paper from the photocopier feeder tray and put it on the table between us.

'Coolaroo,' she said, drawing an elongated circle with a black marker pen. 'An aboriginal word meaning "the Balkans".' She drew a second circle, overlapping the bottom edge of the first. 'Melbourne Upper.'

She hatched the circles with a series of crosses. 'Coolaroo's got about a thousand party members spread across ten branches. Four of the branches are down here, inside

Melbourne Upper. Those four only account for about a quarter of the total membership.' She jabbed her pen into the top circle. 'Anybody considering a run will need major support here.'

'In other words, somebody acceptable to the Turks, the Lebanese and the Greeks,' I said.

'An Anglo,' confirmed Ayisha. 'Somebody neutral who can balance out the competing sensitivities of those wonderfully inclusive communities.'

'I guess we'll know soon enough,' I said, glancing at my watch. 'Won't your kids be wondering if their mother's still alive?'

'Shit!' Ayisha grimaced and dashed for the door. 'Mail's on your desk. Usual bumph, nothing urgent. Bye.'

I ambled into my private office, a glass-walled cubicle distinguished only by a view across the K-Mart carpark towards the Green Fingers garden centre. I yawned, sprinkled some slow-release fertiliser granules on my African violet, plonked myself in my ergonomic executive chair and waded into my overflowing in-tray.

Even in opposition, the flag must be flown, the good fight fought, the flesh pressed, the creed recited, the candle kept burning. Over the next couple of weeks, according to the priorities flagged by Ayisha's multi-coloured post-its, my presence was required at the Housing Justice Roundtable, the Save the Medical Service Action Committee, a performance by the Glenroy Women's Choir, the Greening Melbourne Forum, Eritrean Peace Day, the Sydney Road Chamber of Commerce, the Free East Timor Association and a citizenship ceremony at Coburg Town Hall.

I checked the dates against my parliamentary schedule, then moved on to constituent matters, correspondence for signature and an urgent memo on Y2K compliance.

Apparently some inbuilt computer glitch was going to cause planes to plummet from the sky and hospital operating theatres to black out at the stroke of midnight on 31 December 1999. This global catastrophe was still more than two years away but meanwhile an incessant stream of paperwork had to be completed, with the usual object of ensuring that nobody could be blamed.

I stared down at the pages of techno-babble, thoughts wandering. I was going to miss Charlie Talbot. He'd been one of the good guys. Spent his life getting us into power, keeping us there when we won it and reminding us why we made the effort.

'If we don't do it,' he'd say, 'some other bastards will, and they'll be even worse bastards than us.'

Bastardry, in Charlie's language, was a political attribute, not a personal one. He bore no personal animosity towards his opponents. Not even back in the snake pit of the Trades Hall, back when he was state secretary of the Federated Union of Municipal Employees.

Then, as now, Labor was out of power, state and federal. Whitlam had crashed in a blaze of futile glory and we were back in the wilderness. Blind Freddie could see that we'd be there forever if we didn't get our house in order. Pronto. It was the Reformers versus the Shellbacks. The arena was the union movement and the battle was long and bitter.

Charlie's tolerance must have been sorely tested on quite a few occasions during those decisive tussles. But it was all ancient history now, water over the dam, a mere footnote. The millennium was approaching, bringing new and urgent challenges. I focused on the computer compliance paperwork.

Come the apocalypse, nobody could say it was my fault.

One by one, the afternoon-shift shelf-stackers trickled through the employees' door of the Bi-Lo food barn. When Red appeared, I gave him a bip and a wave. He sauntered over to the car, school backpack slung across his shoulder, shirt-tail hanging out his pants.

'Good funeral?' Red knew Charlie. Sporadically over the years, Charlie had taken a vaguely avuncular interest to which Red had responded in a vaguely nepotal manner. Gifts had never been exchanged.

'His best yet.' I started to open my door. 'Want to drive?'

Red looked around and scanned the scene. 'Now?'

On quiet Sunday afternoons, Northcote Plaza carpark was a perfect spot for introductory lessons in three-point turns and parallel parking. But this was a midweek evening at the intersection of homebound rush-hour and pre-dinner shopping flurry, dusk blurring the visibility, road courtesy somewhere between endangered and extinct. Out on High

Street, the trams were crawling, every stop a stop, the backed-up traffic seething with latent rage.

Red got into the passenger seat. 'Not worth it,' he said.

'I thought you wanted some practice.'

He rolled his eyes and snorted. 'Proper practice. Not ten minutes shitting myself in peak-hour traffic.'

We were built to the same genetic design but Red was half a head taller and two shoe sizes up. And when he was exasperated he was every inch his mother, Wendy.

'You sure?' I said. 'It all adds up.'

'Shut up and drive,' he said. 'I'm starving.'

He'd had his learner's permit for three months and he knew the basics, but it'd take more than an occasional inner-city shuffle to clock up the hundred hours recommended by the Transport Accident Commission. He'd need a few decent runs up the freeway, some night driving, a bit of wet-weather work, the odd long haul. It wasn't going to happen tonight.

'Suit yourself,' I said. 'Can't say I didn't offer.'

I moved into the traffic flow and turned at the corner where the Carters' Arms Hotel had once stood. The spot was now occupied by Papa Giovanni's Pizza and a branch of the Bank of Cyprus. In the olden days, back when I was younger than Red, my father was the licensee at the Carters'. We lived upstairs, hotel-keeping then being a family business. A peripatetic one, in our case, my father being my father.

A crawl-line of tail-lights stretched ahead. I dodged down the first side street, opting for the longer but less congested route. The dusk had taken a Turnerish turn, the clouds tinged with pink, the fresh-lit lamps of the outspread suburbs glinting in the gloaming, flecks of mica in a slurry of wet sand. In the far distance, the Dandenongs were a low bulge blurring into the horizon. There was a damp chill in the air, harbinger of the encroaching winter.

'Payday, eh?' I said, slowing for a speed bump.

'Uh-huh,' he nodded. '$81.60, after tax.'

I extracted four twenties from my shirt pocket. The supermarket job was Red's idea, a token of his commitment to self-reliance and financial independence. But his wages, notionally earmarked to buy a car, tended to get frittered on six-packs, taxi fares and mobile phone top-ups. Still, the gesture was laudable, parentally speaking, so I matched his earnings dollar for dollar.

'Don't drink it all at once,' I said.

We hit Heidelberg Road, crossed the Merri Creek bridge and turned down a short cul-de-sac abutting the parkland leading down to the Yarra.

The neighbourhood dated from the beginning of the century, built to cater for the Edwardian petit bourgeoisie. From its neat brick maisonettes and double-storey terraces, shopkeepers and artisans who had risen above the proletarian morass of nearby Collingwood could turn their aspirations towards the big houses across the river, the boom-era mansions of Kew.

Our place was a single-storey duplex, half of a matched pair. Its interior had been considerably remodelled over the years but the original façade remained intact, complete with a fretwork arch above the front door and leadlight magpies in the windows.

It was smaller than the house in Thornbury I'd bought with Lyndal not long after my election to parliament. But with Lyndal gone, the Thornbury place felt like an empty shell, an echoing reminder of her and the child she was carrying when she was killed.

Over time, my rage had burned itself out. I'd learned to live with my grief, to mourn and to move on.

Or at least to move house. So what if Clifton Hill was outside the boundaries of Melbourne Upper where, convention dictated, I ought to reside among my constituents? Such scrupulousness was more honoured in the breach these days, and Clifton Hill was only a spit and a piddle from the electorate anyway. More to the point, it was very convenient for Red, what with the network of bike paths just beyond the back gate, the railway station and the bus to school a few minutes' walk away.

Not that he'd need bike paths and public transport for much longer. Or me, for that matter. Come the end of this final year of school, the bird would fly the coop, hurtling towards the new millennium in the car I'd helped him buy, leaving me in an empty nest.

But that was months away. I parked at the kerb and Red hauled his books and laptop inside and retreated to his room on the pretext of homework. Doubtless this would entail much tele-conferencing and net-surfing.

I exchanged my suit for jeans and a sloppy joe, poured myself a short snort, stepped through the sliding glass doors onto the back deck and fired up the gas barbecue. In the dying light, the sky was the colour of ancient rust and I stood for a moment, drinking it in.

'At the going down of the sun,' I said to myself, 'we will remember them.'

I went back into the all-purpose eating-living area and pointed the remote-control at the television for the ABC news headlines. The Prime Minister was refusing to say sorry for something. Bill Clinton's penis was facing impeachment. Peace talks, astonishingly, had collapsed in the Middle East.

I gave some rocket a spin, ran the sniff test on a block of feta, sliced a cucumber and nuked a couple of kipflers. By then, the hotplate was ready. I seared two slabs of rump and hit the mute.

'Grub's up.'

Red materialised at the refrigerator door and scouted the interior, his broad shoulders filling the open gap. Physically, he was nearly a man, the stuff of gladiator sports and conscript armies, bulletproof and bound for glory. But as he crouched there, contemplating the cling-wrapped leftovers, tousle-haired in an oversize sweatshirt and bare feet, he was once again a little boy.

'Beer or wine?' he said.

It was five years since he'd opted to join me in Melbourne rather than remain with his mother and stepfather in Sydney, and it felt like five minutes.

Five years, three houses, two schools, one major freak-out and a fair smattering of the ups-and-downs that come with having a politician for a father. A loser politician, at that.

'Don't forget to call your mother,' I said, watching him set the table. 'It's her birthday tomorrow, you know.'

'It was yesterday,' he said. 'I already rang.'

I dished up and we ate in companionable silence. Two honest toilers, home from their workbenches, tucking into a manly repast of meat and potatoes accompanied by a tossed mesclun salad lightly drizzled with extra-virgin olive oil and served with crusty ciabatta and fresh-broached Stella Artois.

The television was burbling in the background, volume low. Half-way through the news, the reporter caught my attention. A big-eyed, round-faced blonde named Kelly Cusack. It wasn't often that she made the prime-time bulletin. Her usual gig was anchoring 'On the Floor', a weekly round-the-nation digest of state political affairs that went to air after the religion show on Sunday nights. Question Time kerfuffles in Hobart, redistribution brouhaha for the Nationals in Queensland, men in suits go yakkity-yak.

It was a program strictly for the hard-core politics junkies. But for Kelly Cusack it was a foot in the door of current affairs, a step up from her previous gig as host of a gee-whiz techno-buff show.

'Hello?' Red was leaning sideways to block my view of the set.

'Say again?'

He tapped the side of his head. Wake up. 'Driving lesson? Saturday?'

'Haven't you got a rehearsal? Bunking off won't get you into NIDA, you know.'

'It's just a run-through,' he said. 'We'll be finished by one o'clock.'

Red's ambition was pointed in the direction of drama school. Theatre Studies was his top subject and a lot of his off-hours went into a youth theatre based in an old knitwear sweatshop in South Melbourne. It was a semi-professional operation with a resident grant-funded dramaturg; more than one alumnus had gone on to feature in a distinctively quirky Australian film.

His mother, of course, took a dim view. Her idea of a proper career was law, medicine or one of the other money-harvesting professions. But the kid was hot to tread the boards. He'd already scored a walk-on in 'Heartbreak High' and two lines in 'Blue Heelers', and in my wild erratic fancy visions came to me of him holding aloft a gold statuette and thanking the father who'd backed him all the way. If only to give his mother the shits. Currently, he was codpiece-deep in an upcoming production of *Rosencrantz and Guildenstern Are Dead*.

'Dunno why you're pissing around with this poncey thespian stuff,' I said. 'What's wrong with plumbing? Steady work and the money's good. You could start by learning how to operate the dishwasher, not just fill it up with concrete-encrusted cereal bowls.'

'Don't change the subject. If you haven't got a fete to open or a ship to launch, we could put in a couple of hours.'

If memory served, my schedule was clear.

'Let's call it a strong maybe,' I said. 'Die young, stay pretty. Worked for James Dean.'

Well pleased, Red microwaved a brace of individual self-saucing butterscotch puddings which we ate on the sofa watching 'The Simpsons'. When he drifted back to his homework, I pulled a cork and retired to my hermitage.

Ah, gentrification. What started life as a laundry at the rear of the building was now a snug little hideaway, just big enough to accommodate my Spooner cartoons, archive boxes, books and music, and an authentic op-shop Jason Recliner. Its side door opened onto a small patio—a bed of white pebbles beside the ivy-clad wall of the next-door neighbour's garage.

I kicked off my shoes, cued an audio cassette and declined on the davenport. There was a hiss, then a male voice spoke.

'Μαθημα Δεκα,' it said.

'Μαθημα Δεκα,' I responded.

Melbourne swarms with Grecians. And having spent half my life up to my taramasalata in the progeny of Hellas, I'd decided it was high time I learned how to order my souvlaki in the demotic. So, earlier in the year, I'd enrolled in a beginners' course in Greek.

'Στο σταθμο του τραινου.'

So far, by diligent application, I'd managed to acquire the conversational skills of a speech-impaired three-year-old. On the up side, most of my classmates were female. And a man in my situation takes his opportunities wherever he can find them.

One classmate in particular had caught my eye. Her name was Andrea Lane, but she was Lanie to her friends and that was the tag by which she'd introduced herself to the class. Our teacher mistook it for Eleni. It was an apt elision. Helen, she who eloped with the Trojan Paris.

Lanie's may not have been the face that launched a thousand ships, but it definitely floated my little rubber duckie. She was cheerful, sardonic and fetchingly full-figured. Naturally, she was already taken.

Hubby had picked her up after one of the first classes, their pubescent daughter in tow. He was a dopey-looking dork, reeking of academia. With any luck, he'd be struck by some fatal skin disease, turn into a mass of weeping pustules and retire to a leper colony. I would comfort his lonely wife and one thing would lead to another. Until that happened, I could only put my hopes for conjugation on hold, try not to ogle her too obviously during class and buff my conversational skills.

'Εχεις πολυ ωραια ποδια,' I recited. '*Ti ora fevgi to treno?*'

After thirty minutes and four glasses of Penfolds Bin 28, my concentration was flagging. I stopped the tape, took my wine out to the wrought-iron table in the pebbly courtyard and fired up an ultra light. SMOKING KILLS, it said on the pack.

So does an out-of-the-blue coronary occlusion in the

dining room of the Mildura Grand Hotel. Funny thing, I thought, Charlie dying in front of me in a restaurant. We first met in a restaurant. Toto's, a pizza joint near the Trades Hall.

In 1978 I was a political science graduate, still in my twenties. I'd been working on a health and safety campaign for the Combined Metalworkers, a futile attempt to convince welders at the naval dockyards to stop getting shitfaced at lunchtime and falling off their gantries. My tenure had just fizzled out and I was pondering my employment prospects.

Charlie was sitting at a table up the back, having lunch with Colin Bishop. Purged from the public service in the aftermath of the Whitlam dismissal, Col was carving a niche for himself as education guru to the unions. From time to time, he'd employed me as a casual teacher at the Trade Union Training Authority. He waved me over and introduced me to Charlie.

I knew him by reputation, of course. He was state secretary of the Federated Union of Municipal Employees, elected on a reform ticket. A former bible basher, he had a reputation among the more hard-nosed blue-collar types as a bit of a boy scout. Somewhere in his forties, he was a stocky, sandy bloke. Teddy-bearish, you might say. Soft spoken, no side, real smart. I liked him straight up.

We made some chit-chat, ate some spaghetti, drank some coffee and I walked away with a job. Assistant Publications and Training Officer. Six days a fortnight, beginning immediately.

My job was producing the monthly newspaper that went out to the Municipals' fifty thousand-odd members. Boilerplate stuff—a paste-up of reports from the state branches, advertisements for the credit union, updates on award negotiations. Between issues, I slaved over a hot photocopier, organising the schedules and study materials for Colin Bishop's weekend seminars for shop stewards. Spiral-bound folders with diagrams of the Conciliation and Arbitration Commission, that sort of thing.

I worked out of the state office, a modern, low-rise building in Queensberry Street, not far from the crumbling mausoleum of the Trades Hall. Our queen bee was Mavis Peel, a woman of indeterminate age and towering coiffure

lirected the daily ebb-and-flow from behind a golf-ball
ric, a PBX and a Rothmans.

vis had been with the union since the days of the
men and she brooked no cheek from anyone. In her
t and diamante frames, she looked like a character
Ealing comedy, fielding calls from shire clerks with
ficiency and guarding our two typists, Margot and
ith the ferocity of a mother lioness. Never mind that
grown women, both already into their thirties, and
to look after themselves. To Mavis, they were her
rgets of opportunity in the blokey world of the

ater I wondered if Mavis had registered what was
between Charlie and Margot. If so, she certainly
close to her twin-torpedo chest. I definitely didn't
id anyone else at the time, far as I was aware.

t I was paying much attention. My relationship
y was moving inexorably towards cohabitation,
rship and parenthood and it simply didn't occur
hidden fires might be burning behind Charlie
l-ironed shirtfront. He was just too straight for
hing. Too married. And Margot, lovely Margot,
than enough to keep her hands full elsewhere.

And then there was the quite unlovely Mervyn Cutlett. Merv had ruled the union since the mid-fifties. He was a wily old throwback, half class warrior, half lurk merchant. A product of the Depression and the War, he regarded the Municipals as his personal property, maintaining his tenure by sheer bloody-minded intractability and a sharp eye for potential challengers.

When he wasn't interstate, shoring up the loyalty of the various state secretaries, he was ensconced in his nicotine-drenched, pine-panelled, shagpiled lair in the basement of the Trades Hall, holding court with his well-stocked bar fridge, his kitsch collection of wartime memorabilia and his attendant gopher, an ageing rocker named Sid Gilpin.

Merv and Charlie were the union's yin and yang, its past and future. As one of Charlie's appointments, yet another university-educated smartarse, I was bound to be viewed by Merv as an object of suspicion.

'Just make sure his picture appears on every page of the union news,' Charlie counselled. 'And try to keep out of his line of sight.'

I took his advice. And later, after he made the switch to parliament and I'd become a minister's minder, I kept taking it. No matter how busy, Charlie was always good for a word of wisdom when I needed one. That was something else I was going to miss about him.

I finished my cigarette, took the bottle back inside and restarted the tape.

'Ας ξαναρχισουμε παλι.'

Lesson Eleven. Future Conditional.

The Premier stood on the topmost step of the broad terrace leading to Parliament House. His chest was thrust forward, his chin tilted upwards, his hands on his hips. The tuft of his trademark cowlick stood erect, the comb of a strutting cockerel. A great strutter, the Right Honourable Kenneth Geoffries. He could strut standing still. All this is mine, his stance announced. The legislature behind me, the city at my feet.

'This cutting-edge development will guarantee Melbourne a place in the front row of the world's leading cities for generations to come,' he declared.

A semi-circle of reporters and photographers clustered around him, scribbling and snapping. Flunkies patrolled the perimeter of the scrum. Tourists paused to observe the goings-on from between the Corinthian columns of the portico.

'...enhanced competitive advantage...international landmark...'

It was nine-thirty the following morning and I was on my way to a caucus meeting. The sky was clear and the morning fair. Mild sunlight suffused the rich, contented lawns of the parliamentary gardens. The forsythia were still in bloom but the shrubbery borders had begun turning to russet.

The end of the autumn session was imminent and the legislature was dawdling towards its winter hibernation. Not that Joe and Joanna Public would take much notice. Parliament was a dull spectacle at the best of times and its current configuration made for monotonous viewing. The Liberals had an iron-clad majority, a steamroller legislative agenda and a bullet-proof leader. They outnumbered us two to one in the lower house, five to one in the upper house. We weren't just a minority. We were an endangered species, a puny splinter with little option but to keep our heads down, our seatbelts buckled and our powder dry. Not that we had any powder. We'd lost the formula two elections ago.

I trudged up the steps towards the main door. Skirting the mini-scrum, I paused for a second to catch the topic of the Premier's spiel.

'The massive contribution of the gaming industry to the people of this state…'

He was barking for the new casino, one of his pet projects. Hyped as a magnet for tourists, a generator of jobs and an all-round good thing, the casino had been slowly taking shape on the south bank of the Yarra. Its grand opening was now only days away and media interest was intense. Mick and Keef were rumoured to be flying in, Wham had got back together and Freddy Mercury was rising from the dead for the occasion.

And the Premier, you could bet on it, was claiming his share of the limelight.

'This is the kind of vision that drives my government...' he was saying.

Trotting up the last of the steps, I went into the grand old pile. The entrance was crowded with management types. They were queueing for admission to the Queen's Hall, the main parliamentary lobby. I nodded hello with the doorman, stuck my head through the door and took a quick squizz.

Fifty or so suited figures were milling around the swathe of red carpet between the two legislative chambers, helping themselves to coffee at a temporary muffin buffet. Many wore V-shaped gold lapel pins, the official insignia of the Premier's insider-trading, head-kicking, nest-feathering regime. Public service mandarins and Liberal backbenchers were mixing and mingling, not a spine among them. A rostrum had been set up, framed by banners. 'Victoria—On the Move', they declared.

On the take, more likely, I thought. You could smell the greed in the air.

The Premier's presidential style, an innovation in Australian politics, was built on events like this. Announcements of landmark accomplishments. Policy launches. New initiatives. *Son-et-lumière*. Colour and movement. A torrent of proclamations and pronouncements that kept his highness on the front page and his critics scrabbling to keep up.

Towards the rear of the room, beside the statue of Queen Victoria, camera crews were uncoiling cables and erecting tripods. Senior members of the parliamentary press corps stood nearby, idly rocking on their heels, waiting for the curtain to go up. Among them was Kelly Cusack, the presenter of *On the Floor*.

She was standing with the other hacks, half-listening to

the half-wit who did the rounds for Channel 10, her gaze skimming the room. Without the television make-up and studio lighting, she had a sexy-librarian quality, the look emphasised by her pairing of a dark suit with a form-fitting, pastel-yellow cowl-neck cashmere sweater.

She noticed me looking her way. She held my gaze, tilting her head to one side as if trying to place me.

At that exact moment, a hand clamped itself around my elbow. It jerked me abruptly sideways as the Premier swept into the room, flanked by a phalanx of ministers and minions.

'Out of the way, sonny. Who do you think you are, standing in the way of progress?'

I turned and found myself looking down at a tubby, leprechaun-faced man with wiry grey hair and twinkly eyes. He wore a crumpled tweed jacket and a cord around his neck with his spectacles attached.

'Let's rush him, Inky,' I said. 'I'll grab him, you bite his knees.'

Dennis Donnelly, universally known as Inky, was a Labor Party institution. A spin doctor *avant la lettre*, he'd been press secretary to prime ministers and premiers, and eye witness to the rise and fall of more Labor governments than I'd had taxpayer-funded taxi rides. Officially retired but impossible to keep away, he was our roving media watchdog, a sniffer-out of potentially damaging press stories.

'I been looking for you.' His voice was a whispery undertone that sounded like two press releases being rubbed together. 'Got a tick?'

I checked my watch. The caucus meeting was still fifteen minutes away.

'For you, Inky,' I said. 'Any time.'

His hand still gripping my elbow, he shunted me into the

corridor outside the Legislative Assembly. 'I understand you worked at the Municipals at one point.'

'Long ago,' I nodded. 'In a galaxy far, far away.'

He pulled a folded copy of the *Herald Sun* out of his jacket pocket and handed it to me. 'Seen this?'

The tabloid was folded open at an inside page. It had a furry, handled feel. Most of the page was occupied by a photo of a lanky young footballer with blond tips in his hair and a cast on his arm. A horde of grinning kids were jostling to sign the plaster.

'It's a cruel world,' I said. 'I've been praying to the Blessed Virgin for a speedy recovery.'

Inky and I were Lions supporters. And if the forced merger of our club with an interstate team was not indignity enough, the loss of our most promising new recruit to a shattered ulna in the first quarter of the first game of the season had rubbed salt into the wounds.

'Bugger the Blessed Virgin,' said Inky. 'Check the sidebar.'

The column contained a half-dozen brief news items. One of them was circled with an orange felt-tip pen. It was headed *Remains Found in Lake*.

> *Human remains were discovered in Lake Nillahcootie in central Victoria yesterday afternoon. They were found in the bed of the lake which has been recently drained as part of maintenance work on the dam wall.*
>
> *Consisting of bones and a skull, the remains were removed by police for examination at Melbourne's Institute of Forensic Medicine. Police said it could take some time to identify them.*
>
> *'They appear to have been at the bottom of the reservoir for a considerable period of time,' said Detective Acting*

> Senior Sergeant Brendan Rice. 'Items recovered from the
> scene suggests that they belong to the victim of a drowning
> which occurred at the lake a number of years ago.'

Inky watched me read, head slanted sideways, an expectant expression on his classic Hibernian dial.

'Well, well,' I said. 'It took long enough, but it looks like they've finally found Merv Cutlett.'

'You reckon it's him?'

'The odds would have to be pretty good. There can't be too many other bodies on the bottom of Lake Nillahcootie, can there?'

'You wouldn't think so,' he rasped. 'Is this first you've heard about this?'

'News to me.'

Inky reached over and laid a stubby finger on the date line at the top of the page.

A memory flashed before me, so fresh I could smell the bacon and eggs. A breakfast table at the Mildura Grand, Charlie tearing at the buttons of his shirt, vomit at the corners of his mouth, his open newspaper cascading to the floor.

'Last Thursday,' I said. 'The day Charlie Talbot died.'

What with one thing and another, I realised, I'd never got round to finishing the papers.

'Ironic, isn't it?' said Inky. 'Charlie being there when Merv drowned, then carking it on the very day the body turns up, twenty years later.'

I nodded, sharing the old flak-catcher's appreciation of life's little quirks. 'You wouldn't read about it, would you?'

Inky gave a world-weary sigh. 'If only that was true, Murray,' he said. 'Thing is, I've had a call from a journalist.

He's picked up on the unidentified remains discovery, put two and two together, come up with Merv Cutlett. He's got the idea there might be a story in it.'

'*Union Boss Slept with Yabbies*?'

'Something like that,' he said. 'He's keen to rustle up some background on the union. Problem is, I spent the late seventies in Canberra, scraping Whitlam-flavoured egg off the face of the national leadership, so I'm a bit behind the eight-ball on the twilight of the Municipals. Right now, you're the horse's mouth.'

Mouth? It was usually the other end. I glanced through the double doors at a buffet laden with coffee dregs and muffin carnage.

'Tell you what, Inky. Buy me lunch and I'll spill my guts.'

Inky patted his paunch and made a mournful face. 'My lunching days are over, mate. Gastric ulcer. Talk about guts, mine are completely cactus.'

The name Inky Donnelly was synonymous with the long Labor lunch. I puffed my cheeks in astonishment and gave a doleful shake of my head. 'No wonder the party's rooted.'

As if on cue, a handful of listless suits shuffled through the entrance archway to Queen's Hall. The remnants of my decimated tribe massing thinly for the scheduled caucus meeting.

'Tell this journo, whoever he is, he's wasting his time.' I handed Inky back his *Herald Sun*. 'Merv Cutlett's death is old news, bones or no bones.'

Inky took the paper. 'It's Vic Valentine,' he said.

I pricked up my ears. 'Accidental drowning's a bit prosaic for Vic, isn't it?' I said. 'All this gangland action going on, you'd think Melbourne's ace crime reporter would have more newsworthy leads to pursue.' We strolled out onto the clattering mosaic of the Parliament House vestibule.

'You can see where he's coming from, though,' shrugged Inky. 'A union official. An influential senator. A recently-deceased former minister. Three men in a boat, one of whom goes to a watery grave. It's got to be worth a sniff.'

'He sniffeth in vain,' I said. 'It was just a stupid accident. And Merv Cutlett wasn't exactly Jimmy Hoffa.'

Inky gave a pessimistic shrug. Crime or politics, a story was a story. And stories had a tendency to grow legs and start running in all sorts of undesirable directions.

'You know him? Personally, I mean.'

'We've talked on the phone a couple of times,' I said. 'Struck me as an okay sort of bloke.'

In the aftermath of Lyndal's death, the cops were beating the bushes, hoping to flush out the maniac who ran her down. Valentine rang me for a quote. Later, when a group of teenagers were taken hostage, Red among them, he asked my permission to interview my son. It was a messy business and I didn't want the kid turned into grist for the media mill. Valentine had respected my wishes.

'They tell me he's a straight shooter,' nodded Inky. 'But once the police ID the body, it'll be open slather. Rumour and insinuation, the Liberals can say anything they like under parliamentary privilege. They'll have a field day. Mindful of which, I think it'd be advisable to stay ahead of the pack, not risk getting blind-sided.'

In the doorway, a man in a somewhat better suit than mine was batting back a routine pleasantry from one of the Parliament House staff. Alan Metcalfe, star attraction of the imminent party meeting. He took a deep, bracing breath, inflated his chest to leaderly proportions and advanced on the staircase.

Inky retrieved some folded sheets of paper from the inside pocket of his tweed. 'I happened to be down the State Library, doing a bit of work on the memoirs, so I took a quick gander at the original newspaper reports.' He tapped his wrist with the sheaf of photocopied clippings. 'They cover the drowning, but they're a bit thin on context.'

I nodded at Metcalfe as he strode by and checked my watch. It wouldn't do to be too much later than the boss.

'Context?' I said. 'In other words, you want to know if the union was corrupt?'

'Was it?'

'There might've been the odd little fiddle here and there, but nothing systemic. The employers were government agencies, so there wasn't much scope.'

'And there was never any question that the drowning was an accident?'

'Nope,' I said. 'Not that I heard.'

'Three blokes go fishing, one of them falls overboard, that's it?'

'Pissed as a parakeet, probably,' I said. 'Cutlett.'

'Consistent with form,' Inky said. 'And Charlie Talbot was state secretary, right?'

I nodded. 'The way I heard it, Charlie jumped in, tried to save him.'

'They were pretty thick, were they?'

'Chalk and cheese,' I said. 'Mortal enemies, so to speak. Charlie was trying to drag the union into the twentieth century. Merv preferred the early nineteenth.'

'But pally enough to go fishing together?'

I tried to imagine Charlie Talbot in an aluminium dinghy with a bucket of worms and a six-pack. The image didn't come readily to mind.

'That's another irony,' I said. 'Charlie wasn't the outdoor type. Merv must have twisted his arm. Probably dragged him along just to give him the shits.'

'The union had a place on the lake, right?'

'The Shack,' I nodded. 'Notionally a training and recreation facility for the members. In reality, it was Merv's private retreat.'

Inky put on his specs and quickly flipped through his collection of newspaper cuttings. 'So what was Barry Quinlan doing there? I can't see him and Merv Cutlett as mates.'

'They weren't,' I said. 'Quinlan was working for the Public Employees Federation. He had some nebulous title like development officer or liaison co-ordinator or some such. Essentially, he was their mergers and acquisitions man. The PEF was very pro-active on the amalgamation front, always on the lookout for a takeover target. Charlie knew that amalgamation with a bigger union was the only way forward for the Municipals. He and Quinlan were working a tag team, trying to swing Merv on the issue.'

Inky nodded along, connecting the union dots to the bigger political picture. 'The PEF backed Quinlan onto the Senate ticket for the 1979 election. That would've been his pay-off for bringing the Municipals into the fold. The amalgamation must have increased its membership by a hefty swag.'

'A well-trod route,' I said. The more members, the more votes a union has at party conference.

Inky patted his pockets, found a half-gone roll of Quik-Eze and peeled away the foil.

'Tell you what,' he popped a couple in his mouth and started to crunch. 'How about we have a drink with your mate Valentine? Nip this thing in the bud. How're you set tonight after work?'

It was a rare Friday night that Red didn't have a social engagement. Tonight was no exception. Come knock-off time, I'd have no reason to go rushing home to an empty house.

'Sure,' I shrugged. 'I'll shout you a glass of milk.'

'I'll give Valentine a call, get back to you with the when and where.'

I was already turning away, pushing it to make the meeting on time. Inky grabbed my sleeve and thrust his collection of cuttings into my hand.

'Extra! Extra!' he rasped. 'Read all about it.'

The party room was a grand salon on the first floor, all neo-classical architraves and french-polished sideboards. I arrived just as the pre-meeting burble was dying down and found a seat in the back row.

The entire parliamentary party was there. All twenty-nine of us.

As usual, the Right sat on the left and the Left sat on the right. An apt demarcation since the two factions were indistinguishable in both principle and practice. The Right had long been dominant, having successfully pinned responsibility for our demise on the Left, a situation akin to the cocktail waiters blaming the dance band for the sinking of the *Titanic*. They called themselves the Concord faction, thereby staking out the moral high ground. The Left, demonstrating its usual measure of political imagination, just called itself the Left.

Those without factional affiliation, myself included, sat

at the back. In due course, if I wanted to retain my endorsement, I'd probably be forced to choose a side. For the moment, however, I was content to keep my entanglements to a minimum. Even if it meant sitting at the back.

Up front, facing us, sat Alan Metcalfe, along with his deputy, Peter Thorsen, and a select group of senior front-benchers. Metcalfe stood up, cleared his throat and called the meeting to order.

'*Harmf*,' he said. 'Let's get on with it, then.'

Metcalfe was a former federal MP who'd been shoe-horned into state politics after losing his safe seat in a redistribution. He was capable, earnest, deeply ambitious and utterly boring. He had the head of a shop dummy, the mannerisms of a robot and the charisma of a fish finger.

Notwithstanding these excellent credentials, the electorate had failed to warm to our glorious leader. Under his tutelage, our state-wide primary vote had plummeted to new depths. Nobody, probably not even Alan himself, believed that he could reverse this trend in time for the next election. In the most recent preferred-premier poll, he'd rated somewhere lower than viral meningitis. But what he lacked in voter appeal he more than made up in tenacity. He clung to his job with fingernails of steel, a testament to inertia disguised as stability.

'Fair to say, and I think you'll all agree with me,' he started, 'we've put up a pretty good show in recent weeks. The public is tiring of this government's high-handed attitude. It's looking to us to keep up the pressure.'

Metcalfe was whistling dixie. The fact was, we'd been comprehensively trounced in every fight we picked. And successfully painted as a rat-pack of financial incompetents who couldn't be trusted to run a primary school tuck-shop.

As Metcalfe continued, chopping the air for emphasis, an air of lethargy filled the room. In the seat beside me, Kelvin Yabbsley, the member for Corio East, lowered his chin to his chest and closed his eyes.

He was dreaming, I fancied, about his superannuation payout. After twenty-two years on the back bench, Yabbers was due to retire at the next election. With his parliamentary pension and a pozzie on the board of the Geelong Harbour Trust, he would want for nothing for the rest of his natural life.

Play your cards right kid, I told myself, and one day that could be you.

Eventually, Alan Metcalfe's air-karate pep-talk petered out. 'Fair to say, all things considered, we've got our work cut out for us,' he concluded. 'And on that note, I'll hand the floor to the shadow ministers who'll brief us on their respective portfolio areas.'

Shoulders sagged lower and backsides sank deeper into seats. Con Caramalides, our point man for planning and infrastructure, began to outline his plans to stick it up the government over a raft of issues connected with increased domestic electricity charges. If anybody needed a raft, it was Con. He sounded like he was drowning in molasses.

'…the flow-on of cross-ownership to low-voltage…'

I did my best to stay awake, just in case there was any mention of my current parliamentary duties. Shadow Secretary for Ethnic Affairs, Local Government and Fair Trading. Acting assistant manager of opposition business in the upper house, *pro tem*. Various other bits and bobs. With our numbers so short, it was all hands on deck.

And what a motley crew of deck-hands we were.

Most of our frontbench were yesterday's heroes, so busy undermining one another that they'd lost sight of any other reason for existence. Circling each other like burned-out suns, they were kept in place only by the centrifugal force of their mutual loathing. Of the fresher faces, few stood out as foreman material. For my money, our best hope was Peter Thorsen, the deputy leader.

Thorsen was a cleanskin, untarnished by our period in government. Not yet forty, wheaten-haired with the hint of a tennis tan, he was the very picture of a golden boy on the cusp of middle age. One of the Concord faction, he carried himself with a breezy self-confidence that played well on television. He'd scored some hits on the floor of parliament and he was popular with the troops. But so far, he'd given no indication of having his sights set on the top job. Whether motivated by caution or timing or loyalty, he seemed content to play second fiddle to Metcalfe.

'Natural gas, on the other hand,' said Con, 'is a two-edged sword…'

Thorsen had one arm draped across the back of his chair, browsing a document. He glanced up, saw me looking his way, and gave me a sly grin. Ho-hum, it said, here we are again. I replied with a resigned shrug and put a balled fist to my mouth, stifling a yawn.

By eleven-thirty, the shadow ministers' round-ups had ambled to a conclusion. The room came out of its collective coma. Members began gathering up their papers. Kelvin Yabbsley opened his eyes, blew his nose and pulled up his socks.

'Fair to say that covers the overall thrust,' said Metcalfe, raising his voice above the resurgent murmur. 'But before I close the meeting, I've got a brief announcement to make.'

There was a communal deflation and bums again descended onto seats.

'We're all deeply grieved,' said Metcalfe, 'fair to say, at the untimely death of Charlie Talbot.'

'Hear, hear,' murmured a smattering of voices.

Metcalfe signalled for silence, then raked us with his sternest stare. 'And I believe the best way to honour his memory is to avoid a distracting and divisive preselection brawl over the seat he left vacant. Accordingly, I've assured our federal colleagues that the Victorian branch can be relied on one hundred percent to adhere to the current agreement regarding the prompt filling of the vacancy in Coolaroo.'

There was a low burble of assent from the Concord ranks.

'So who's the lucky boy?' chipped in Nanette Vandenberg, one of the independents. 'It *is* a boy, I presume.'

Heads swivelled, then turned back to Metcalfe. 'I've been given to understand that the choice is Phil Sebastian,' he said. 'He'll bring a strong background in policy development to the federal team.'

In other words, he was a policy wonk with fuck-all experience of ground-level politics. He also happened to be Barry Quinlan's chief-of-staff. At least now I knew which particular finger the good senator was giving the voters of Coolaroo.

A lukewarm murmur of approval wafted from the thin ranks of the Left. The choice had evidently not been met with unanimous enthusiasm among the comrades. Nothing remarkable there. Nelson Mandela would've got the same reception.

'I'm confident I can rely on you all,' said Metcalfe pointedly. 'A hundred percent.' He brought the edge of one hand down hard on the open palm of the other. 'Understood?'

All heads nodded in unison, a row of toy dogs in the rear

window of a slow-moving vehicle.

'In that case, I declare this meeting closed.'

As the room began to empty, Peter Thorsen caught my eye. Angling his head slightly, he twitched his chin upwards in the direction of his second-floor office.

Whatever it is, I thought, it can wait until I've had a cup of tea. I headed for the urn on the sideboard to dunk myself a bag. Jenny Hovacks, a Concord spear-carrier, was ahead of me in the queue. She'd been buttonholed by Eric Littler, one of the Left.

'We're not unhappy with the result,' he was saying fiercely. 'It's the process we don't like.'

'Murray,' Jenny turned to greet me. 'What do you think of your chances tomorrow?'

Jenny was an Essendon supporter. The Lions would be up against them at the MCG, their first Melbourne match since the merger.

'I think we'll make a good showing,' I said. 'Then you'll shit on us from a great height.'

'Just as well you're used to it, eh?' said misery-guts Eric, snaffling the last of the teabags.

I didn't like the turn this conversation was taking. I settled for a butternut snap and trudged upstairs to Thorsen's office.

His admin assistant, Del, was busy at her keyboard, fingers flying. 'Go on in, Murray,' she said, flipping a wrist towards the open door of the inner sanctum.

Thorsen's office overlooked the Gordon Reserve, a triangle of lawn studded with memorials to dead poets and imperial warriors. He was standing at his desk, a massive block of native hardwood incised with an *art nouveau* gum leaf motif. His jacket was draped over the back of his chair and he'd loosened his tie. A cluster of silver-framed photographs was arrayed in a semi-circle on a credenza behind him, family snaps of his barrister wife and their brood of tow-headed children, four at last count. A phone was pressed to his ear.

'Yup, yup,' he said into the mouthpiece, waving me inside and signalling that I should shut the door. 'Yup.'

Peter's political base lay on the other side of town, in socially liberal seaside suburbs that had long since traded their working-class credentials for off-the-rack bohemianism, grouchy gentility and rampant property speculation. Our relationship was cordial, but it had yet to be tested where the poop meets the propeller.

He hung up, nodded for me to sit down, ambled across to the window, propped his backside against the sill and stuck his hands in his pockets.

'Everybody appreciates the job you did with Charlie Talbot, Murray, the funeral arrangements and so forth. It must have been pretty rough.'

'The least I could do for an old mate.'

'Big shoes to fill,' he said. 'You know Phil Sebastian, do you?'

'We've met in passing,' I said. 'But I imagine I'll be seeing a lot more of him from now on. Squiring him around the shire, familiarising him with the southerly boroughs of his new fiefdom,' I fluttered a regal hand. 'Introducing him to the peasantry.'

'Will the folks in the local branches be welcoming?'

'There's bound to be some bitching about being taken for granted,' I said. 'Always is.'

'Think any of them will feel aggrieved enough to take a tilt?'

I shrugged. 'Somebody might have a rush of blood to the head, but I doubt they'll go the distance. The result's a foregone conclusion after all, isn't it?'

'Alan certainly hopes so. The push for a change of leadership is building up steam. Keeping this cross-factional deal on track will be the litmus test of his authority. But if the wheels come off, he'll have laid himself open to a challenge.'

'Only if there's a challenger,' I said.

A wolfish glint flashed in Thorsen's eyes. Hello, I thought. Could he be making a move at long last?

I looked around, mock furtive, and dropped my voice to a conspiratorial whisper. 'Strictly between you and me, Peter,' I said. 'Nobody could be worse than Metcalfe. Not even a ponce like you. And if you can cook up a spill, you've got my vote.' I put my hand on my heart. 'True dinks.'

He gave a sardonic smile. 'The Murray Whelan seal of endorsement.'

'But,' I said. 'Throwing the Coolaroo deal off the tracks, that'll take some doing. You'd need a spoiler candidate, the fly in Metcalfe's ointment.'

'Do you think there's any chance such a person might emerge?'

'Anything's possible. Plenty of wannabes out there. What you're after is a kamikaze pilot.'

'Quinlan has the numbers on the panel, so they'll get creamed in the final count,' he agreed. 'The important thing is to make a decent showing in the first round, the district plebiscite. The ideal stalking horse would be some local identity with a branch or two up their sleeve.'

The description fitted Mike Kyriakis to a tee.

'Somebody encouraged to run by a friend in the

parliamentary ranks?' I said. 'A hidden hand to steer him in the right direction.'

'Precisely. An MP without a vested interest in the current arrangements. Somebody committed to the renewal of the party. Somebody with an eye to the future.'

'Put away the trowel, Peter,' I said. 'What's in it for me?'

'Assuming this all pans out,' he said. 'How does a shadow ministry sound?'

'Like a hollow carrot,' I said. 'More work for very little gain.'

'But an assured seat at the grown-ups' table when we get back into office.'

'*If* we get back into office.'

Thorsen smiled placidly, conceding the point. 'Sooner or later the pendulum will swing back our way. And when it does, we'd better be ready. Not sitting around with cobwebs up our quoit.'

He went back behind his desk, the loyal deputy leader once more. 'We're speaking hypothetically, of course.'

'Naturally.'

If Peter had finally decided to take a shot at the boss cockie's job, he was approaching his target at a very acute angle. In all likelihood, he was simply testing the waters, sniffing the wind, flying a kite, laying some pipe. Whatever the case, I felt no pressing temptation to sign up for the ride.

Wait and see, that was the motto emblazoned on my escutcheon. Head down, tail up. There was fuck-all mileage in getting sucked into the machinations of the upper echelons.

Thorsen scrutinised my face with a look of bland innocence. I chuckled, shook my head slowly and stood up.

'Before you go,' he said. 'Brian McKechnie is heading off on a study tour of Europe at the end of the month. Looking into export opportunities for the alfalfa industry. We'll need somebody to cover his portfolio.'

'Agriculture?' I said. 'What do I know about agriculture?'

'Messy business, apparently. Sometimes you have to get your hands dirty.'

I went downstairs to the back door, heading for my office in the prefab annexe behind the House. The Henhouse, we called it. A cool front had arrived from the west, turning the sky into a roiling mass of rain clouds. The temperature had dropped ten degrees and gusts of damp wind whistled across the carpark. As I hunched my shoulders, bracing for the dash, my mobile phone rang.

'Mr Whelan? It's Kelly Cusack from the ABC. I wonder if you could spare me a moment of your time?'

She was perched on one of the banquettes in the vestibule, a laptop open on her knees, too deeply immersed in her work to cast more than a cursory glance at the comings and goings around her. From time to time, she compressed her telegenic lips and looked up absently, as though hunting an elusive phrase. I ambled past in the slipstream of a tour group, then detoured into the now-empty Queen's Hall, confident that she'd registered my presence.

Thirty seconds later, she found me waiting beside the statue of Victoria Regina, concealed from casual view by the royal plinth. A press pass was clipped to the lapel of her jacket and her laptop case was slung over one shoulder. She was all business.

'I don't have long,' she said. 'I'm on a flight back to Canberra at three. Is there somewhere we can go?'

Heavy drapes hung on brass rails across the archways at the back of the hall, separating it from the gallery outside the parliamentary library, an area off-limits to the public. I checked the way was clear, we slipped through the curtains and I led her down a carpeted corridor past the office of the Usher of the Black Rod, closed for lunch. Ten steps along, I pressed my shoulder against a section of the wood panelling. It swung open, revealing the dimly lit chamber of the Legislative Council.

The shop was shut, the portals locked, the lights switched off. A pale wash of daylight spilled through the high transom windows, illuminating the elaborate plasterwork of the barrel-vaulted ceiling and the gilt finials of the Corinthian columns. Reflected off the crimson plush of the benches, it bathed the whole space in a rosy glow. I shepherded the journalist inside and slipped the latch on the door, a discreet hatch used by the clerks when sittings were in progress. Up close, I could smell her perfume, musky and elementally feminine.

My hands found her hips and guided her back against the scalloped canopy of the President's podium. Her peripherals slid to the floor as I took one of her lobes between my lips and sucked her pearl stud.

She pushed me away, hoisted her skirt and peeled off her pantyhose. In the five seconds this took, I shucked off my jacket and tossed it across the back of the President's chair.

With a quick glance to double-check that we were still alone, we went back into our clinch. Her response was eager, a real buttock-gripper. As my lips slid over her cheek, she ran her palms up my chest and ground her hips against me. 'Is that a ceremonial mace in your pocket or are you just glad to see me?'

Too glad for words, I lunged for her earlobe again, running my hands up the inside of her jacket, one cupping the contents of her cashmere, the other savouring the sexy slither of her back, my fingers splaying as they neared the nape of her neck. 'The hair,' she squirmed. 'Don't muss the hair. You know the rules.'

No kissing was the other rule. It played havoc with her lipstick, she said.

Obediently, I slowed my pace, allowing things to take their time, what little time we had. Lust-flushed in the half-light, we gazed glassily into each other's eyes, confirming our mutual understanding of the situation.

This wasn't romance. It was an itch. And by Christ we were scratching it.

'Saw you at the Premier's casino thing.' My breathing was heavy with anticipation. 'Not exactly hard news.'

'Not as hard as something I could name.'

'Name it,' I begged. 'Name it.'

She did more than that. She put her mouth to my ear and tendered some encouraging recommendations regarding its employment. My fingers delved beneath her skirt. She was likewise engaged, negotiating a break in my strides. As I found the passage I sought, she seized upon the pressing issue.

'I hear there's a spill in the offing.'

With a handshake like that, she should have been in politics. She definitely had my vote of confidence. Maintaining her grip on proceedings, she edged towards the despatch table, towing me along behind.

'You want spill,' I muttered through clenched teeth. 'Keep glad-handing me like that, I'll give you spill.'

She shoved aside the chief clerk's chair and bent forward across the despatch table, cheek pressed to the baize. 'Thorsen's almost got the numbers, I hear.' She widened her stance, toes gripping the carpet, fingers curled around the bevelled edge of the hardwood. 'He's making all sorts of offers, they say. Thinking of putting your hand up?'

Not just my hand. I hefted her skirt, exposing her ivory orbs. My head spun with the sheer recklessness of it, the wanton folly. We could be sprung at any moment. The main doors would burst open and the chief steward would usher in a tour party of school children. It was utter madness. Again I scanned the room, confirming that we were unobserved.

'Who's this "they"?' My trousered thighs slid forwards into a valley of bare skin.

'My lips are sealed.'

'Liar,' I gasped, pressing home my point.

The slap of flesh on flesh, the carnal squish of congress, urgent and rhythmic, ascended to the chandeliers. Regal beasts, the lion and the unicorn, stared speechless from atop the President's podium. Mythic champions brandished their frescoed spears. The locomotive of progress hurtled onward, pistons pumping.

We'd been at this, intermittently, for almost a year. It had begun with a spur-of-the-moment, alcohol-fuelled shag on the fire stairs at the Meridian during some interminable awards dinner, something to do with medicine and the media. She was there to accept a Golden Goitre for a doco on pharmaceutical kickbacks. I was there as the shadow of the Shadow Minister for Health, who was recovering from a colonoscopy.

Introduced at the pre-dinner booze-and-schmooze, we'd let our eyes do the talking across the floral centrepiece during the leek tartlets, given our dates the slip half-way through the pan-seared spatchcock, and found ourselves going the slam against a concrete wall in the emergency exit somewhere between the Most Outstanding Contribution to Obesity Awareness and the Best Jingle in a Cough Suppressant Commercial. Fifteen minutes later, she was stepping onto the stage to accept her trophy, not a hair out of place.

No visible hair, at least. Several of her short and curlies were stuck to the roof of my mouth, a piquant textural counterpoint to the passionfruit panacotta.

Ours was a no-strings, no-promises, no-assumptions arrangement. It suited us both. She was married, I was amenable. If Kelly Cusack needed attention, I was happy to provide it, even at short notice and close quarters. We hardly ever talked politics. Or much else, for that matter. Too busy with the wham-bam.

Although she was fastidious about her appearance and circumspect in regard to our assignations, Kelly had a taste for quickies. What stoked her fire were knee-tremblers in risky locales, situations with a high prospect of having our coitus interrupted in flagrante. Since the episode in the hotel stairwell, we'd abandoned caution in the kitchenette of a corporate box at the tennis centre during the mixed doubles final of the Australian Open, in a fitting cubicle in the Myer menswear department, in the back of an ABC outside-broadcast van and between the buttress roots of a Moreton Bay fig in the Fitzroy Gardens. On the solitary occasion we'd taken a hotel room, she'd unpacked my lunch in the lift on the way upstairs.

But going the goat on the despatch table in the Legislative Council really did redefine the parameters of parliamentary privilege. My heart was thumping. My loins were pumping. My pulse was ringing in my ears. Ring-ring, ring-ring, ring-ring.

Not my pulse. A mobile phone. Close. Very close. Kelly abruptly jack-knifed upright, bucking me off at the exact moment my honourable member reached the climax of his oration.

She dived for her carry-all and tore it open. 'Helloo,' she warbled, chest heaving. 'Oh hi, darling.' She rose from the carpet, Eriksson pressed to her baize-burnished cheek. 'What? No, fine, just run up some stairs, that's all.' She mouthed her husband's name, as if I needed telling. 'What, right now?'

I teetered unsteadily, my legs jelly, my lap a swamp, my standard at half-mast, and plonked myself down in the President's chair. Kelly continued her conversation, domestic and therefore private, simultaneously wiggling back into her hosiery, counting her earrings, fluffing her cashmere and otherwise repairing her dishabille.

By the time I'd reclaimed my wetlands, zipped my fly and run my tie back up the flagpole, she'd finished her call and traded the phone for a vanity purse. She reapplied her lippy, checked herself in the mirror, then turned to me for confirmation that she didn't look like she'd just been schtupped in the consistory.

'You're a true professional,' I said. 'Best interview technique in the business. Pumping while you're humping.'

'I didn't get much out of you.' She patted her hair and smoothed her skirt.

'More than you realise,' I said. 'Miss Lewinsky.'

She reached for her rump, then jerked her hand back. 'Ick!'

I crouched behind her and sponged away my memorandum with a spit-wetted handkerchief, copping a feel while I was at it. 'Now what's this about Thorsen?' I said.

'I'll call you later.' She scooped up her kit. 'Must rush.'

I surveyed the corridor and gave her the all-clear. She sidled past, giving my bum a squeeze and my cheek a parting peck, then glided away, not a backward look, poised and purposeful. I plopped down in the place customarily occupied by the government whip, heaved a sigh and waited for my blood to settle. Seven minutes twenty-nine seconds had elapsed since we entered the chamber, a zipless PB.

As the coital fog ebbed, I contemplated Kelly's crack. The one about putting my hand up. What did she mean about Thorsen and the numbers? Was she working up a story? Was the cat already out of the bag, or was she just fishing?

I'd have no answer until she called me back. Even then, I'd be lucky to get anything out of her.

I consulted my watch. One o'clock. No wonder I was feeling peckish. Time for a smidge of the fast and easy.

Outside on the front steps, a photographer was posing a wedding party at one of the antique light stanchions, the bride's gown billowing. Nearby, a pair of teenage constables were keeping a bored eye on a cluster of subversive geriatrics, a thermos-fuelled vigil against the Formula One circuit in Albert Park.

I joined the lunchtime throng on the Bourke Street footpath, and spotted an empty stool at the window-bench of Tojo Bento.

Equipped with a plastic tray of yakitori nori and a squishy-fishy soy-sauce sachet, I parked myself at the bench and pried open a pair of disposable rainforest-timber chopsticks. As I sank my fangs into the seaweed, I unfolded Inky Donnelly's slim collection of photocopied newspaper clippings and began to read.

Alert and purposeful, Merv Cutlett stared into the middle distance, his jaw clenched in unwavering resolve, steely determination glinting in his gimlet eyes. His hair, thin but tenacious, was slicked back over his scalp and deep lines were etched into his sentinel face. He looked like a cross between a fox terrier and a sack of hacksaw blades.

The photograph was Merv's personal favourite. His Great Leader shot. He also liked Merv at Work, which showed him at his desk, staring out importantly from behind a redoubt of papers, important files weighed down by a hefty ring of keys, his emblem of office. For lighter stories, he favoured Merv Shares a Laugh, in which he appeared surrounded by a mob of admiring garbologists at the annual union picnic.

All three were regular features of the *FUME News* during my stint as editor. I'd not been at the Municipals long when the incident at Lake Nillahcootie occurred. Six months or so. Thinking back, I had no firm recollection of hearing the news about Merv's disappearance. No JFK moment. Many concerns occupy a man in his twenties, and the office is sometimes the least of them. Cutlett's drowning was a notable event, of course, but all I could recall with any certainty was the almost palpable sense of relief it brought to the Queensberry Street office.

As I studied Merv's photograph, tears flooded my eyes. Bloody wasabi. Honking into a paper napkin, I turned to the next photocopy.

It was a page from the *Herald*, Melbourne's long-defunct evening broadsheet. The date was written in the margin in Inky's shorthand scrawl. Saturday 27 July 1978. Refugee Influx Raises Fears, I read. Terrorist Bombing Shakes London. Record Profit for Qantas. Unionist Feared Drowned.

> *A search has failed to find any trace of prominent union official Mervyn Cutlett, 58, who disappeared this morning while fishing on Lake Nillahcootie north of Alexandra. According to police, Mr Cutlett was reported to have fallen overboard in rough weather conditions. Despite repeated attempts, his companions were unable to pull him from the water. Police said that heavy rain at the scene has hampered the efforts of emergency services to locate Mr Cutlett, who is head of the Federated Union of Municipal Employees. The alarm was raised by fellow union officials Barry Quinlan and Charles Talbot. Mr Talbot was treated at the scene for hypothermia.*

The story concluded with a statement from the officer in charge about the police being short-handed due to a call-out to assist victims of flooding in other parts of the district.

I'd forgotten about the weather, I realised. Even by Merv's standards, it was particularly perverse to drag a pair of reluctant fishing companions out onto a lake in what must have been miserable winter conditions. No wonder Charlie had copped a dose of hypothermia. The water must have been freezing.

The next report was lifted from the *Herald*'s stable-mate, the *Sun*. It was dated two days later, the Monday morning edition. It described a more extensive search, including the use of divers and a line search of the shore, but the headline summed it up. *Hunt fails to find unionist's body.*

A similar story appeared in the next day's *Age*. It was slightly better written but contained no fresh information.

Out on the street, the lunch crowd was thinning, scurrying back to the grind, shoulders hunched against the breeze. A young woman of the Oriental persuasion materialised at my elbow, washcloth in hand. A Chinese student, probably; about as Japanese as a California roll.

'Jew finish?' she said, whisking away my plastic tray and giving the benchtop a perfunctory swipe. 'July a trink?'

I ordered green tea. When it comes to coffee, the Nips are the pits. While I waited, I pondered the newspaper reports. Although they told me nothing I didn't know already, they'd begun to prime the pump of my memory.

Now that I thought about it, I seemed to remember that there were others up at the Shack that day. Colin Bishop? Someone else, too, but it eluded me for the moment.

In any case, the incident had faded into the background pretty quickly. With Merv out of the picture, the amalgamation proceeded apace. By the end of the year, FUME had been absorbed into the PEF. The Municipals' staff being surplus to requirements, jobs were slated for slashing and mine was high on the hit list. Charlie saw me right, though. Found me a full-time spot at the Labor Resource Centre, a policy think-tank tasked with cooking up a strategic vision to be enacted in the event that Labor ever got itself elected into government.

Which, in due course, it did. By then, both Charlie and Barry Quinlan had seats in federal parliament, Charlie in the Reps, Quinlan in the Senate. Our glory days were upon us. I was married to Wendy and Red was on the way. And Mervyn Cutlett, like the stegosaurus, had receded into prehistoric oblivion.

My green tea arrived, pallid but piping. While it was cooling down, I sucked air over my scalded tongue and ran my eye over the last of Inky's pages. An obituary from the *Labor Star*, official organ of the ALP, it summarised the salient features of Merv's biography.

> *Born 1920, youngest son and third child of a slaughterman. Apprenticed as a motor mechanic, then worked at Footscray Council maintenance dept before volunteering for the AIF in 1940. Service in North Africa, repatriated, rejoined the council. Shop steward, then elected to union executive in 1948. Sailed close to the communist wind but never carried a card. Emerged from the splits and ructions of the fifties as national secretary, a position he continued to hold for the next two decades. One of the longest-serving union officials in Australia, survived by wife and daughter, to whom the labour movement extends its sincere condolences.*

As intimate and revealing as your average obit, it revealed nothing about his personality, such as it was. On that subject, the Great Leader photo offered more clues.

In line with Charlie Talbot's advice, I'd kept my contact with Cutlett to the bare minimum. But once a month, I was compelled to enter his office in the Trades Hall to get his approval for the layout sheets of the *FUME News*.

'Look out,' he'd say. 'It's Scoop Whelan, our very own Jimmy Olsen.'

That'd get a big guffaw from Sid Gilpin, his spivvy sidekick. 'Charlie Talbot's bum boy,' he'd chorus.

Low-grade monstering, it might have got a rise out of a first-year apprentice. But it was like water off Merv's Brylcreemed comb-over to me. I wasn't there to bat the breeze. I was there to get the national secretary's sign-off so I could send the union newsletter to press.

Merv would put on his thick, big-framed reading glasses and carefully study the layout boards, all the while eyeballing me as if I was trying to pull a swiftie on him. Once he'd confirmed that his photograph did indeed appear on every second page, he'd grunt grudgingly and reach for his signing pen.

The pen was part of a brass desk-set fashioned from an expended shell casing. Merv's desk was a repository of such items. An ashtray on bullet legs. A cartridge cigarette lighter. A letter-opener with an anti-tank round for a handle.

At first I'd assumed Merv's cherished collection of museum-quality trenchware was a souvenir of his war service, a reminder of his front-line participation in the global conflict against fascism. But not according to Col Bishop.

'Merv never heard a shot fired in anger,' Col once told me. 'He was in the sanitation corps. The Royal Australian Shitshovellers. Got clapped up in Cairo then invalided home after the provos beat him to a pulp in a street brawl. But that's not something Merv cares to advertise. He just happens to like that sort of crap. And if people want to jump to the wrong conclusion, that's hardly Merv's fault, is it?'

Nor, contrary to the suggestion in his obituary, was Cutlett much of a family man. The wife might have survived him, but she was long gone. Gave him the flick some time back in the fifties, according to office rumour. The daughter—her name escaped me, perhaps I'd never known it—was sighted in his office occasionally, a listless lump of ageless frump whose resigned demeanour reinforced the assumption that old Merv was not worth breeding off.

He was definitely a dinosaur in his general attitude to women, for all his leftist posturing. The office 'girls', Margot and Prue, clearly did not relish their frequent trips to the Trades Hall to fetch or deliver documents. It was not for nothing, apparently, that they called him Merv the Perv.

I had no idea how his daughter felt about his disappearance, let alone the prospect that his remains had been resurrected from the mud at the bottom of Lake Nillahcootie. If identification of the remains involved DNA tests, she'd probably already had a visit from the police.

I pocketed the clippings and downed the dregs of my tea. Like I'd told Inky, Merv Cutlett's disappearance was a non-story. Even the most imaginative journalist would be hard put to suggest otherwise. If and when the ownership of the remains was confirmed, the whole business wouldn't be worth more than a couple of paragraphs, a historical postscript.

Vic Valentine, crime beat specialist, was probably just giving the trees a passing shake, see if anything interesting fell out. I'd be telling him not to waste his time.

As I was standing at the register, paying for lunch, my mobile rang. It was Inky.

'Re that drink with Valentine,' he rasped. 'He suggested somewhere in Fitzroy, a place called the Toilers Retreat. You know it?'

Valentine obviously had a sense of humour. The Toilers Retreat was a watering hole in Brunswick Street, a former milk bar that had been refurbished in the faux proletarian style. The name was part of the design. At least it wasn't the Hammer and Tongs or the Rack and Pinion.

'I used to live around the corner,' I said. 'What time?'

'Six-thirty,' he said. 'If your car's at the House, I'll cadge a lift with you. See you at six in Strangers Corridor, okay? Oh, and by the way, the odds have shortened on the deceased being Merv. Nothing official yet but I've just picked up an interesting bit of static from a mate at the Peaheads.'

The Peaheads were the PEA, the Public Employees Association, the government sector super-union. Originally the Public Service Association, it had become the PEA after absorbing the Public Employees Federation subsequent to the PEF's amalgamation with the FUME.

'Couple of days ago, they had a call from the constabulary wanting to know if they've still got the Municipals' old records.'

'Something in particular?'

'Membership rolls, payroll, financial accounts, that sort of thing,' he said. 'Circa 1978.'

'You reckon it's got anything to do with Merv Cutlett's bones turning up?'

'No names mentioned. A routine enquiry, whatever that means. Nobody at the Peaheads seems to have joined the dots. The Municipals were three amalgamations ago and corporate memory doesn't exactly run deep at the PEA. Lucky if they can remember as far back as breakfast.'

'They give the cops the records?' I said.

'In my experience, unions are reluctant to hand over their internal documents,' said Inky. 'But being a helpful lot, the

Peaheads said they'd have a poke around, see what they can find. Which will be exactly zip. The old FUME records were definitely BC. Before Computers. Nobody's got the faintest idea where they ended up. Long gone, probably.'

'How can twenty-year-old financial records help identify an old skeleton?' I said.

'You tell me, Murray,' said Inky. 'You tell me.'

Not much was happening in the Parliament House library.

A pair of dust motes were dancing a slow waltz in the air beneath the crystal chandelier. A century of Hansard was snoozing on the shelves, silent in its calf-leather covers. A scatter of documents and a writing pad lay unattended on the big octagonal reading table beneath the cupola.

The duty librarian, a studious-looking, carrot-haired young man in a boxy suit and tiny diamond ear-stud, was languidly staring into a monitor, occasionally tapping a key.

'G'day, Pat,' I said. 'Busy?'

'Frantic,' he said, deadpan, then tore his attention away from the screen. 'How may I assist you today, Mr Whelan?'

The parliamentary library prided itself on its ability to hunt down and capture almost any publication in the global vastness of the public domain. And do so with absolute confidentiality. I could have asked for the Olympia first edition of *Swedish Stewardesses on Heat* and Pat wouldn't have batted a pale-pink eyelid.

'I'm after the findings of a coronial inquest,' I said.

'That shouldn't be a problem.' He was clearly disappointed that it was not something more professionally challenging. 'Recent?'

'1978,' I said. 'Sorry.'

On my way back from lunch, it'd occurred to me that I might be able to rustle up a tad more information on the circumstances of Merv Cutlett's drowning than the sketchy outline provided by the newspaper reports.

At its last meeting, the Scrutiny of Acts and Regulations Committee had considered a slate of recommendations from the State Coroner regarding the mandatory wearing of life-jackets. Too many teenagers were dying in canoeing accidents and the rules on mucking around in boats needed tightening. Supporting documentation had included inquest summaries pertaining to accidental deaths on inland water-ways, some going back twenty years. The proposed legislative amendments were uncontentious, so I hadn't bothered wading through the files.

'It might even still be here,' I said. 'Pending return to the Coroner's office.' I gave Pat the details and he jotted them down.

'I'll get right onto it.' His attention was drifting back to the monitor.

'ASAP will be fine,' I said.

By then it was two-fifteen, time for the monthly meeting of the Public Accounts and Estimates Committee. I went upstairs to the conference room and took my seat at the table. It was a bi-partisan conclave, with Labor outnumbered six to two. The other Labor member was Daryl Keels, our

Shadow Finance Minister and chief number cruncher.

The meeting was chaired by the Treasurer, an abrasive, pug-faced Liberal dry with eyebrows like cuphooks and a Gorgon's stare guaranteed to freeze the wee in a Liberal backbencher's underpants. The main agenda item was gambling revenues.

In other states, poker machine licences were issued to sporting clubs, the earnings earmarked for community facilities. In our case, the Liberals had dished them out to friendly plutocrats in return for a slice of the action. And the action was going ballistic. Hundreds of millions of dollars were slipping through Lady Luck's fingers and into the state's coffers.

Social consequences be damned, it was money for jam. A bottomless goodie-bag that no future Labor government would be able to keep its hands off. As a policy issue, gambling was a lost cause. We were all sons of bitches now. All that remained was to dicker over the distribution of the whack, and Daryl did the dickering. Labor wanted more of the revenue allocated to health and education. As usual, we were defeated on party lines.

The meeting finished at four and while we were all packing up our papers, I chatted with Keels.

'Get your invite to the big event?' he said, shovelling a small mountain of facts and figures into his briefcase. He meant the casino opening. The proprietors had invited all state MPs and every federal MP from Victoria, irrespective of party.

'You bet,' I said.

As I spoke, I realised that I still didn't have an escort for the evening. What with Charlie's death, the whole thing had slipped my mind. It wasn't like I could ask Kelly. I knew who

I'd like to invite, but she was unavailable. Unattainable, I told myself sternly. My classmate from Greek lessons was not a potential date, she was a married woman. I should stop fantasising about her and get serious about finding somebody else.

It couldn't be too difficult. Even Keels had managed it, for all his bony arse and non-existent hairline. Recently divorced, he was putting himself about a bit, or so the gossip went. Doing okay, too, apparently. As the last of the Liberals left the room, he lowered his voice.

'This Coolaroo business,' he said. 'Alan's very keen that it goes without a hitch. This is no time for disunity. You're pretty close to the ground out there. No one's got it into their heads to play funny buggers, I trust.'

'You know me, Daryl,' I shrugged. 'Nobody ever tells me anything.'

When I got to my cubicle in the Henhouse, a couple of phone message slips were waiting for me. I returned Ayisha's call first.

'Barry Quinlan's office called,' she reported. 'The senator would like a word at your earliest convenience. I imagine he wants us to organise a meet-and-greet for the soon-to-be member for Coolaroo.'

'You've heard?'

'Phil Sebastian?' she said. 'It's going through the grapevine like a dose of the salts.'

Phylloxera, I thought, or sap. That's what runs through grapevines. Not doses of salts. 'Mike Kyriakis? Any word there? Is he still planning on making a run?'

'Far as I know.'

'Do me a favour,' I said. 'Press your shell-like a bit closer to the terra firma. Find out if any other hopefuls are lurking in the woodwork.'

'Sounds like you've been promoted to boundary rider,' she said.

'Let's just say I like to keep abreast.'

Just as I hung up, the phone rang. It was the library.

'I've got your report,' said Pat. 'Do you want the summary or the full transcript?'

As I'd hoped, the files had not yet been returned to the Coroner's office. Even better, some included the evidence tendered at the inquest in addition to the finding itself. I told Pat I'd come straight over.

'We close in half an hour.'

'I'll read fast.'

But first I called Barry Quinlan's office. I flipped open my diary as I dialled, expecting one of his buffers to organise the meeting with Phil Sebastian. The buffer, it transpired, was Phil himself.

'Murray,' he cooed. 'Listen mate, I'm sorry I missed you at Charlie Talbot's funeral. It must have been a shocking experience, you being there when he, er, went and everything. I wanted to personally tell you how much everybody here appreciates the job you did with the arrangements.'

'Yeah, well,' I mumbled. 'It wasn't the best of days.'

'Anyway,' he moved right along. 'As you've probably heard by now, I'll be his replacement.' He managed to make it sound like an onerous but inescapable burden, one he'd agreed to shoulder out of duty. 'So Barry suggested we get together, the three of us, and have you brief me on some of the specifics of the demographic. He's in Sydney at the moment, Telecommunications matters, but he'll be back in Melbourne on Monday. How does ten-thirty sound, here at Barry's office?'

One time's as good as another when you're being taken

for granted. 'It's in the book,' I said, scribbling it into my diary. 'See you then.'

'Before you go,' he said quickly. 'This thing on Sunday at Broadford town hall. I was thinking it might be a good opportunity to meet some of the locals. And to pay my final respects, of course. Two birds with the one stone, so to speak.'

'*Broadmeadows*,' I said. The idea of him working the room at Charlie's wake was too appalling to contemplate. 'I can see where you're going, Gil. But Sunday'll be very much a family affair, know what I mean. Bit of a closed shop.'

'Point taken,' he said. 'Monday, then.'

We kissed goodbye, I hung up and headed over to the library. The weather had changed yet again. The wind had dropped and the cloud ceiling had lifted to a high grey sheen. To the west, beyond the office towers of the central city, it was breaking open to reveal clear skies. By the look of it, Red would get his hoped-for wheel-time. As I walked, I fished out my mobile and dialled the other call-back number on my list. It belonged to Charlie's electorate officer, Helen Wright.

Helen had been hit pretty hard by her boss's death. Not only because they'd been friends and workmates for many years, but also because she was now facing an uncertain future. Phil Sebastian owed her nothing and once he was securely installed, he'd probably dump her and use the job to buy some local personal loyalty. Such was the nature of political patronage, and Helen knew it.

She'd called, she explained, to ask my advice.

'You've heard about Phil Sebastian getting the guernsey, I take it? Thing is, he's been trying to get in touch with me. The electorate office is closed for the duration, so he's been leaving messages on my voicemail. He wants us to meet as soon as possible, and for me to line up some introductions with branch secretaries. And, get this Murray, he wants to come to the wake.'

Helen was not just a brick, but a mate. I'd do my best to steer her right.

'It's up to you, Helen,' I said. 'You can always lie low for the weekend, plead family matters or whatnot while you make up your mind what you want to do. As for the wake, I've already spoken with him about that.'

'What did you say?'

'I told him to fuck off.'

She laughed. 'Nah, you didn't. You're better brung up than that, Murray.'

Since she was on the line, I asked if she knew of any other possible contenders. She didn't, but she'd heard talk that Dursun Durmaz, a state lower house member whose seat also overlapped Coolaroo, had been sniffing around, asking the same question.

Durmaz was a Concord faction footsoldier, Turkish by birth and thicker than chick-pea dip. If the Metcalfe forces were using him as their watchdog, they obviously weren't expecting problems.

'See you Sunday,' I said, ringing off as I stepped through the back door of Parliament House.

Climbing the stairs to the library, I wondered if Durmaz, too, had been made an offer by Peter Thorsen. He wasn't the brightest bauble in the bazaar, but he was a political opportunist of the first water. If the tide was beginning to turn against Metcalfe, Durmaz would be among the first to jump ship.

Up in the library, Pat handed me the coroner's file and

pointed to the clock, a reminder that my time was limited. I pulled up an antique chair, flipped open the file and began to read.

Thirty minutes later, as arranged, I found Inky Donnelly waiting in Strangers Corridor, an elongated antechamber that served as a public restaurant area for Parliament House visitors. He was nursing a coffee, absently gnawing a shortbread as he studied that morning's *Australian*.

'Hold the presses,' I said. 'Breaking news in the Cutlett carcase case.'

Inky peered up at me, biscuit poised in mid-air, waiting.

'He's not dead,' I said.

Inky stubbed out his coffee and brushed the crumbs from his lapels, and we plunged into the entrails of Parliament House, weaving our way along corridors lined with portraits of forgotten politicians and bronze busts of colonial mugwumps.

As we steered for the rear exit, we were met at every turn by the hail-and-farewell of scarpering MPs, pub-bound young staffers and home-heading bureaucrats. Five-thirty on a Friday night and the joint was emptying faster than a pensioner's pocket at the pokies.

'Officially, Mervyn Cutlett is not dead,' I repeated. 'He is merely missing.'

Inky grunted impatiently. 'I've got that much,' he said. 'I'm not fucking senile, you know. What I'm asking is why the inquest?'

The sooner I got that glass of milk into the grumpy old codger the better.

'Normally, the proceeds of an estate can only be distributed on production of a death certificate. No corpse, no certificate.'

'No certificate, no probate.'

'Exactly,' I said. 'Only way to expedite execution of his will was have an inquest.'

'Who were the beneficiaries?'

We went out the back door into the carpark and I pointed my keys at the Magna. 'No idea,' I said. 'The family, presumably.'

Inky made a pained face, lowered himself into the passenger seat, popped an antacid and eased the seatbelt over his dyspeptic midriff. The boom gate rose and I turned towards Fitzroy, joining the line of cars backed up at the lights beside St Patrick's cathedral.

'The Coroner's verdict was death by misadventure,' I said. Inky gave a belch of relief. 'An interim finding,' I added, '*Pro tempore.*'

'*Coitus interruptus*, eh?'

'In theory, I suppose. But for all intents and purposes *consummatus est.*' The lights turned green and we inched forward. '*Per omnia secula seculorum.*'

'Let's hope so, Murray.' Inky eyed me sideways. 'Let's just fucking hope so.'

At any other time, Brunswick Street was a five-minute trip. Peak hour, the traffic was moving with all the urgency of a sedated sloth. To aggravate the situation, a fire engine emerged from the Eastern Hill fire station, sirens blaring. As I negotiated a stop-start crawl through the fray, I gave Inky the gist of the testimony in the coronial record.

The Benalla magistrate heard the case eight months after the event. Under oath, the witnesses confirmed their original statements to the police and answered detailed questions.

According to Charlie's testimony, the purpose of the weekend trip to the lake was to discuss work-related issues at the union's purpose-built country retreat. They travelled there in separate parties, making the three-hour trip from Melbourne in two cars, one driven by Charlie, the other by Quinlan.

Charlie and Merv got to the Shack about eleven-thirty in Charlie's union-issue Falcon. Barry Quinlan and Col Bishop arrived half an hour later in Quinlan's car. Sid Gilpin had been left behind, due to a mix-up about the departure time.

Immediately prior to leaving Melbourne, Merv had been drinking at the John Curtin Hotel. He was 'somewhat intoxicated' when Charlie picked him up at the Trades Hall. Charlie, who had not been drinking, did the driving. Merv slept for most of the trip. On arrival, they each had a can of beer, then several more when Quinlan and Bishop turned up at midnight. Before retiring for the night at one a.m., Merv took a nightcap of rum and cloves.

'Yum, yum.' Inky smacked his lips. 'The working man's all-purpose tonic.'

Cutlett woke the others about seven and proposed that they go out in the Shack's boat and catch some redfin for breakfast. Despite the cold and fog he insisted, claiming the conditions were perfect for fishing. Colin Bishop refused but 'for harmony's sake', as Charlie's testimony stated, the other two reluctantly agreed. Under Merv's direction, the boat was wheeled from the shed, launched and tied up at the Shack's short jetty. Merv consumed a 'phlegm cutter' of Bundaberg rum but appeared to be in full control of his faculties.

All three were dressed heavily against the cold and they took along a thermos of coffee laced with rum. Nobody wore life-jackets. Merv drove the boat, a 6.3 metre Catalina with a half-cabin canopy. Visibility on the water was poor, but Merv was familiar with the lake and navigated the boat confidently into an area some two hundred metres from the jetty, then stopped the motor and tied-off to a dead tree projecting from the water. They fished for around fifteen minutes without success before moving to another spot, again tying off to a tree. The fog began to rise and a heavily timbered section of the shoreline was visible, but neither Quinlan nor Charlie had a definite sense of their exact location.

After about twenty minutes, the fish still weren't biting and they had finished the coffee. Prompted by questions from the court officer assisting the Coroner, both Charlie and Quinlan stated that it contained 'a high proportion' of alcohol. The weather was rapidly becoming threatening and they decided to immediately return to the Shack. As Merv was casting off from the dead tree, a squall front hit. Torrential rain began to fall. As Merv hurried to untie the rope, the boat turned in the wind and he toppled overboard.

He thrashed wildly in the widening gap, the wind pushing the boat beyond his reach. Quinlan and Charlie tried to grab him, but he went under almost immediately. While Quinlan tried to get the boat started and bring it back around, Charlie jumped in and attempted to reach him but he'd disappeared beneath the surface. Charlie duck-dived, trying to find him, but his efforts were futile. The water was pitch black, lashed by the rain and freezing cold.

By the time Quinlan got Charlie back into the boat, he was shivering uncontrollably. They returned immediately to the Shack to get help. When they got there, they found that

Colin Bishop had been joined by Sid Gilpin, who had arrived while they were out on the lake.

Gilpin tried to ring for help, but the phone at the Shack was locked—standard procedure when the place wasn't in use—so he drove to the nearest roadhouse and raised the alarm. While this was happening, the other two helped Charlie out of his wet clothes and thawed him out in front of the fire.

A police constable on traffic patrol near Mansfield was directed to attend. On the way, he stopped off at the home of the regional State Emergency Services captain and within forty minutes there were six boats on the lake. They included the Catalina, which Gilpin had taken back out on his return from summoning help. Charlie and Quinlan gave fairly precise directions to the scene of the accident, but the wet and blustery conditions doomed search efforts to failure.

By the time the diving team arrived the next day, the worst was assumed. Efforts to locate the corpse were fruitless. Underwater visibility was zero and the compression ratios at that depth limited dive times to a matter of minutes. According to the officer in charge, there'd have been a better chance of winning Tattslotto than finding a body. Weighed down by clothing, lungs filled with water, it would soon discharge its gases and settle on the bottom, between five and fifteen metres down, depending on the precise location.

Citing alcohol and the absence of life-jackets as contributing factors, the magistrate handed down his interim verdict and consigned the case to the files.

'Straightforward enough,' summarised Inky. 'But it doesn't tell us why the cops want to get their hands on the Municipals' old records.'

We cleared the tangle of traffic and I cruised down Brunswick Street, scouting for a parking spot.

'Maybe this sensation-mongering jackal of the gutter press can shed some light on the subject,' I said, slowing as we neared our destination.

'Yeah but let's keep it under our hats for the moment,' said Inky. 'See what Valentine has to say about it first.'

Spotting an opening, I threw a U-turn in the face of an oncoming tram and snaffled a spot directly across the road from the Toilers Retreat.

In the five years since I'd moved from Fitzroy, its landmark strip of pubs, funky cafes, knick-knackeries, record stores, bookshops and kebab boutiques had continued to creep up the hill towards the city. With their usual eye to the revenue potential, Yarra Council had jacked up the parking meter fees and erected time-limit signs of such baffling complexity that a team of Philadelphia lawyers armed with atomic clocks would've been hard put to escape a ticket. I double-checked the sign and fed every coin I possessed into the meter.

The Toilers Retreat was buzzing with a boisterous Friday evening crowd. Young persons on heat, the weekend ahead, anticipation in the air. Over-loud music ratcheted up the drinking rate and pool balls clicked. Vic Valentine wasn't hard to identify. Apart from us, he was the only one in the joint over thirty.

He was tending a beer at a corner table, eye to the door. By way of identifying himself, he raised his chin.

The journalist was a spare, spindly type with a sharp-featured rodent face. His head, almost perfectly spherical, was shaved as clean as a burnished hazelnut. He wore a hairline moustache, a faint, self-deprecating smirk and a black leather motorcycle jacket. He was maybe forty.

'Fuck me,' muttered Inky. 'It's Zorro.'

I nodded towards Valentine's glass. He held it up. Beer, almost empty. Same again, thanks. While Inky elbowed his way to the bar, I went over, sat down and introduced myself. Valentine asked after my son and explained how he'd picked up on the Merv Cutlett connection. At the time of the drowning, he was a cadet, working general rounds at the *Herald*. One of the more senior journalists had covered the original search, but the discovery of the remains rang a bell when Valentine picked it up in the daily feed from police media relations.

Inky arrived with two beers and a Guinness, its foamy head as close as he was prepared to come to a glass of milk. '*Sláinte*,' he said.

We all took a convivial sip. Then Inky put his glass down, wiped the foam from his lip and leaned across the table towards Valentine. 'Ground rules,' he rasped. 'This conversation is strictly off the record. Background only.'

Valentine stared around, innocence itself. 'Noisy, isn't it? Can hardly hear myself think.'

That settled, we got down to it.

'What do you want to know?' I said. 'There's slim pickings in the Municipals for a crime reporter.'

'Maybe,' said Valentine. 'But if those bones turn out to be Mervyn Cutlett's, there might be a three-course banquet.'

He paused while Inky and I exchanged wary glances.

'Go on,' said the Ink.

Valentine took a sip. 'Two-way street,' he said. 'I'll show you mine if you show me yours.'

'Okay,' said Inky. 'Show.'

'You first,' said the journalist. 'What can you tell me about a bloke named Sid Gilpin?'

'He was one of the union's organisers,' I said.

'And what exactly did he organise?'

I shrugged. 'The usual stuff, I assume. Resolved minor workplace disputes. Liaised with the shop stewards. Kept an eye on membership subscriptions. Out and about, on the road, maintaining a presence.'

As I said it, I realised something that didn't quite gel. All the other organisers worked out of their respective state offices. Gilpin reported directly to Merv Cutlett. Whatever his job description, it wasn't on the organisational chart.

'Mate of yours?'

I made a noise like I'd swallowed a fly. 'Not my speed. I was mid-twenties. He was a fair bit older. One of the safari-suit squad. University of Life and don't you forget it, pal. He thought I was an over-educated, up-myself nancy boy.'

'How about him and Cutlett?'

'Thick as thieves, so to speak,' I said. 'Matter of fact, he was on the scene the day Merv drowned. The first to go out looking for him.'

Inky shot me a warning glance, reminding me not to get ahead of the game. 'What's your interest in this Gilpin, Vic?' he said.

'He rang me. Unsolicited. He said he'd heard of me, asked if I was aware of the recent discovery at Lake Nillahcootie. Flagged the name Cutlett. When I expressed interest, he claimed he had evidence that Cutlett was the victim of foul play.'

He took a long, slow sip, studying our reaction over the rim of his glass.

Inky snorted dismissively. 'What evidence?'

'Proof of corruption, he said. But he wouldn't go into specifics, not without being paid. Started talking telephone numbers. I told him it didn't work that way. If he had reason to believe a crime had been committed, he should go to the cops.'

I glanced at Inky. Could this explain the police visit to the Peaheads?

'And did he?' Inky pondered his Guinness. 'Go to the cops?'

'You'd have to ask them,' Valentine shrugged. 'I was hoping you might be able to shed some light on the subject.' He meant me. 'Any intimations at the time?'

The bar was getting noisier and more crowded by the minute, all elbows and belt buckles and tribal tattoos. I wondered why Valentine had chosen it.

'If there were, I never heard them,' I said. 'Which isn't to say there might not have been some pub talk. It was the seventies. Conspiracy theories were thick on the ground.'

Valentine took a tin of baby cigars out of his motorbike jacket, unwrapped one and tapped the end idly on the lid. 'And the Municipals were clean, you reckon?'

'As the driven?' I said. 'Maybe not, but the opportunities for graft were minor league. As for foul play, the idea's got whiskers all over it. The cops were there within minutes. There was a full-on search of the scene. Anything suss went down, somebody would've noticed something. And Gilpin testified at the inquest. He uttered not a peep about anything untoward.'

'Perhaps he found out later.'

'Perhaps he's pulling your chain.'

'Why would he bother?'

'Buggered if I know. He got the bum's rush from the

union soon after Cutlett's demise. Maybe he's been pining for revenge. Maybe he's just trying to hustle up a dollar.'

'Fishing in troubled waters?' said Valentine. 'Stirring up the mud?'

Inky grunted. 'Mud's got a tendency to stick. What's this Gilpin do now? Who does he work for?'

'He's a dealer.'

'Drugs?' I was genuinely surprised. Sid had chancer written all over him, but drugs were something else entirely.

'Junk.' Valentine smirked. 'Rubbish.'

He waved a demonstrative cigarillo at the Toilers Retreat's tone-setting collection of blue-collar nostalgia. Bushells Tea and Castrol Oil signs adorned the walls. An old Bundy clock stood on the bar. Toolbox assortments embellished the bottle shelves.

'He did quite well for himself in the eighties, I hear. He had a big old barn of a place up Upwey way. A former foundry or superseded smithy or some such. Stuffed it full of brass doorknobs, cast-iron lacework, Golden Fleece petrol bowser lights, all the usual crap. Called it a flea market and made a killing in Australiana.'

Sid would've been ideally placed to go into the junk business, I thought. The Municipals' members included garbage collectors and rubbish tip attendants. The Outcasts of Foolgarah. Gleaners and fossickers with their treasure troves of the cast-off and chucked-away. A man with Sid's connections could really clean up. Buying the stuff at fifty dollars a trailer-load, recycling it into instant authenticity and selling it for whatever the market would bear. Turning old tin into pure gold.

'About ten years ago, the joint burnt down,' Valentine continued. 'Suspected arson. Nothing proved but the insurance company wriggled out. Gilpin lost the lot. Lock, stock and Early Kooka. After that, everything turned to shit. Wife left him, children turned their backs, dog died. He hit the skids and hit the bottle. The whole country music ball of twine. These days, he's down to his uppers, flogging dross out of an old nissen hut across from the cargo sheds at Victoria Dock.'

I vaguely remembered a rusting wartime relic half lost in the eyesore industrial jungle between the wharves and the railyard.

'Has he tried to sell this so-called story to anyone else?' said Inky, back to the point.

'He spoke to some of my esteemed colleagues. We all told him the same thing. If you've got evidence, take it to the police.' Valentine shook his head, benignly amused at the human capacity for self-delusion. 'People read something in the paper, they start seeing dollar signs.'

'But you're not dismissing him out of hand,' said Inky. 'So either you've got a lot of free time or there's something you haven't got around to sharing with us.'

Valentine eyed me sideways. 'Is he always like this?'

'Dyspepsia,' I said. 'It makes him crabby as all hell.'

Valentine twiddled his Wee Willem. 'What happened to our quid pro quo?'

Inky picked up his stout, poured a long draught down his throat, wiped his mouth with the back of his hand and nodded.

'I've been given to understand the rozzers are making enquiries about the Municipals' old membership accounts,' he said.

Valentine was nonchalant, wheels turning in his hairless head. 'Interesting.'

'Is it?' said Inky. 'Why?'

The journalist made a show of mulling his response. Then he leaned forward and dropped his voice, drawing us into his huddle.

'Because it might tie into something else the boys in blue are keeping very close to their silver-buttoned chests. Something a little birdie told me about those remains.'

Inky and I leaned closer, elbows on the table, all ears.

'It's a dry argument.' Valentine sat back and surveyed the bottom of his glass. 'A man could perish.'

As I fought my way back through the press of bodies, crab-gripping three glasses, the corner of a bag of peanuts clenched between my teeth, my phone began to ring.

I let it ring off to voicemail and deposited my load.

Inky had gone for a slash, leaving Vic to hold the table. The journalist picked up his beer and nodded towards a guy coming through the door, a beefy young lump in a buzz cut and Cockney-crim pinstripe suit, tie loosened, eyes darting around the room like startled goldfish.

'My next appointment,' he said. 'Jason's in the wholesale pseudoephedrine business, or so it's been alleged in a slate of charges currently before the County Court. He's taking me to see a man about a dog. Or maybe it's vice versa.'

Jason spotted the journalist's chrome dome and began homing in. Vic flashed him ten fingers, buying us some time, and the speed-vending slugger veered off to join a group of hyperactive boyos who were hogging the pool table.

Inky returned, drying his hands on a handkerchief. 'So, Vic,' he said sceptically. 'You were saying?'

Valentine tore open the bag of Nobby's finest, laid them out on the table. 'You know the Institute of Forensic Medicine? AKA the morgue?'

I'd done the tour, part of some committee or other. The place was new, state-of-the-art, disaster-ready. It was housed in the same complex as the Melbourne Coroner's Court.

'Did they tell you about their in-house wireless communications network?'

I nodded, then explained to Inky. 'There's an internal radio link between the autopsy suites and the typing pool. By the time the pathologist has rinsed his scalpel and binned his gloves, a print-out of his notes is ready for checking and signature.'

Valentine moved his head forward, again drawing us into a conspiratorial hunch. 'That little birdie I mentioned, he's a technology buff. He's also a forensics fan. He likes to combine his two hobbies. He sits outside the Institute with a scanner and a set of earphones.'

He paused while we conjured the image.

'Sick, isn't it? I really should report him to somebody. But he's harmless enough and whenever he picks up a transmission he thinks might interest me, he gets straight on the blower. Which is what happened last week after they brought in the hessian sack from Lake Nillahcootie.'

Inky's eyes were growing less twinkly by the second.

'For what it's worth, I've got the tape,' continued Valentine. 'The examination is categorised as preliminary but what it boils down to is this. Only the larger bones remain—pelvis, thighs, upper arms, cranium. Reasonably well preserved considering the passage of time and the ravages of the creepy-crawlies. The owner was a mature male aged somewhere over fifty, approximately 170 centimetres tall with mild osteoporosis. Teeth in the upper jaw were long gone, indicating the corpse wore dentures.' He paused and flicked a peanut into his mouth. 'How are we doing so far?'

'Fits Mervyn Cutlett's general description,' I said. 'Shortish, right age group, probable chopper wearer.' Dentures were virtually standard issue for members of Merv's class and generation. You got a full extraction and a pair of clackers on your twenty-first birthday, save yourself further trouble and expense.

'Now here's the interesting bit,' said Valentine. 'Wear on some of the bones consistent with rope friction. Plus trauma to the parietal plate in the form of a circular perforation of approximately six millimetres diameter.'

He leaned low over the table, displaying the bare back of his depilated noggin. Using the tip of his miniature cigar, he gave it a sharp, demonstrative tap.

'Conclusion,' he said. 'He'd been tied up and shot in the back of the head.'

My eyes widened in disbelief. 'You've got to be kidding.'

I tore the parking ticket off my windscreen and read the penalty by the light of the lava lamp bubbling in the nearest shop window. Fifty bucks, straight down the toilet. Inky shovelled a handful of Quik-Eze into his face and grunted.

Across the street, outside the Toilers Retreat, I could see Vic Valentine getting into an illegally parked BMW, his dope-dealing informant Jason behind the wheel. 'It's extortion, pure and simple.' I squinted up at the four paragraphs of fine print on the parking sign.

The implications of Valentine's startling revelations about the pathology examination were still sinking in. They were alarming, unfathomable and as welcome as a prawn cocktail in a kosher deli.

'The whole idea's ludicrous,' I said. 'If the remains are really Merv Cutlett's, then Charlie Talbot and Barry Quinlan must've shot him and dumped the body in the lake.

Assisted by Colin Bishop. We've got two MPs and the pro vice-chancellor of a university guilty of murder and criminal conspiracy. It beggars belief. Did they kill him somewhere else? Did they lure him up to the Shack and do it? Did something happen while they were there that escalated? Where did they get a gun? Who pulled the trigger? It's patently absurd.'

Inky nodded. 'You don't kill somebody over a union amalgamation,' he pointed out. 'No matter how tempting.'

Which was what we'd told Vic Valentine when he dropped his bombshell. And he admitted that it did seem an unlikely scenario. Fortunately, for the moment at least, he wasn't actively pursuing the story. For a start, the pathology report wasn't publishable, given its provenance. And the remains were yet to be definitely identified as Cutlett's. Matters were now in the hands of the Homicide Squad and he was content to let the story play itself out before writing it up.

Meantime, he had the imminent outbreak of a gang war to occupy his attention. The Beamer peeled away and we watched it disappear down the street.

'What do you think Gilpin's playing at?' I said, pocketing the poxy parking infringement notice.

Inky's mind was elsewhere. 'I think it might be a good idea if you had a word with Barry Quinlan,' he said.

'Me?' I asked. 'Why me?'

He crunched his antacid and gave a choleric scowl. 'Me and Bazza aren't exactly Bogie and Bacall. It's a long and tedious story dating from the Hawke–Keating showdown. Suffice to say, I wouldn't get through the door.'

'Yeah, well,' I said grudgingly. 'So happens I'll be seeing Quinlan on Monday. You think it can wait until then?'

'It's been waiting for nearly twenty years, it can wait

another couple of days. No point getting our underwear in an uproar. Like the man said, it's still provisional.'

'If this is what it looks like…'

'If this is what it looks like, it's going to be the shitstorm from hell. We don't want to find ourselves anywhere near it.' He held out his arm and a taxi pulled up. 'You hear anything else, let me know.'

And on that less-than-illuminating note, the leprechaun climbed into the cab and fucked off, leaving me holding the crock. And it most definitely wasn't full of gold.

The street was coming alive with dreadlocks, pierced appendages and ravenous vegans. I fished out my mobile and called Red. The lad was at home, divesting the refrigerator of its remnant leftovers before heading to a farewell party. His mate Tarquin was flying out on Sunday for six months' study in Japan.

'Say sayonara from me,' I instructed. 'Don't get wasted. Don't take any of my beer. And be home by one-thirty.'

'Are we still on for the driving thing tomorrow?' he said. 'The weather report says fine and mild.'

'We'll see,' I said. 'But all bets are off if you're not home before curfew.'

I checked my voicemail. I got the last caller first.

'This is Detective Constable Stromboli, Mr Whelan,' said a male voice. 'Homicide Squad. If you get this message before eight, please call me back this evening.'

By ten to eight, I was at the northern limits of the Coolaroo federal electorate, out where the tract housing finally gave way to market gardens, stud farms, small wineries, golf courses and bare paddocks. Tullamarine Airport was ten minutes behind me, a phosphorescent glow in my rear-vision mirror.

The house stood at the end of a gravel driveway, both sides planted with rows of vines, a curtain of natives shielding it from the road. As I turned off the asphalt at the letterbox marked TALBOT–FOLLBIG, my headlights swept the outbuildings.

First the old dairy shed in which Charlie turned his minuscule *vendage* into Chateau Coolaroo, a quaffing red guaranteed to put fur on the tongues of his Christmas list of friends, colleagues and constituents. Then a triple carport, swathed in Virginia creeper, where his maroon Lexus was parked beside Margot's Audi and a little red Mazda 323 that

I assumed belonged to the young woman who looked after Margot's daughter Katie. And finally the chateau itself, low, sprawling and unostentatious, the brick of the original homestead rendered in whitewash.

Katie heard my car arrive. She was waiting behind the screen door, her chubby face beaming.

'Mum, Mum,' she called. 'It's Muh-ree.'

I waited for her to open the screen, knowing she liked to do it herself. She was almost thirty, stocky in a dusty-pink tracksuit, with the slanting, ageless eyes that announce Down Syndrome.

'Hello, Katie.'

As I stepped inside, I touched the back of her plump hand. She went shy, blushed and gave me a disconcertingly coquettish look. I followed her rolling gait into the living room, a welcoming space with muted lighting, soft cushion-strewn couches and a large refectory table from which Margot rose to meet me.

Her eyes were tired, her face was scrubbed and her ash blonde hair was drawn tight behind her ears but she was still easily recognisable as one of Mavis Peel's girls from the FUME office. The original Charlie's Angels, the big-hair brigade.

'Murray,' she said. 'Good to see you.'

We hugged gently, motionless in each other's embrace. Television sounds came low from somewhere deeper inside the house and Katie's carer appeared.

'Hello, Sarah,' I said, remembering the girl's name. She was a serious young insect with bobbed hair and glasses, a part-time student who lived in a self-contained flat attached to the house.

'Hi,' she said. 'C'mon, Katie. Let's say goodnight to Mr Dobbs.'

They disappeared, off to the stall where Katie's elderly pony was stabled.

Between them, Charlie and Margot had done well. Their pooled resources had funded a comfortable set-up and Margot would never need to worry about money. But it had been a struggle for her, especially in the early years. A single mother, a disabled child, no formal education past secretarial school. And now what? Picking up the pieces, facing the future alone, the material comforts scant compensation.

'Help yourself to a drink,' she said, sliding open one of the glass doors onto the flagged patio that overlooked the side lawn. 'Let's have a fag.'

There was an open bottle of white on the table beside a heap of unopened envelopes. I got a glass from the usual cupboard.

We stood, wine in hand, smoking and staring into the darkening space where they'd pitched the marquee that summer day, eight years earlier, when she and Charlie finally tied the knot.

'How's Katie taking it?' I said.

'She's still waiting for him to come home, I think. It's all a bit much for her to grasp.' Margot exhaled hard and sucked her cheeks, holding herself back. 'I think I'm still waiting, too. But that's normal, isn't it?'

A dead partner, that was something else we had in common.

'You never really get used to it,' I said. 'But you get on with it.'

'I'm sorry,' she said. 'It's just…' The sentence trailed off and silence hung between us, more expressive than words.

She abruptly extinguished her cigarette, screwing it into a terracotta pot-plant saucer on the heavy redwood garden table. 'You'll stay for dinner, I hope.' She started back inside. 'I've got a lot of casseroles need eating.'

The refrigerator was stacked with funerary meats. Gestures of sympathy in plastic tubs and floral pattern Corningware, the offerings of neighbours, friends and constituents. A fortnight's supply at least.

'Got any tuna mornay?' I scanned the collection. 'Apricot chicken?'

'Don't be mean,' tutted Margot. 'You'll eat what you're given and you'll like it. Open another bottle while I heat something up.'

She blitzed some condolence stew in the microwave and we sat at the big refectory table and poked at it. I asked about her plans.

'Back to work,' she said. 'Everyone's been wonderful, of course. Staff, clients, everybody. But the place won't run itself. Or maybe it will, which would be even worse.'

She owned a travel business, Fliteplan. A niche outfit with three staff in the Melbourne office and two in Sydney. Together with Prue, the other typist at the Municipals, she'd set it up when the amalgamation made them redundant. Charlie helped arrange finance, making good on his promise that he'd see everyone right. With their experience of organising travel for FUME officials and their contacts among the women who did likewise at other unions, the pair soon had a thriving operation. They broadened out into the corporate sector and by the late eighties they were doing well enough for Prue to sell her half to Margot and take early retirement.

'So, you're not tempted to pack it in?' I said.

'And do what?' She swept the air with the back of her hand. 'Revive my career as an international supermodel?'

I shrugged. 'Something different.'

'Maybe,' she conceded. 'Eventually. But it's not something I want to think about right now.'

'No, no,' I said. 'Of course not.'

She gave me a reassuring smile. 'How's your goulash?'

'Rubbery,' I said. 'Dericious.'

'Gina Schiavoni's tiramisu might be a safer bet.'

I ate two helpings and made some coffee to finish off. While it was perking I asked if she was going to the wake. She shook her head firmly. That side of Charlie's life was now a closed book. 'But tell them thanks for all the support,' she said.

The bottle I'd opened with the alleged goulash was almost empty. Margot was out-drinking me, two to one.

'Snort of port with your coffee?' she said.

'Better not. Run into a booze bus on the way home, it's more than my job's worth.'

Katie came through the archway leading to the bedrooms. She had Sarah by the hand, as if for moral back-up.

'We've come to say goodnight,' announced Sarah. 'Say goodnight, Katie.'

Katie blushed furiously. 'Goodnight, Muh-ree,' she declared, then scuttled away with the ambivalent finality of a woman terminating an over-long engagement.

While Margot went off for the bedtime ritual, I took a cup of coffee outside for a smoke. After a few minutes, she joined me once more on the terrace. I nodded towards the lawn, a rectangle of deep darkness where the lights of the house bled out into the night.

'You were like a couple of teenagers that day,' I said. 'Prancing around the dancefloor, that god-awful cover band playing old Buddy Holly tunes.'

'Teenagers?' she snorted. 'Hardly.'

'Okay, thirtysomethings.'

'That's better. Barefaced flattery, but closer to the mark.'

She lit a cigarette and tapped the ash on the edge of the terracotta saucer. I screwed my courage to the sticking point.

'I don't know if you heard about it,' I started, 'but they found part of a skeleton up at Nillahcootie. The lake's been drained apparently, some sort of maintenance work. They're still working on the ID, but it looks like it might be Merv Cutlett.'

'So I understand,' she nodded. 'As a matter of fact, the police came to see me this afternoon about it. A man and a woman. Plainclothes. They were very nice, sorry to intrude at a time like this and all that. They asked if Charlie had told me much about the accident. They're trying to get a more precise picture of exactly what happened. To help with the identification, they said.'

She inhaled deeply, as if catching her breath, and looked upward towards the faint engine roar of a northbound plane. Its wingtip lights were pulsing pinpricks of red in the encompassing void of the sky.

'I don't think I was much help. Charlie never really spoke about it, not back then and not after we got together properly. I think he felt guilty.'

'Why would he feel guilty?'

'You know what Charlie was like,' she said. 'Probably blamed himself, thought he should have done more.'

The moon was rising, a pale crescent above the raked vines. Margot shivered slightly and wrapped her arms around herself.

'Did they know you were working at the Municipals when the accident happened?'

'They didn't say. I was Margot Barraclough back then, of course.'

I knew the story. Barraclough was Katie's father's name. When she fell pregnant, Margot had told her parents they were married. She and Barraclough had gone their separate ways by the time the child was born, but Margot continued with the pretence. It was only when she was starting the travel business that she went back to Follbig, her maiden name.

'It's just that I've had a message to call them,' I said. 'I think they might be doing the rounds of anyone who was at the union at the time.'

Margot furrowed her brow. 'Why?'

'You remember Sid Gilpin?'

'Oh yes,' she said. Her tone made it clear she remembered him only too well.

'Thing is, he's bobbed up in the wake of these remains, trying to flog some yarn about corruption at the union.'

She turned to me, fierce. 'That little weasel. He's not saying Charlie was corrupt is he?'

I patted the air, a mollifying gesture. 'So far nobody's taking him seriously. But Charlie not being here to defend himself, you never know what kind of bullshit might find its way into circulation.'

'The union was a long time ago.' Her voice had taken a flinty edge. 'But I'll tell you one thing for sure. If I ever hear anyone cast the slightest doubt on Charlie Talbot's honesty, I'll wring his neck, so help me. Charlie was the finest, most ethical man I ever met. He could've had me anytime he wanted. An affair, anything, and he knew it. But he was married to Shirley. He'd made his vows and he kept them. Never so much as touched me until he was a free man, more's the pity. You think somebody like that is going to put his hand in the till for a few dollars? Sid Gilpin wasn't fit to tie his bootlaces.'

I sat there, abashed, until the heat went out of her.

'I'm sure it'll all blow over, Margot,' I said. 'I just thought you should know, that's all.'

She sighed wearily, then reached over and squeezed my forearm. 'I know, Murray,' she nodded. 'I'm sorry.'

She took her hand away and used it to brush her eyes. Then she stood and gathered up my cup, her glass and the ashtray.

'Anyway,' she said. 'It wasn't Buddy Holly. It was Chuck Berry.'

'It wasn't Jimi Hendrix,' I said. 'That's for sure.'

She walked me to the front door, pausing on the way to press a Pyrex dish of non-specific pasta bake into my hands.

'If there's anything,' I said. 'Anything at all.'

'I know.' She smiled tightly. 'I know.'

We embraced again. This time, she seemed as fragile as a sparrow. And when I stood at the car door and waved back at her, framed there in the doorway, she looked brittle enough to snap in half.

At six the next morning, I tossed back an orange juice and laced up my trainers.

Twice a week for three years, I'd risen in the dark to drive Red to rowing, then run for thirty minutes on a treadmill in the gym at the City Baths, reading the newspapers while I jogged. It wasn't much but at least I was making an effort. After Red switched from dipping his oar to treading the boards, I slipped out of the habit of regular exercise. Another winter of puddings and gravy and my decline would be irreversible.

It was do or die. I went out the back gate and began thumping down the path to the river.

A heavy dew had fallen and the lawns were dark and sodden, still untouched by the pearly tinge spreading from the eastern horizon. By the time I reached the bottom of the slope, my lungs were raw and I was dizzy from exertion. Where the grassy slope ended and the path entered the trees,

I stopped for a second to catch my breath.

On the high ground across the river, the old lunatic asylum was taking shape against the dawn sky. It, too, would soon be luxury apartments. A waste, I thought, what with madness on the rise.

I jogged for half an hour, easing my body back into the groove. As I ran, I thought about the scraps that had blown across my path the previous day. Politics abhors a vacuum, and Charlie Talbot's death had created one. Ambition was being sucked in from all directions. And despite myself, I could feel the inexorable tug.

It was a dead-set certainty that we'd lose the next state election. If we were lucky enough to win the one after that, I'd have spent ten years in opposition. Even if I entered government as a junior minister, I'd be shin-deep into my fifties, my future behind me. It wasn't an encouraging prospect. On the other hand, I wasn't exactly spoiled for choice, career-wise. After a lifetime in politics, I was ruined for useful work.

And then there was the business of the Nillahcootie bones and Sid Gilpin's mischief-making. Having slept on it, I was even more convinced that I'd been slipped a tinfoil sixpence. The remains might not even be Merv's. Even if they were, there could be any number of explanations for the hole in his head. And anyway, Sid Gilpin had no credibility. The coppers would soon have it sorted.

The day was shaping up as forecast, the opening act of what might be the last weekend of fine weather before the onset of winter.

As I staggered through the back door, aching in unaccustomed places, a girl was coming out of the bathroom. She was bleary-eyed and tousled and creeping softly so as not to wake anybody. Glancing back down the passage, she noticed me, gave a little wave and let herself out the front door.

Her name was Polly, or perhaps Molly, or Milly. She was one of Red's school friends, part of the gang. Her parents, if I remembered right, were both medicos of some kind.

Red had arrived home just after midnight, a small entourage in tow. He'd stuck his head around the bedroom door, found me reading and we'd made our goodnights. Around one-fifteen, my sleeping ears registered muffled shushes and heavy-footed tip-toes at the front door. Evidently, not all of Red's visitors had departed at that point.

By the time he emerged from the Stygian gloom of his bedroom, I'd showered, donned my Country Road casuals, breakfasted and almost finished working my way through the weekend broadsheets. It was pushing nine and he was running late for the train that would get him across town to the Knitting Mill Youth Theatre.

'All systems are go for your driving lesson,' I said, watching him simultaneously inhale a muesli bar, fall into his clothes, brush his hair, find his travel card and grab his script. 'I'll pick you up at one, okay?'

He nodded enthusiastically, gave me the thumbs up and rushed out the door. I checked the number on my voicemail and rang DC Stromboli.

'Thanks for getting back so promptly, Mr Whelan,' he said. 'We're attempting to identify some human remains recently found at Lake Nillahcootie which may possibly be those of Mervyn Cutlett, the former secretary of the municipal employees' union. In the course of our enquiries, we're seeking the assistance of a number of people who used to work for the union. Is there a convenient time in the next few days for me to ask you a few questions?'

'Fire away, Constable.'

'I'd prefer to speak with you in person, if possible.'

He didn't need to explain how he knew that I'd worked at the Municipals. I'd had enough dealings with the law over the years, not least during the business with Lyndal and matters arising, to warrant an entry in the police database. A keyword search of the union would've thrown up my name. Not everybody who worked there would be quite so easy to track down, I suddenly realised. Which possibly explained the police interest in the old union records.

'Your place or mine?' I said. 'Whichever you prefer. I'll be catching up with some paperwork at my electorate office between ten and twelve this morning if that's convenient for you.'

It was. I gave him the address and rang off.

Larder, refrigerator and cellar were all looking wan, so I ducked into Safeway on the way to the office. As instructed, Red had refrained from nicking off with my last half-dozen cans of beer. He'd simply invited his friends home to consume them *in situ*. I made a mental note to dock his allowance and give him a sound thrashing. Just as soon as I'd interrogated him about his overnight guest.

I'd made some work-related calls and shuffled some paper around my desk by the time Detective Constable Stromboli knocked on my door around eleven-thirty.

He was younger than he sounded on the phone. A tall, solid man with close-cropped hair that was starting to whiten, he wore his suit like he still trying to get the hang of it.

'Robert Stromboli,' I said. 'I did wonder about the name. You're the bastard cost us the 1985 semi-final, aren't you?'

A Robbie Stromboli had played three seasons with Collingwood in the early to mid eighties, one of those patchy footballers who has his occasional dazzling moment, then fades away. Stromboli's flash of glory happened when he snatched the ball from the pack at the first bounce of the 1985 semi, went through the Fitzroy backline like cod-liver oil and booted it straight between the big ones. Twenty seconds, go to whoa. We stayed behind for the rest of the game.

'I did my bit,' he said. 'But I can't claim credit for the entire thirty-seven-point margin.'

'You broke our spirit,' I said, extending my hand. 'Come in, Detective Constable, tell me how I can be of assistance.'

He gave me a brief pump and a resigned, collegial look. The sooner we get this nonsense out of the way, the sooner we can get back to our proper work. The manner was relaxed but the shake was all copper.

'I won't keep you long, Mr Whelan,' he said, settling into my visitors' chair and taking out a small notebook. 'If we could begin with a brief outline of your history and duties at the union and the extent of your contact with Mr Cutlett.'

I obliged, trying to keep it succinct. He nodded along and made a few scribbles.

'Do you happen to know if Mr Cutlett wore a wrist-watch?' he said.

I thought for a moment and answered truthfully. 'Can't say I ever noticed.'

The detective took an envelope from his jacket pocket and handed me two Polaroids.

'Anything here jog your memory?'

The photos showed a yellow-metal watch, front and back views.

'A number of items were found in the vicinity of the remains,' explained Stromboli. 'Buttons, some one and two cent coins, but this was the only personal object. We're hoping somebody might recognise it.'

It was a sports watch, a thing of winders and knobs and subdials. The clasp-lock band was undone and the hands were stopped at 11:17. Seiko Sports Chronometer, read the name on the face. Limited Edition.

'Still under warranty?' I said. 'It says "Guaranteed water-proof to 60 metres".'

Stromboli smiled. 'It's a knock-off.'

I studied the Polaroids carefully. The watch face had a distinctive rotating bezel, day and date, and an alarm function, but it didn't ring any bells. I shook my head and handed back the snaps. 'I thought it was all DNA and whatnot these days.'

'In the works.' Stromboli pocketed the Polaroids. 'But it takes time. We're still in the process of locating family members.'

The sentence ended on an interrogative note. I shook my head again. Sorry, couldn't help there either.

'Meanwhile, it's old-fashioned methods,' he said, the foot-slogger who'd copped the door-knocking job.

'But you're pretty sure it's Merv Cutlett?'

He crossed his legs, keeping it conversational. 'On the balance of probabilities, it seems likely. The only other reported disappearance in that area was a child who drowned back in the sixties. The nature of the remains rules that one out.'

He consulted his notebook, flipped some pages then asked if there was anybody else connected with the union who I thought might be able to assist. 'Interstate officials and so forth?'

I thought for a moment and gave him some names. Three of them were still involved in union and public affairs. One worked for an employer organisation. Stromboli noted the names and details.

'I assume you've talked to Barry Quinlan and Colin Bishop,' I said.

He nodded. 'It's a pity we can't speak with Mr Talbot, who was also there at the time,' he said. 'I understand that you had a close relationship with him over a number of years. Did you ever talk about the incident?'

I put my elbow on the desk, rested my chin on my balled fist and had a think.

'Not that I can bring to mind,' I said, eventually. 'I was well down the union totem pole. Our friendship developed later. By then, we'd both moved on a fair distance and the subject never came up.'

'How did Cutlett get along with his associates, the ones at the lake the day he disappeared?' He consulted his notebook. 'Colin Bishop?'

'They had a reasonable working relationship, far as I know.'

'Charles Talbot? Barry Quinlan?'

'Likewise.'

'I understand that there was a degree of friction in the union.'

Understood from where, I wondered? 'Friction?'

'Cutlett was a bit of prick, wasn't he?'

I had to laugh. 'Obstreperous, let's say. And, yes, there were differences of opinion concerning the direction of the union. Management issues. Nothing of a personal nature, if that's what you're getting at.'

'And the assistant secretary, Sid Gilpin?'

'Gilpin wasn't assistant secretary,' I corrected him. 'That's an elected position. Gilpin was a sort of personal assistant. I wasn't privy to their relationship.'

He scribbled something in his pad. 'One last question, Mr Whelan. Were you ever at the union place up at Lake Nillahcootie?'

'The Shack?' I said. 'Afraid not, Constable. The decadent pleasures of Lake Nillahcootie were the preserve of the elect, not minions like *moi*.'

The detective pocketed his notebook, uncrossed his legs and stood up. 'Thank you for your time, Mr Whelan.' He indicated the clutter on my desk. 'I'll leave you to it.'

I showed him to the door and waved him off, hoping I'd played it right.

Stromboli wasn't giving anything away, which was only to be expected. But our little chat had raised more questions than it answered, at least for me.

There'd been no mention of the forensics, for a start. Was that because they'd arrived at a different explanation from the one Vic Valentine was trying out? Something a bit less melodramatic?

The questions about relationships within the union, on the other hand, didn't seem relevant to ID-ing the remains. So were the cops going with the shooting scenario, but still not showing their hand? Were they looking for a possible motive?

And the watch. What the hell was that about?

It was true I'd never noticed if Merv wore a timepiece. But I was damned sure of one thing. If he had, it wouldn't have been a flashy chunk of tomfoolery like that boy-bangle in the Polaroids.

Merv was the sort of bloke who wore a cardigan with his suit. For special occasions, he might've had a Timex Oyster self-winder with an expandable strap. Day-to-day wear was more likely to have been a Casio digital one-piece with a black plastic band. Merv, to strain a threadbare metaphor, wouldn't have been seen dead in a Seiko Sports Chronometer with stopwatch, day/month calendar and phases of the moon.

So who did the watch belong to?

I slid back my cuff and examined my own timepiece. It was ordinary but accurate. The time had arrived, it told me, to extract my digit.

Red's grip loosened a notch and the blood flowed back into his knuckles. We both heaved a sigh of relief as the massive semi-trailer moved further ahead of us, taking its buffeting slipstream with it.

'Speed,' I said.

Red flicked a glance at the dash, checked the rear-view mirror, eased back on the accelerator and turned his head just far enough to give me a wide smile. Pilot to co-pilot. So far so good.

The first half-hour had been stressful, both of us anxious during his neophyte negotiation of the cross-town traffic. Still, I thought, anxious was good. Better than overconfident. When I proposed a spin up the Hume, some open-road motoring, he'd jumped at the chance. Now that we were on the dual carriageway, he was cruising, pace steady, alert but not alarmed, enjoying himself. There was even scope for conversation.

'So what's this play about?' I said. 'Rosybum and Goldenpants Are Deadshits?'

'*Rosencrantz and Guildenstern Are Dead*, by Tom Stoppard,' he said. 'You know *Hamlet*?'

'Not personally. But I'm familiar with the type. Chronic existential indecision interspersed with fits of violent rage. You see a lot of it in my line of work. You're drifting into the emergency lane.'

He corrected his steering. 'Well, this is a play about the play within the play.'

This Stoppard geezer should be writing for the Labor Party, I thought. Red took a hand off the wheel for a second and jerked his thumb back over his shoulder, indicating the dog-eared script on the back seat.

'Hear me my lines,' he said. 'I was fluffing big time at the walk-through.'

'Hands at ten-to-two,' I said sternly. 'Stay in the left lane, no faster than eighty, and watch out for dickheads. We're in the country now.' Bypassing Kilmore to be precise, seventy kilometres north of town. Not exactly the mulga, but you can't be too careful once the houses run out. 'And no fluffing in the car.'

I flipped through the script, a mass of scribbled annotations and post-it notes.

'Tell me again, which one are you?'

'The Player.'

'Ah, yes,' I said. 'Which reminds me. That little friend of yours I noticed leaving the familial premises at the crack of dawn. Ellie? Polly? Molly?'

'Madeleine,' he said. 'Maddie.'

'I knew it was something like that. The point being, is this something serious?'

'Or what?' he said. 'Am I just using her for sex?'

'Well, are you?'

'Maybe she's just using me.' He eyed me sideways. 'Are you giving me the third degree?'

'That comes later,' I said. 'For the moment I'm simply exercising some natural parental interest in your activities.' Jesus, I thought. Listen to yourself. You'll be talking about your roof next, insisting on your right to know what goes on under it. 'You're being careful, I hope.'

'I won't knock her up, if that's what you mean.'

I winced at his bluntness. But Red's age-group had been raised on condoms, so to speak. If nothing else, AIDS had reconnected sex and consequences, two concepts my generation thought it had sundered forever. But it wasn't the idea of an unwanted pregnancy that worried me as much as the prospect that he'd mistake the ride for the destination. That what began as a fumble on the futon would end with a stomped-on heart. His.

'Abstinence has a lot to recommend it,' I said.

'The voice of experience?' He put his hand on the indicator lever and checked me sideways for the go-ahead to pass a puttering tractor.

I cleared him to overtake. 'The old dog's got life in him yet.'

'Yeah?' Red did the Groucho eyebrow dance. 'Anyone I know?'

We were going places I'd rather avoid. As we swept around the Massey Ferguson, I gave the driver a cheery wave. The constipated old cockie ignored me. Probably a One Nation supporter. Didn't he know tractors aren't allowed on the freeway?

'I'm glad we had this little chat, son. I'll reassure

Madeleine's parents next time I see them.'

Red moved back into his lane. 'They don't mind.'

Oh well, great then. Clearly, I was the last to know. As usual. I flipped through the pages. 'So where do we start?'

'Page 17, half-way down. You're Rosencrantz.'

The place was marked. '*What's your line?*' That was the line.

'*Tragedy, sir,*' declaimed the young Olivier. '*Death and disclosures, universal and particular, denouements both unexpected and inexorable…*'

The speedo was creeping towards ninety. 'Ease back a little,' I instructed.

'No, it's supposed to be hammy,' he said. 'I'm in character.'

By the time we were shot of Elsinore, he'd been behind the wheel for two hours straight and we were almost in Benalla.

'Need a break?'

He gave his head a vigorous shake. Nothing short of a crowbar would've got him out of the driver's seat. 'Then hark us hence homeward via the scenic route, what sayeth thou?'

'Aye, my lord.'

We turned south along the Midland Highway, two lanes of blacktop that curved through open, rolling farmland and scrubby bush, double lines for long stretches. The traffic was light, but the driving took all of Red's concentration.

We were coming back over the hump of the Divide. The Strathbogies lay to our right and the peaks of the High Country reared distantly to our left, bare bouldery shapes emerging from thick timber. The radio commentary had the Lions down 51–77 and the weather was looking iffy. The sky had turned from high and hazy to low and broody. I was splitting for a piss.

'Pull in here,' I said. 'We'll stretch our legs and I'll spell you for a while.'

Red eased it back nicely and turned into the landscaped picnic area at the Lake Nillahcootie weir. I directed him along an unpaved track between some big shade trees until we reached the high-water mark.

'Wow,' he said. 'Somebody pulled the plug.'

The bare bottom of the lake sloped away to dark, wind-rippled water at the sheer concrete cliff of the dam wall. The waterline reached no more than a quarter of the way up the 25-metre embankment, leaving the spillways at each end gaping uselessly, high and dry.

The water extended for half a kilometre or so, then narrowed to an elongated tadpole-tail that snaked away across the exposed lake-bed. An intermittent picket of long-dead trees marked its path. Those closer were footed in water, the more distant fully exposed.

We got out and drained our personal reservoirs against the trunk of a big redgum. No call for modesty. We had the place to ourselves.

'Let's check out the weir,' I said.

Access to the dam wall was barred by the chained gate of a cyclone fence. The construction camp was locked down, its cluster of Porta-sheds and heavy equipment deserted for the weekend. YOUR TAXES AT WORK, read the sign. KEEP OUT.

'So, Dad,' said Red. 'What are they doing?'

Once upon a time, I'd been a policy advisor to the Minister for Water Supply, so I was able to give him the benefit of my expertise.

'Buggered if I know,' I said. 'But I guarantee it's both

necessary and expensive.' Necessary, most likely, to the ongoing job security of the local National Party member. Expensive in that it cost a packet.

The weir had been thrown across a choke-point where the Broken River narrowed to a gorge. From the footpath above, we looked down into the rocky cleft, thick with trees and undergrowth. The clouds were glowering and the wind, heavy with the smell of rain, was rattling the treetops. I didn't know why I was there.

We went back to the car. I slid the driver's seat forward a notch and drove further along the highway, its course running parallel to the elongated bed of the lake. Trees marked the far shoreline, a kilometre away, thinning to pasture. The situation at the MCG had not improved, 64–91 at three-quarter time.

'A bloke I knew was killed out there,' I said. 'A couple of years before you were born.'

'How?'

Good question.

'Fell out of a boat while they were fishing. He'd been drinking and he wasn't wearing a life-jacket.'

'Let that be a lesson, young man.'

''ken oath,' I said.

The Shack, in whatever form it now took, lay somewhere on the far side, invisible up a short inlet formed by the undulations of the terrain. The inquest papers I'd scanned in the Parliament House library included a sketch map of the lake showing the location of the Shack and the spot where Cutlett was last seen. A photocopy would've been handy but I hadn't thought to make one. Why would I?

'They never recovered the body,' I said. 'But about ten days ago a couple of blokes found bits of a skeleton while they were poking around out there, looking for old stuff.'

'Yeah?' Red was interested. 'Where?'

'Let's have a squizz,' I said, 'see if we can work it out.'

The road and the lake diverged, separated by a low rise capped with a cluster of buildings surrounded by trees. A school camp, some sort of private religious college. Just past it, a weathered sign announced BARJARG ROADHOUSE 300M, the paint peeling. An unpaved side road led back towards the lake. I turned down it and found the claypan again.

Despite the general dryness of the season, Melbourne had seen two rainy days and a smattering of intermittent showers since the middle of the previous week. Up here, it had possibly been even wetter. In any case, it was impossible to miss the churned-up margin and the deep ruts running about two hundred metres out towards a cluster of bleached tree-trunks and a string of shallow pools.

'Over there,' Red pointed. 'See the bits of plastic tape?'

The ground was gouged open and the tracks included deep caterpillar treads. I wondered what sort of equipment the police had brought in to sift the sludge.

'Looks like they did a pretty thorough job of trying to find all his bits and pieces,' I said.

I tried to conjure up a mental picture of the Coroner's sketch map. If I had it right, the Shack was somewhere in the trees beyond the fence line where the edge of the cleared paddocks ran ruler-straight to the shoreline. But Charlie and Barry had certainly got their geography skewiff. The place they reported losing Merv was a good five hundred metres closer to the dam wall. The search had been concentrated in the wrong area.

I cruised along the road another couple of hundred metres, hunting for the turn-off to the Shack. A well-maintained road led in the right direction but it was barred by a locked gate. Private Property. Trespassers Prosecuted. Cows lifted their heads and loped towards the fence. I turned the car around and we went back to the highway.

The Barjarg Roadhouse was somewhere between picturesque and primordial, a weatherboard throwback that looked like it had been erected to cater to the passing bullock-dray trade. In front of a bull-nosed veranda enclosed by expanding garden trellis, the petrol bowsers stood naked on a raw dirt apron. The only concession to amenity was an arbour at the side, an outdoor eating area roofed in shade cloth with a tan-bark floor, two pine-log tables and a green wheelie bin.

'If we can't get a sausage roll here,' I said, 'I'll eat my socks.'

'If I don't get something into me soon,' Red replied, '*I'll* eat your socks.'

The interior was a dim, lino-floored general store whose main lines were apparently fishing tackle, dust and jumbo tins of Pal. A man in a faded flannel shirt with a beer gut and a head like a pontiac potato sat on a stool behind the counter, talking to a man in a faded flannel shirt with a beer gut and a head like a glaucomic wombat. Strangers to the service economy, they ignored us.

I peered across the counter at the pie warmer. Its solitary sosso roll looked like it had been smuggled through customs in a body cavity. 'See if they've got any chocolate-coated socks,' I told Red.

We hunted up a late lunch of BBQ crisps and lolly water and piled our selections on the counter. Flannel-back number one broke off his riveting monologue about what he'd told Kev about Brian's attitude to Goose for long enough to ring up the damage. $7.85. I took a five out of my wallet, emptied my pants pocket onto the counter and sifted through my small change for correct weight. Red gathered up the comestibles and went out to the car.

I caught up with him as he was opening the driver's-side door. The little bugger had snaffled my keys. 'Hold up,' I said. 'You've done okay so far, but it's getting dark and looks like rain. Let's not push it.'

'Just a bit longer,' he pleaded.

'Give,' I said, holding out my palm.

He stood his ground. 'Just a few more kilometres.'

As we faced off, a fully loaded logging truck barrelled past, spitting volleys of gravel in our direction. A few seconds later, we heard the crunch as it shifted down a gear.

'You want to sit behind that monster for half an hour?' I said. 'Or are you planning on overtaking it?'

Red considered the options, shrugged and slapped the keys into my open hand. 'Worth a try.'

I floored the pedal, hit the radio button and we laid into the carbohydrates. The final siren was two minutes away but it might as well have been two hours for all the difference it made. At the close of play the score was 71–102. Our nineteenth consecutive loss at the MCG, said the word from the commentary box. Not bad. After all, this was our first season, *per se*.

We overtook the logging truck in good order and headed back through Mansfield.

'Any plans for the evening?' I asked.

'Videos at Max's.' He was making an early night of it, due to a shift-swap deal that would have him shelving cornflakes for most of the following afternoon.

'Seeing Madeleine tonight?'

He waggled his hand, *que sera sera*. 'You?'

'Probably not,' I said. 'She's playing hard to get.' This was greeted with the silence it deserved.

'Since you're asking, I'm presenting the trophies at the Somali Youth Association regional basketball finals.'

'Hope your arms are long enough,' he said. 'Some of those kids are so tall they have to reach down to shoot for goal.'

My gig was at seven-thirty. I sat on the speed limit and took no prisoners as dusk descended around us. I kept thinking about the lake, wondering how Charlie and Quinlan had managed to be so far off the mark. Even allowing for the lack of distinctive landmarks, it was a wide margin of error. Yet both swore that's where Merv went down.

On a long straight strip just before Tallarook, crows were picking at a carcase by the side of the highway. A fox maybe, or a possum. They flapped upwards at our approach, and when I glanced back in the mirror, they'd settled again, beaks in the mess. It was an image that stayed with me until the sky broke open and torrents of rain threw themselves against the windscreen.

After that, there was no room for thought of anything but the way ahead.

Obsessive punctuality is a vice rarely practised by those who have fled to these shores from the war-torn Horn of Africa, so nobody at the Somali Youth Association was fussed by my slightly tardy arrival at its northern region basketball final. The official start time was merely indicative, after all.

Abdi Abdi, the association president, showed me to my place with the other dignitaries in the Fawkner Park Sports Complex gymnasium just as the whistle sounded. On the bleachers opposite sat an undemonstrative crowd of snaggle-fanged Mogadishu matriarchs, egg-shaped and taffeta-swathed, each attended by a retinue of long, lissom girls with oval faces and gazelle eyes. The menfolk of the community were not much in evidence. Presumably they were busy driving taxis and drinking glasses of tea.

The collective clout of Melbourne's Somali population was yet to be tapped but its potential had not gone unnoticed. The evening's fixture had attracted a number of representatives of the body politic whose interest in both Somalia and basketball was tangential at best.

I, of course, was one of them. As was the mayor of Darebin, whose bailiwick included the housing commission estate in West Heidelberg, and the Legislative Assembly member for Yorta Yorta, Ken Crouch.

Ken sat two seats away, on the other side of the imam from the Brunswick mosque. The holy sheikh was blind and wore dark glasses. He spent the match smiling wildly and rocking in his seat, Stevie Wonder in a green turban. Ken spent most of it on the phone, a frown on his dial and a finger jammed in one ear.

At the half-time break, he unbuttoned beside me in the urinal and revealed the reason for his distraction.

'This fucking preselection deal,' he groused. 'It's turning pear-shaped.'

Ken was the Shadow Minister for Community Services and a steadying hand on the tiller of the Left. His state lower house seat overlaid the Coolaroo federal electorate to an even larger extent than mine, so he had a territorial as well as a factional interest.

'ALP preselections don't turn pear-shaped, Ken,' I said. 'They're born that way.'

In this case the paternity of the pear rested with Barry Quinlan.

As soon as word of Charlie Talbot's death got around, Ken explained, the party's national executive was besieged by aspirant replacements. Every come-again kid, voter-ousted ex-minister, wannabe-politico union official and me-next machine oiler was knocking on the door, flourishing their credentials. All claimed to be perfect for the job, due to either proven experience, self-evident talent, string-pulling

123

skills or the principles of affirmative action.

Sensing a major affray, and constrained by the deal already cut guaranteeing the next federal vacancy in Victoria to the Left, the executive handballed the fingering job to Barry Quinlan. Barry had dibs on the spot, but nobody specific lined up to fill it. Finding common cause with Alan Metcalfe, who didn't want a drawn-out brawl in his backyard, Barry nailed down a fast-track timetable and shoe-horned Phil Sebastian into the slot. Phil's major qualification being that he wasn't owed or owned by anyone else.

All this had happened while I was escorting Charlie Talbot's corpse from Mildura, seeing it into the tender hands of Tobin Brothers Family Undertakers and conferring with the various stakeholders as to the manner, location and scheduling of its interment.

'Made sense at the time,' said Ken, directing himself to the stainless steel. 'And it still makes sense.'

But no sooner had the bell sounded on round one than the would-be contenders were up off the mat and shaping up for round two. Quinlan had exceeded his brief, they were muttering.

Unsurprisingly, the loudest mutterers were those he'd given to understand could count on Barry's support whenever the next vacancy arose. And Barry being a master of the dangled expectation, there were plenty of those. All of them members of his own faction.

'I've been on the blower 24/7 since Phil Sebastian's name came out of the hat,' complained Ken as he shook the drops off the end of his dick. 'Hosing down half the Left.'

'You're in an unenviable position, Ken,' I said, hitting the flush button.

'I think there's a very real chance of a split.'

'In the Left?' I zippered up. 'You're kidding. You've already split more times than a hyperactive amoeba. Do it again and you'll be holding your meetings in a Petri dish. For Chrissake, Ken, there's only eight of you still standing.'

'Not the *state* Left, Murray.' He spoke as though to a particularly obtuse child. 'The *federal* Left. If the right candidate steps forward, he or she could drive a wedge through Barry's numbers on the selection panel. Split the Left wide open.'

'The right Left candidate?' I said.

'That's right. And that'll leave the Left in a right mess.'

'I see,' I said, washing my hands. 'Better get back to the game. I think the Kensington Giraffes stand a very real chance of a comeback in the second half.'

But Ken was already back on the blower, damping down the embers of smouldering discontent.

By ten o'clock my duty was done. I'd stood with assorted Abdis, the shadow minister, the mayor and the mufti and handed cups and trophies to a line of slope-shouldered, toothy youths. I'd shaken the tips of their feather-light fingers, partaken sparingly of the potato-crisp and Fanta supper and called it a medium-long day.

While performing my bedtime ablutions, I studied my face in the mirror. More shop-worn cases walked the earth, to be sure, but my lifelong battle with gravity was entering its decisive phase.

At fifty, they say, a man has the face he deserves. Fifty wasn't far away, almost as close as the millennium. What had I done to deserve this particular countenance?

'At least you've still got your own teeth,' I reassured myself. I took a closer look. 'Most of them.'

As I fell into that slumbering state that passes for the sleep of a parent—a sober one, anyway—a sharp sound cut the faint swish of the distant traffic. The jarring, metallic screech of brakes.

It sounded like an axe being ground.

The rain that sluiced the roof that night had cleared to a persistent drizzle by seven-thirty, so I togged up and hit the exercise track again, drawstring tight on the hood of my lightweight nylon slicker.

Where it wasn't drizzling, it was either dripping from the trees or leaking through my elastic. A pair of kayakers hurtled downstream, chasing thrills down the Yarra's swollen bacterial brew. Head down, I focused on the way ahead, mouth working as I pounded the pavement.

'Γρηγορα,' I croaked, pushing the guttural γ from the back of my throat onto my palate, then rolling the ρ across the tip of my tongue. 'Ο γατος γρηγορα ηπιε το γαλα.

'The cat drank the milk,' I translated for my own benefit. Bloody wet cat, this morning.

On Sunday mornings, an informal gathering of my class-mates from the Greek course met for coffee, cakes and conversation practice at the Archeon Cafe in Lonsdale

Street. My participation was intermittent at best, but I'd missed the last three lessons, so it would be a way of getting back into the linguistic swing. That's what I told myself anyway, as I sloshed along the riverbank, sweating into my slicker and performing unnatural acts with the fleshy folds of my maxillary tuberosity.

By the time I'd showered, downed my cereal, read the papers and made my leisurely way into town, Lonsdale Street was parked out by the first-sitting yum cha crowd streaming into Chinatown. I wasted twenty minutes cruising for a vacant space, then put the Magna in the carpark under the Daimaru cookware department and walked the two blocks to the Archeon. At the hoardings surrounding the Queen Victoria Hospital site, I couldn't resist looking through one of the viewing windows into the massive hole which had once been the maternity wing. Eventually, an international hotel would arise in the spot where Red had first drawn breath. Or a shopping complex, or an office tower, or some indispensable combination of all three. For the moment, it was just an empty, puddle-dotted crater and the prospect of a year's work for a thousand construction workers.

Finally, fully half an hour late, I reached the intermittent string of tavernas, pastry shops, worry-bead emporia and travel agencies that constitute Melbourne's official Greek precinct. In fine weather, we had our practice chit-chats at one of the tables on the footpath outside the Archeon. But the rain-specked tables were deserted. Even by hardy Melburnian standards, this was no day to go alfresco.

I peered through the window and scanned the interior, a tasteful combination of chrome-frame chairs, ripple-glass tabletops and mirror-tiled walls. Wogarama Deluxe. The

Archeon was a popular Sunday brunch spot and business was brisk. The place was chockers. Women with brass hair, men in expensive tracksuits, their fat kids and people who couldn't get into yum cha.

I spotted our little *kafeneon*-klatsch at its usual table in the back corner, away from the worst of the bustle and shielded from the turbo-pop blare of the ceiling-mounted television. There were six of them, a good turn-out.

I could make out Terri, a children's book illustrator who claimed to have picked up a smattering of Greek on Mykonos during her hippy days. Her smatter was long scattered but she was doing her best to round it up again. As she spoke, she rotated her wrist in the air, as if uncoiling the tentative thread of her thoughts. The others were leaning forward, the better to catch her drift. I recognised one as Simon, a palliative-care nurse in his early thirties with plans to explore the Peloponnese. And some of the Peloponnesians, too, I assumed. The others, three females and one male, had their backs to me.

Lanie, I registered immediately, was not among them. My shoulders sagged and I mouthed a silent curse. *Malaka.*

I shouldn't have come. I'd been bullshitting myself. Truth be told, it wasn't the prospect of refreshing my feeble, faltering Greek that had lured me to the Archeon. It was the dumb, wistful hope that Lanie would be there.

My gaze dropped to the display of pastries. The syrup-drenched *kataifi* cocoons, deep-fried *loukoumades* and sugar-dusted *kouranbiethes*. The moist walnut cake and flaking *bougatsa*. The oozing babas and sticky halva. The suppurating *galaktoboureko*.

Butterflies danced a lead-footed Zorba in my stomach. I started to turn away, back the way I'd come.

Jesus, Murray. Behave yourself. Get a grip. So what if she's not here? You hardly know the woman, for Christ's sake.

But I did know some things. She had a wide, confident mouth and heavy-lidded sensual eyes. She was pleasingly full-figured and her thick mane of chestnut hair went down to her shoulders. She didn't get impatient when other students slowed down the class because they hadn't done their homework, even though she always did hers.

I knew she was a piano teacher. In the first lesson, she'd told us so, fluttering her fingers across an imaginary keyboard. From our practice dialogues, I knew she lived in Abbotsford in an apartment near the river. So I didn't know nothing.

Which didn't excuse the fact that I was pining after her like some smitten teen. I slapped some sense into myself and turned back towards the door.

But my appetite had gone. For cakes, for company, for coffee. This whole conversation thing was a waste of time. I'd be better off alone, working on my vocabulary or taking dictation from a tape.

So, was I staying or leaving? A wispy drizzle began, not quite heavy enough to qualify as rain. Even the weather couldn't make up its mind.

A Daihatsu hatch-back pulled up, double-parking in the inside lane. The passenger door flew open and a woman jumped out, a flurry of seasonal browns and burgundies. A chunky adolescent girl clambered from the back and took the empty seat. Hasty goodbyes were exchanged, and the car drove away.

Lanie Lane, looking a little cross, flung her scarf back over her shoulder and marched towards the coffee shop.

'*Ti kanis?*' I said brightly. '*Kala?*'

'*Kala.*' She twitched her mouth, erasing the frown.

'Better late than never, eh?' I said.

She grimaced and tossed her chin in the direction the car had taken. 'My bloody ex. You'd think an IT expert could tell the time, not turn up an hour late.'

'I've just arrived myself,' I said.

Her ex! Things were looking up. Potentially.

I held the door open, then followed her into the filo-and-cinnamon scented fug of the coffee shop. 'Θελετε καφε κυρια?'

'Latte, *parakalo*,' she smiled, 'as they say on Santorini.'

We joined the others. Space was made, greetings exchanged. '*Kalimera, kalimera. Kala?*'

Everybody was *poly kala*. Simon, the palliative-care nurse, was explaining that he had been to the *kinimatografos*. Was it *enhromo* asked Julie, the florist, or an *aspromavro*? It was a *komodhia*. Yesterday, I informed them, I had visited *exohi*. I had not gone by train. I went there by *aftokinito*. Lanie had been to a *sinavlia*. Her friend played the *klarino*. Friend, masculine. Just who was this tootler, I wondered?

After half an hour of mangling our generatives and spraying our fricatives, slipping in and out of English to encourage and correct each other, our number began to dwindle. Other customers were impatient for tables and the waitress confiscated our chairs as fast as they were vacated. Eventually, it was down to me and the object of my desire. We dawdled, guarding our cups, neither of us in a hurry.

A waitress started clearing the table. I scooped up the book illustrator's leftover baklava as the plate was whisked away. Nothing wrong with my appetite now.

'Abbotsford, eh?' I said.

She nodded. 'Bought if off the plan. Saved a fortune in stamp duty.'

There are places in the world where conversation revolves around subjects other than real estate. Melbourne is not one of them. Lanie told me about her place. I told her about mine. In the process, we sketched the bones of our personal histories.

She'd bought her apartment, she told me, with her pay-out from the Education Department. A high school music teacher, she was one of the thousands made redundant in the wave of school closures initiated by the incoming Liberals. As well as her job, she'd lost her husband. Given him the flick for fooling around. He was now shacked up with a marketing consultant. No great loss, she said, and the divorce had left her with half their house in Balwyn.

'Fifteen years of capital gain, tax free,' she said, scraping the bottom of her coffee cup and licking the spoon.

She'd bought the Abbotsford place because she liked the location and it had enough room for her grand piano.

'It's leased. But nothing impresses the customers like a grand. Means I can charge twenty dollars an hour above market rates to teach little Griselda her scales.'

Talk came easy to us. We got and gave in equal measure, and Lanie learned at least as much about me. From real estate and work, we moved to children and education. Her daughter, Nicole, was in year seven at McRob Girls' High. She had the second bedroom in Abbotsford, plus a room at her father's place in Prahran. I reciprocated with the potted history of Red and Wendy.

The only subject I deliberately elided was Lyndal, but I read in Lanie's eyes that she had an inkling. Many people did. The murder had generated a fair amount of press.

The waitress came back, a bottle-blonde dragon with a cat's-bum mouth. She stared at our empty cups and flicked her towel. We were getting the heave-ho. But there was still one subject yet to be broached.

'Stop me if I'm speaking out of turn or making a fool of myself,' I said. 'But I wonder if you'd be in a position to accompany me to a sort of semi-official, semi-social event thingo on Thursday evening?'

Lanie smiled at the construction. 'A semi-official semi-social event thingo?'

I made a sheepish face. 'The casino opening, actually.'

'I thought the Labor Party didn't approve of the casino?' Her tone was teasing.

'It's a reconnaissance mission,' I said.

We stood up and made for the cashier, my eyes on the sway of her hips. She looked back over her shoulder. 'So a hand of blackjack and a spin of the roulette wheel would be out of the question?'

'Fan tan, craps, two-up, you name it,' I said. 'We can even pull some slots with the hoi polloi if you like.'

I tried to pay for her coffees. She wouldn't let me.

'Is this a dress-up event?'

'Whatever you like. Long as you're not wearing a balaclava and carrying a sawn-off shotgun.'

She chewed her lip, hesitant. 'Thursday evening, right?'

'I could ask them to change it,' I said. 'But Mick and Keef might get shitty.'

'Could take a bit of juggling,' she said. 'Can I let you know in a day or two?'

I nodded, a little too eagerly, and borrowed the cashier's pen to write my home number on the back of a business card. Lanie glanced at the number, then read the other side.

'Parliament of Victoria.' She shook her head dolefully. '*Malaka.*'

Broadmeadows Town Hall was a vision of drear in the afternoon rain, a brick monolith distinguished only by its lack of distinction. As the venue for a wake, it was hard to imagine anywhere more depressingly institutional.

I directed the cab to the agglomeration of buildings between the K-Mart and the municipal library, hoping that Mike Kyriakis had at least laid on an adequate supply of grog. A wake is not a wake without booze. It was basic multicultural courtesy. The rites were over. The tomb was sealed. It was time to get ragged and maudlin.

When I was a teenager, Broady was the very end of the earth. Beyond lay only factories and thistle-infested paddocks. Its residents were blue-collar workers, their feet tentatively planted on the first rung of the ladder to affluence. Many were recent migrants whose oily-rag thrift had allowed them to scrape together the deposit on a stake in the Australian Dream.

Community facilities were basic. The opera rarely performed there. Ballet classes were few and far between. Childbirth often preceded wedlock. The mullet ruled supreme. Sheepskin moccasins were high fashion. Broady boys were generally not a calming presence.

In the following decades, however, the frontier of suburbia galloped further north. Target and K-Mart colonised the council carpark, school retention rates had risen and a tertiary campus sprang up. It had got to the point now where real estate agents were describing the place as a 'desirable location' without the faintest hint of irony or even deception.

Pity there wasn't a decent pub in the area. Still, there's a limit to what social engineering can achieve.

I paid my chauffeur and followed the hand-lettered signs up the Prussian-blue polypropylene pile to the council chamber, the locus of the gathering.

The chamber had recently been decommissioned following a forced rationalisation of local government by the state Liberals. While the surrounding offices continued to operate as an administrative centre, decision-making had moved elsewhere. It was now a general function room and storage area for municipal artifacts. Honour rolls of mayors previous. Mementoes from sister cities. Winning bushscapes from the annual acquisitive art award.

About fifty people had turned up. They were milling around the room, drinks in hand, chatting and raising a gratifyingly loud hubbub.

Somebody had taped old campaign posters and press photos to the walls. Serious-faced Charlie in front of the party colours. Dark-suited Charlie opening the Community Health Centre. Hard-hatted Charlie inspecting progress on the Meadow Heights adventure playground. Just-folks Charlie living large at the Upfield Senior Cits dinner dance.

Mike Kyriakis spotted me the moment I arrived. He beckoned me over to a bunch of old ducks who were stripping the buffet of four-point sandwiches and meatballs on toothpicks. At their centre was Mavis Peel, former doyenne of the Municipals' typing pool. Her bosom had vanished and her hair had thinned to a blue-rinsed wisp. She was deaf as a post and didn't know me from Adam. But she remembered Charlie Talbot, all right.

'Such a nice young man,' she reminisced. 'So considerate.'

Her companions from the Craigieburn Home for the Terminally Bewildered nodded agreement and sank their talons into the pink salmon sangers.

'Have you got a drink, love?' asked one of them.

I couldn't tell if she was cadging or inviting. Mike grabbed me like a life preserver and steered me to a trestle table where a council hall keeper in a clip-on bow-tie and a neat blue mohawk was pleased to offer me something from his comprehensive selection of wines, beers and spirits.

'This is a fine thing you're doing, Mike,' I said, hoisting a stubby of VB. 'Here's to Charlie.'

A lead weight descended on my shoulder. It was the open hand of Sivan Demiral, one of Charlie's office auxiliaries. He was an old mate, a Kurd who'd helped run the Turkish Welfare League alongside Ayisha when I was the electorate officer for Charlene Wills, many moons prior.

'Murray, my friend,' he boomed. 'We have lost a good man.' He raised his stubby and I seconded the motion.

An ebullient optimist with the build of a Hittite shithouse, Sivan was forever launching ill-fated business ventures, all the while keeping his hand in local Labor politics. His current project was a Turkish video store, its precarious earnings underwritten by a part-time job in Charlie's electorate office. Customers with a valid ALP membership card got a ten percent discount.

We swapped some Charlie Talbot anecdotes and I gravitated towards Helen Wright. She was part of a trio that included Ayisha and a woman from the Broadmeadows Neighbourhood House toy library. They were taking a punt on the white.

'Courtesy of Domaine Diggers Rest, the winery just up the road from Charlie and Margot's place.' Helen puffed her cheeks, swished and swallowed. 'An argumentative little drop with an aftertaste of aviation exhaust.'

I accepted a glass and took a tentative sip. Helen wasn't just a fine electorate officer. She had a cast-iron stomach. Perhaps these facts were not unrelated. Ayisha was downing the stuff like a trooper.

'Margot sends her apologies and her thanks,' I said. 'If you ladies will excuse me, I think I'll stick to the suds.'

I collected a cleansing ale and made the rounds. I knew perhaps half the people in the room. Ron Tragear, secretary of the Anstey branch and C-grade juniors football coach. Signor Panebianco, the Cicero of the Calabrian Club. Lauris Foxe, deputy principal of Strathmore Primary. Doug and Vera Ahern of the Anstey Progress Association. Ada Ahmet from the Disability Resource Centre. Working-bee regulars and old-school true believers, bedrocks of their communities. As big a pack of dags and busybodies as you could ever hope to assemble. The more I drank, the more I loved them.

'Your attention for a moment, folks.'

I was saved from total immersion in the well of sentimentality by Mike Kyriakis. He rapped on the table with a spoon and Helen Wright hauled her low centre of gravity up onto a chair.

She made a short speech, reminding us why we were there. It centred on a funny story about the time computers were first installed in members' offices in the old Parliament House in Canberra. To Charlie's bafflement, the technician sent to explain their operation kept using an acronym current in the computer jargon of the day. WYSIWYG, pronounced Wizzywig. What You See Is What You Get.

'Charlie Talbot was a Wizzywig man,' she said, drawing her tale to its point. 'What you saw was what you got. A man who knew what he stood for, did what he could to the best of his abilities, recognised his limitations and honoured his obligations. The sort of person who restores your faith in politics. I'm not sure if they make 'em like that anymore.'

And we all drank to that, and shared a silent sniffle. I realised my stubby was empty and, as I turned towards the bar, banged into a vaguely familiar middle-aged woman. She clicked her tongue and gave a reproving shake of her head.

'Jesus, Murray Whelan,' she said. 'Still as hopeless as ever, I see. You don't recognise me, do you?'

'Course I do.' I smiled widely and racked my fibbing brain. A committee? A delegation? A primary school pageant?

'Nadine,' she said. 'Nadine Medlock.'

'Of course, Nadine,' I said, my ears turning pink. 'It's been a long time, that's all.'

'Twenty-three years, four months and five days.' She eyed my livid lobes, amused, then appraised the rest of me. 'Don't worry, Murray. I almost didn't recognise you, either.'

The last I'd seen of Nadine Medlock was her bare arse.

I had a force ten hangover and I was crawling out her bedroom window, shoes under my arms, trying to remember where I'd parked the car. She was flaked out on her doona, her bum in the air and her head buried under a pillow. It took me three days to find the car.

'So,' I said, bouncily. 'What've you been up to? What brings you here? Didn't realise you knew Charlie.'

She cupped an elbow in one hand, sipped her wine and slipped into chatty mode. 'Been living in Darwin,' she said. 'Husband, kids, the full catastrophe. No, it's been great, actually. Len's in the PS, Department of Environment and Natural Resources. Transferred back here last year so the girls could finish school. I've been working with young offenders and Charlie was a big help with a program at the Sunbury juvenile centre. Thought I'd drop by and pay my respects. What about you?'

Nadine was, I remembered, a pretty good sort.

'I'm in state parliament,' I said.

'No!' she said. 'You poor bastard. What did you do to deserve that?'

'I'm in it for the glamour,' I said. 'My electorate's just down the road.'

We stood at the plate-glass window, looking down at the K-Mart carpark, and traded ancient gossip about half-remembered acquaintances from our long-gone twenties.

For a while, I recalled, Nadine was a barmaid at the John Curtin Hotel, the watering-hole directly across the street from the Trades Hall.

The Curtin was an institution in those days. ACTU headquarters was just down the road in Swanston Street and it drew thirsty union officials like flies to the proverbial. In its beery swill, sanctified by the name of Labor's most revered and contentious prime minister, loyalties were affirmed and animosities stoked, rumours circulated and deals done, old alliances eroded and new ones forged. Every inch was staked out. The Right sat by the window, the Left near the cigarette machine. The pragmatists held the bar, leaving just enough room for the Maoists. People went there as much to fight as to drink.

'You don't happen to remember Merv Cutlett, do you?' I wondered.

'How could I forget? The old letch cost me my job.'

'Yeah?' I topped up her glass. 'How so?'

Nadine shrugged. 'Usual story.'

'Got a bit frisky, did he?'

'Downright grabby,' she said.

'Tell all,' I said. 'Paint me a picture.'

She heaved a reluctant sigh. But reminiscence, after all, was our pretext for an afternoon on the grog.

'It was a Friday night, right. Bedlam hour. Cutlett was perched at the bar, usual pozzie, with his bandicoot-faced little hanger-on.'

'Sid Gilpin?'

'I forget the name. A cut-price Bob Hawke, always cracking his knuckles and twiddling his pinkie ring and tugging at his earlobe.'

She smoothed back the hair at her temples, mimicking one of Gilpin's grooming gestures. She had him down pat. I laughed appreciatively, egging her on.

'As per usual, the little grease-ball had his head so far up Merv's bum you couldn't see his neck. Anyway, this night, for some reason, the two of them were particularly full of themselves. Carrying on like they'd just pulled a major swiftie. Sold Sydney Harbour Bridge or something. Patting themselves on the back. And hitting the amber pretty hard in the process. Eventually, whatsisname, Sid, got totally legless and lurched off. So Cutlett turned his attention to yours truly. Stupid old fart tried to crack onto me. Really laid on the charm, told me how much he admired my tits.'

Nadine's tits weren't bad, if memory served, but they weren't anything to write home about. My eyes started slipping downwards but I got them back to Nadine's face before they disgraced me.

'Of course sexual harassment was an occupational hazard at the Curtin,' she said. 'Bar work, it's no job for a shrinking violet, but even you proto-SNAGs assumed it was open slather.'

Before she got any further down that particular detour, I steered her back to Merv.

'He was pissed and arrogant and I wasn't in the mood to be nice. So I tried for a swap with Terry, the barman upstairs. He reckoned he was flat out, too, and I should just cop it and carry on. Anyway, Cutlett keeps it up, so I banged his next beer on the bar so hard it slopped into his lap.'

'Bet he loved that,' I said, the scene vivid in my mind.

'Went off like a pork chop. Said he knew exactly what I needed and he was just the man to give it to me. There's a scrum of drinkers three deep at the bar, waving their money in the air, grabbing glasses off me. Every time I lean across the bar, he puts his hands on me. I go to the boss again, said I couldn't work under those sort of conditions, tried to get shifted. He said "Later", so I cracked the shits. "Take this job and shove it," I told him, "I ain't workin' here no more."'

'Johnny Paycheck,' I said.

'Dead Kennedys, the way I did it,' Nadine laughed. 'Felt

good at the time, but I was jacked off about it later. Turned out to be the weekend the old goat got himself drowned. He never went back to the Curtin, so I needn't have quit on his account.'

I shook my head at the injustice. 'And here we are,' I said. 'Twenty-odd years later, at the wake of the man who jumped into a freezing cold lake trying to save the bastard.'

'Yeah, well,' she said. 'That's the difference between the Merv Cutletts of this world and the Charlie Talbots.' She held out her glass and I topped it up with Domaine Diesel. We gave a desultory toast and I sucked meditatively on my stubby. Down in the K-Mart carpark, Sunday afternoon shoppers were dashing though a downpour, their purchases clutched tight.

'Cutlett and Gilpin,' I said. 'You don't happen to recollect what they were so pleased about?'

Nadine gave a derisive snort and eyed me like I was nuts. 'Christ, Murray, it was twenty years ago.'

I tried a little charm of my own. 'Still,' I said. 'You do have amazing powers of recall.'

'Careful, Murray.' Nadine fixed me with a wry look. 'I might start remembering things best forgotten.'

My ears flared again. I racked my brain. What exactly had happened between me and Nadine? 'Yes, well…I, er…'

'Anyway,' she said, letting me off the hook. 'It ended well. I walked straight into a job at the Dan.' The Dan O'Connell was a folkie pub. Wack-fol-the-diddle, electric bush bands and outlaw crossover. 'That's where I met Len. And I'm still with him. Just goes to show that things work out for the best sometimes, eh?'

'Sometimes.'

By seven o'clock it was down to the hard core.

Somnolent, we sprawled among the ravaged platters, devastated dips and knackered plastic glassware. Helen Wright had taken off her shoes and propped her stockinged feet on a stackable vinyl chair. Sivan toyed with a bottle of raki, unscrewing the cap, thinking about it, then sealing it back up. Ayisha began clearing up. Mike Kyriakis told her not to bother, the cleaners would take care of it in the morning. Sam Aboud, the administrator of the Meadow Heights Community Health Centre, managed to scavenge enough sachets of Nescafe to make a round of coffees.

Darkness had fallen outside. One of the fluorescent ceiling lights spluttered sporadically. Mike took the Australian flag from its stand and poked the tube with the pole. It hummed, plinked and expired.

There were a couple of other lingerers, faces I knew less well, their names slightly out of range. A young psephologist with an attempted beard, one of Charlie's part-timers, sat on the floor with his knees cradled in his arms. One of Mike Kyriakis' council confreres, an official with the printing industry union. He'd souvenired one of Charlie's campaign posters, rolled it up like a telescope and was trying to focus down the tube.

We were all somewhat oiled, but I was probably the worst offender, flopped in an armchair and sinking gently into the west.

'I've done my sums,' said Mike, dragging a chair into the circle and dropping into it with an air of finality. 'And I gotta say, I'm more tempted than ever to put my hand up for Charlie's old seat. I reckon he'd want me to, too. What do you say, Helen, how about seconding me? And Sam, you too? Between the lot of you, I reckon there's just about enough signatures for the nomination form.' He gave the flagpole a slow wave. 'It'll be a glorious defeat. Gallipoli all over again.'

Sivan languidly returned the wave with his bottle of raki. 'Didn't we win that one?'

Mike was warming to his theme. 'I've got no illusions about my chances, but I reckon I can make those know-it-alls in Canberra sit up and take notice.'

He'd been though the membership rolls with a fine tooth comb, and he'd come up with a strategy.

'Everybody's been stacking branches for years, right? And both sides have about equal numbers, right? But it's like the nuclear balance. It only works if it isn't tested in practice. As long as they've got the numbers on paper, they never need to actually mobilise them. All they need in any vote is enough to make a symbolic showing. So next Saturday, come the plebiscite of local members, there'll probably be a turn-out of less than fifty percent of the eligible voters, right?'

The question was rhetorical. We settled further into our seats and let him answer it.

'If I can round up three hundred surprise punters, which I think might just be do-able, I really put the cat among the pigeons.'

He paused pregnantly, awaiting a reaction. Eventually Ayisha obliged with the obvious questions.

'Where are you going to get three hundred stray votes, Mike, and how are you going to keep them up your sleeve until Saturday?'

In Coolaroo, as in most ethnically diverse electorates, membership management was a highly developed science. Between the six of us, we knew every trick in the branch-stacking book.

The game had begun in the sixties when party rules were amended to allow branches to conduct their meetings in languages other than English. This, it was believed, would encourage migrants to join.

The Left started the meatball rolling with mass enrolments of Italians and Greeks. For a while, it was all Mikis Theodorakis and Bernardo Bertolucci. Then the Right followed suit by signing up a grab-bag of deracinated Indochinese, irredentist Chetniks and assorted Middle Eastern minaret polishers.

Before long, the so-called ethnic warlords emerged. Bottom feeders with murky affiliations and interchangeable surnames who enrolled hundreds of their most compliant compatriots, paid their membership dues and sold their votes to the highest bidder. All with as little regard for ideological distinction as any other influence peddler.

As they debated the merit of Mike's figures, I rested my

eyes and let the talk ebb and flow around me.

'You can discount the Italians completely,' Mike said. 'For political purposes, they're no longer ethnics. Three generations here, they might as well be skips.'

'Not like the Greeks,' said Helen. 'They don't migrate, they colonise. They could be here forever and never dream of giving up their political muscle.'

She's right about that, I thought. The heirs of Aristotle and Pythagoras know in their bones that politics is all, numbers are everything.

'Yeah,' said Sam Aboud. 'But did you ever try to get fifty Greeks to do what they're told? It's like herding cats.'

'You leave the Greeks to me,' said Mike. 'And what's the story with those Montignards or whatever you call them that you've stacked into the Attwood branch?'

'Hmong,' said Sam. 'A proud warrior people from the headwaters of the Mekong, currently residing in Meadow Heights. They worship me as a god, or at least the guy who can get them on the waiting list for a hip replacement.'

'How many have you got?'

'Sixty.'

'Bullshit.'

'Okay, forty-seven.'

'AK-47 you mean,' cracked Sivan, slapping his knee.

Ayisha said, 'You'd need five times that number to counterbalance the Croatians. With Metcalfe backing the deal, you've got to take the Right into account, too, don't forget.'

'The Croatians'll be a no-show,' said Mike. 'The Right's lost its key Croat head-kickers. They took their fat fascistic arses back to Zagreb when Yugoslavia fell apart. Welcomed with open arms and government jobs by their fellow Ustashi exile, Tudjman. And thanks to Milosevic, nobody wants to know the Serbs, so we can count them out, too.'

'I might only have forty-seven Hmong,' said Sam Aboud. 'But I've also got a minibus to ferry them to the polling point.'

'And somebody in Canberra doesn't know Muslim calendar,' said Sivan. 'Saturday is Miled an-Anabi, birthday of Mohammed. Nobody from Izik mosque gunna vote, too busy having big party.'

'Bullshit, Sivan,' said Ayisha. 'Since when was Miled a feast day?'

'Since new mufti arrive. Very go-ahead feller.'

And so it went, back and forth, as they amused themselves with the speculative scenarios of a theoretical campaign.

'No good without the element of surprise,' said Helen.

'That's where you come in,' said Mike. 'Let's face it, Helen, working for Charlie was a labour of love. You don't really want to end up the housekeeper for this time-server, Sebastian. Be my secret agent. Feed him misinformation, lull him into a false sense of security.'

'Tempting,' she yawned, a smile in her voice. 'Poison the wells. Go out with a bang not a whimper.'

I was drifting off, settling into a boozy miasma, Sam Aboud's instant coffee going cold in my lap. I was thinking about Nadine Medlock seeing Merv Cutlett and Sid Gilpin at the Curtin, their high spirits on the eve of Merv's death. Neither of them was the most demonstrative of blokes. What were they celebrating? More to the point, was it connected to the union?

'What about it, Murray?' The sound of my name dragged me back to the present.

Mike Kyriakis was asking me a question.

'You've got enough pull with those schoolteacher intellectuals and old retired boilermakers in those branches of yours. How about signing up to the crusade?'

I kept my eyes closed. This was Ayisha's department.

'Why would Murray want to stick his head above the parapet?' she said. 'Just so you can get your name in the papers and get a reputation as a man to watch.'

The talk was all still theoretical, the question academic.

'She right, Mike. Better he don't support you. Better he run himself.' Sivan picked up the baton. He'd been doing some thinking. 'Imagine if panel splits. They don't like Sebastian. They don't like you neither, Mike. So Murray, he decides to run. He don't support you. He runs against you. You both draw votes from Sebastian. He gets eliminated. Second round, you give Murray your preferences. He falls over the line. He gets Coolaroo. Thank you, Mike. You can have Melbourne Upper, he don't need it no more. He's in Canberra. He takes Ayisha, big new office up there. Helen, she gets Ayisha's old job, runs Melbourne Upper for you. I get Helen's old job, run Murray's office down here. Everybody happy.'

It was so elegant, so improbable, that they all burst out laughing and gave him a clap.

'What about me?' said Sam Aboud. 'What do I get?'

'You get to be Mayor of Broadmeadows,' said Ayisha. 'But first you get to call Murray a taxi. He's fallen asleep.'

I opened my eyes. 'Huh?' I said.

They poured me into a cab and I got home just in time to crash on the couch in front of the television. The usual ABC Sunday night fare. Women in hooped dresses and long-faced, sinister toffs in top hats. Red woke me when he'd packed up his books at eleven-thirty. 'On the Floor' was just finishing. Whatever Kelly Cusack had reported, I'd missed it.

I was thinking about Kelly as I climbed into bed. But then I was thinking about Lanie. Eleni of Troy.

With whom I had a date. Maybe.

We were on a boat, a sailing boat, skimming across a sparkling sea, the Aegean, destination unknown. The sun was warm. The sky was blue. I was wearing a tunic and sandals. Lanie was wearing a chiton and there was a diadem in her hair. She was standing at the prow playing 'Advance Australia Fair' on a piano accordion. There were others on the boat, somewhere behind us. I could hear them scuffling. Somebody fell into the water. Splash. I turned to look and the sea was gone. Lanie was gone. Everyone was gone. I was alone and the boat was sitting on dry land. I was stark naked and burning up. A parching dryness filled my mouth. I tried to swallow but I was suffocating, dying of thirst.

I groped blindly for the glass on the bedside table. My hand knocked it over, spilling water on the clock-radio. I swung my feet to the floor, stumbled to the bathroom, gulped from the tap, peed, gulped again. The sudden flare of the bathroom light set stars spinning behind my eyes. There was something I was trying to remember. I couldn't remember what.

Then I was standing at the door of my study, looking into the dark, thinking about my archive boxes. All that old paper. The silverfish would be eating it, nibbling it into powder. I'd put mothballs in the boxes, but that was long ago. They'd be gone by now, all used up. Buy mothballs, that was what I was trying to remember.

Mothballs, I told myself. Hold that thought.

And then the alarm clock went off.

Senator Barry Quinlan was advancing to greet me even as the polished glass security door into his reception area was clicking locked behind me.

With a state-wide electorate and therefore no particular constituency to pander to, senators pleased themselves as to where they located their offices. For the Nationals, it was always somewhere in the boonies, where they'd be visible to the cud-chewers. Those from the other two parties hung out their shingles wherever it suited them. Some liked the leafy 'burbs. Others bunged on the common touch, setting up shop at street level and opening their doors to all comers. Some found a comfortable pied-a-terre in the Commonwealth offices in Treasury Place with its ankle-deep carpet and uniformed doorman. In Barry's case, it was a corner suite in a mid-rise office building at the legal and banking end of Bourke Street, a short stroll from nowhere in particular.

He extended his hand, not for me to shake, but to

shepherd me through to his office. As well as the woman at the computer behind the reception desk, I counted four other staffers in small, glass-panelled side offices as we made our way towards the bridge of *HMAS Quinlan*. They looked up as we passed. One of them was Phil Sebastian. He was on the phone and signalled that he'd join us as soon as he finished the call.

Quinlan was well turned out, as usual, minus a jacket. Crisp and businesslike, but cordial. A man who'd spent a long time at the top of his profession. Warm, but not toasty.

'Thanks for coming, Murray,' he said, directing me to one of the comfortable chairs at the small conference table that shared the space with a file-stacked desk.

There was a fairly good painting of a racehorse on one wall, gilt-famed. A whiteboard on the other, erased but bearing evidence of much use. We could have been in a well-heeled bookie's office on settling-up day.

'I appreciate it,' he said. 'I really do. And so does Phil. I was probably a bit out of line the other day at the cemetery. Insensitive, bringing up this preselection business in a situation like that, you and Charlie being close and all.'

'That's all right, Barry,' I said. 'No offence taken.'

'Good,' he said, sitting down across the table, pinching up his trouser leg at the knee so as not to ruin the crease as he crossed one leg over the other. 'I felt sure you'd appreciate the need for a smooth transition. We've got a load on our plates right now, dealing with this Telecom privatisation push, pressing our advantage on the travel rorts scandal and so forth.' His hand swept the air expansively.

I gave an understanding nod. Many are the toils of those who would clean the Augean stables.

'This fast-track decision-making is not ideal I know,' he

said, forestalling any qualms I might have been poised to express. 'Under normal circumstances, we'd've been content for things to take their natural course. But a mid-term preselection tussle, if it gets out of hand, it costs us points at the by-election. That hands the government a chance to say we're running out of steam. It's like pissing in your own pants. Feels pretty hot to you, but the only thing anyone else notices is the smell.'

'I understand the party's concern, Barry,' I said. 'And I share it.'

'Good,' he said, that settled. 'I suppose you wouldn't be here if you didn't.'

Phil Sebastian came into the room. He was slightly younger than me, but he didn't have as much hair. The crown was the thin spot, leaving him with a monkish tonsure. His face radiated intelligence and goodwill. He had a brisk collegial handshake and a slightly harried manner, like the school dux interrupted midway between handing in an assignment and getting togged up for cricket practice. It was hard to dislike him and I saw no reason to try.

'I appreciate this, Murray,' he said. 'I really do.'

It's always nice to be appreciated. We'd met on a handful of occasions, he recalled, naming them. Party conferences and state–federal confabs back when we were in government. He'd worked for the ACTU, I recalled, and I'd read some of the papers he'd written for the Evatt Institute.

From a competence point of view he was no liability, that much was an evident fact. If the world was a meritocracy, Phil Sebastian had a ticket to ride. But that's not the way it works, of course. Sometimes it's down to kissing arse.

'I understand that your opinion carries a lot of weight in

parts of the electorate,' he kissed. 'I'd very much like the benefit of your insights, help steer me right in my approach to the local branches. No doubt they're feeling a bit sidelined at the moment and even though their votes only add up to half the total, I'd like to feel I'm coming into the job with their support.'

I nodded. 'I'm sure if they're handled in the right way, they'll do what's expected of them.'

'It doesn't have to be unanimous,' said Quinlan. 'Just overwhelming.'

We had a chuckle, fine fellows that we were.

'I've just been on the line to Helen Wright,' said Sebastian. He adjusted the knot in his tie, giving me time to send up a flare if one was required. His tie had an oblique dark green stripe on a maroon background. Corporate camouflage, fifty dollars at The Tie Shop.

'Keeping her on then, are you?'

'It's a good idea, I think,' he said, glancing at Quinlan. 'She does know the lie of the land.'

'She does indeed,' I said. 'Lined up some appointments, has she?'

He reeled off a list of names, most unknown to me. The few I recognised were minor players, all points of the Coolaroo compass.

'You'll be a busy boy for the next five days,' I said. 'It's a big electorate, lots of territory to cover. Tell you what, I'll have a chat with my electorate officer, nut out a list, have her call you back later this afternoon. You've caught me on the hop a bit. Parliament's rising this week and I've got my work cut out, but let's see what we can do for you.'

Sebastian handed me a card with his contact numbers. 'Anytime, anywhere. Just call me and I'll be there.' Phil had missed his vocation. He should have been a lyricist.

One of Quinlan's back-room beavers stuck his snout around the door. 'Your car's here, boss. And the select committee papers are ready. Christine'll brief you in the car on the way to the airport.'

Quinlan stood up and donned his jacket, tugging it into good order and shooting his cuffs. 'Sorry to rush,' he said. 'I've got to go and make the case against the full privatisation of a rapacious monopoly. Try to explain why it isn't a great idea to let a five-hundred-pound gorilla out of its cage to a pack of ideologues who'd sell their sisters to sailors and call it asset rationalisation.'

Phil Sebastian stayed seated, clearly anticipating my further assistance.

'Bit pressed myself,' I said. 'I'll come down with you, Barry.'

I followed Quinlan to the lift, just the two of us there waiting for the doors to open, Barry raising and lowering himself on the toes of his tiny, well-buffed shoes.

'Funny thing,' I said. 'I had a visit from the police the other day. Seems they've found Merv Cutlett at long last. What's left of him, at least.'

'Yeah,' said Quinlan, eyes on the floor numbers. 'I heard they were doing the rounds.' One lift went past, going all the way to the top, stopping to take on cargo. The other had taken up permanent residence in the basement. 'They talked to me last week. I was surprised there was anything left after all this time. Odd coincidence, eh, Charlie dying the day after they found him.' He tapped a toe, time-strapped. 'Showed you the watch, did they?'

'Yes. I didn't recognise it.'

'Me neither. I wish I'd had the presence of mind to say I

did, though. I should've told them I'd seen Merv wearing it. Save the taxpayer the expense of further buggerising around. Those forensic tests cost a poultice.'

Quinlan didn't sound like a man with anything to hide. He reached over and pressed the button again.

'I got asked some other questions as well,' I said. 'They wanted to know all about internal relations in the union. How everybody got along and so forth.'

'Yeah?' Quinlan raised an eyebrow. 'What did you tell them?'

'One big happy family. A veritable Woodstock.'

Quinlan snorted. The lift arrived and we stepped aboard, the only passengers.

'I got the impression they were giving the original reports a pretty thorough going over, like they were suspicious of something.'

'Well it was the Homicide Squad, right? That's the found bodies department. If they don't act suspicious, people think they're not on the job.'

The doors opened at the fourth floor and two women got in, talking some kind of finance language. Barry smiled and they smiled back, not drawing breath.

'So,' I said, just chatting. 'How did Merv manage to lure you up there that weekend, middle of winter? My idea of hell.'

'Well it wasn't for the fishing, that's for sure.' Quinlan adjusted his drape in the mirrored wall of the lift. 'That part was just Cutlett being bloody-minded. Actually, we'd gone up there to make him an offer, try to seal the deal on the amalgamation. The old coot had been playing hard to get, seeing how much he could squeeze out of the proposed new set-up before he'd agree to it.'

We followed the two women into the foyer. An officious looking young apparatchik in a navy pants-suit was standing by the door with a briefcase beside her and a fat folder in her hand. She looked towards us expectantly, but Barry signalled her to wait. We continued our conversation beside the tenants list. Orion Investment Planners. Cohen, Bullfinch and McGill. The Marasco Group of Companies. Leicester and Associates.

'It all came down to money and face. The golden parachute and its rate of descent. Cutlett wanted three years' salary, a term on the PEU executive and life access to the Shack. All of which wasn't going to happen. We were prepared to top up his super, which was already generous, and hang his picture in the hall of fame, but we weren't going to let him screw us. If he didn't accept, Charlie would go around him, swing the other state secretaries and he'd end up out in the cold.'

Quinlan was telling me this, his tone implied, for no other reason than to satisfy my curiosity. It was an act of courtesy.

'Cutlett being Cutlett, he would not go gently. Dug his heels in, made the whole exercise as difficult as possible. Always had to have the last word. He was the hairy-arsed champion of the underdog. We were a cabal of limp-wristed pen-pushers. Of course the big irony was that by getting himself drowned, he made the amalgamation both easier and cheaper. Charlie was assistant national secretary, *ex officio*. With Merv gone, he was in charge. The amalgamation sailed through under budget and ahead of schedule.'

'Earning you a seat in the Senate,' I said.

'Indeed,' he said, acknowledging the point with a courtly dip of his head. 'Indeed. And Charlie a place in the Reps. A most fortuitous outcome all round.'

One worth killing for? It would have been impolitic to ask.

Quinlan put his hand on my sleeve, signalling his departure. 'Just before I go,' he said. 'There's nobody out there in your neck of the woods looking to make an issue of Phil, is there? He'll be a real asset, you know.'

'These things are rarely uncontested,' I said. 'Nature of the beast.'

'Anybody in particular?'

'Nobody you need worry about, Barry.'

'But you'll keep your ears open?'

'I always do.' It was simple anatomy.

'Good man.' He patted me again and started for the door.

'Matter of fact, I did hear something might interest you,' I said. Quinlan paused mid-stride and turned. 'Apparently Sid Gilpin has resurfaced. He's trying to peddle some story about corruption at the Municipals, something involving you and Charlie.'

Quinlan creased his brow. 'Sid Gilpin?' He tried to place the name. 'Cutlett's off-sider? What story?'

'Dunno,' I said. 'He approached a journo I know, reckons he's got evidence of dirty deeds. Won't specify what until he sees a cheque-book.'

Quinlan made a world-weary face. 'Sounds like he hasn't changed. Your journo mate buying?'

'I don't think so.'

'Somebody should tell Gilpin we've got defamation laws in this country.'

'Specifically designed to protect politicians.'

'My oath,' said Quinlan. 'Who do you think made them?'

The aide approached, displaying her wrist to urge haste. Quinlan took the folder and gave me a parting nod. I watched them get into the back seat of his Comcar and drive away.

You can't defame the dead, I thought. Not within the meaning of the act. Once a man is gone, you can say anything you damned well like about him. And if you say it loud enough or long enough, it'll find its way into print. And if it's in print, it must be true.

A row of cabs was waiting outside the hotel across the street. I headed for the start of the line, hand raised, and gave a whistle.

The entire area between the waterfront and Spencer Street railway station looked chewed up and spat out. The shunting yards had been uprooted, the cargo sheds demolished, the oily earth churned by bulldozers.

From this blasted heath a glorious future would soon arise. The sod had been turned on an astroturf colosseum with a receding roof and fifty thousand pre-warmed seats, due for completion in 1999. The docks were destined for transformation into luxury apartments, high-rise mortgages with water views. Surprise, surprise.

The old nissen hut was virtually the only remaining evidence of the area's industrial past, a hump of curved tin marooned between dead-end roads and freeway feeder ramps. Grimy engine blocks, gutted washing machines and doorless refrigerators stood out the front with their hands in their pockets, looking bored and propping up weathered signs spray-painted on warped bits of plywood. CLOSING

Down Sale. All Stock Must Go. Last Days.

The big double doors were shut, so I gave the cabbie a twenty and asked him to wait.

A Docklands Authority notice-to-quit was tacked to the splintery timber of one of the doors. Its plastic sleeve was torn and the ink had bled on the tenant's name, rendering it illegible. From inside came the sound of machinery, a cutting or drilling device of some sort. A heavy chain hung loose, dangling an open padlock. I pushed at the door and it moved inwards.

The vaulted interior was lit only by filthy safety-glass windows. Worthless crap of every variety was laid out in aisles on the concrete floor. Obsolete computer monitors. The carapaces of busted stereo speakers. Rough stacks of chipped crockery. Milk crates and plastic baby-baths overflowing with disembodied chunks of kitchen appliances. Cracked wash-tubs. Scaly coils of perished garden hose. Rag-stoppered oil bottles and drip-encrusted paint tins with lids hardened on.

The aisles terminated at a chain-mesh partition running across the rear quarter of the shed. On my side of the wire, a figure was hunched over a bench, his back to me, working the screeching machinery. I waved off the cab and went inside.

I walked down the central aisle past a row of derelict Space Invader machines. Cracked screens, holes punched in their chipboard carcases. Inside the fenced section of the shed was a roofless room, its interior visible through an open door. Television sets were stacked haphazardly on a bench inside. One was running, its volume inaudible. Jerry Springer was working his audience. In front of the sets was a sagging sofa, a repository of yellowed bed linen. A boxy electric radiator glowed red, sending its heat upwards to a row of lights that hung from the ceiling. Their globes were screwed into basin-shaped enamel shades. Probably the only market-able objects in the place.

An open door led out the back. It had a Yale lock on the inside and a heavy-duty bolt on the outside. Standing just inside it was a slide-top ice-cream chiller. Magnum. Cornetto. Paddle Pop. Through the door I could see the tray of a ute and a 44-gallon drum, lidless and toppled. Flattened hessian sacks lined the drum and bleached dog turds surrounded it.

The din filled the shed, amplified by the curve of the walls. Its source was an ancient electric grinder bolted to an oily bench. The hunched figure was oblivious, engrossed in his task. He was picking tarnished brass pipe fittings out of a milk crate, polishing them on a spinning wire brush, then tossing them into another crate. He worked with the point-less mechanical monotony of a man shovelling mercury with a pitchfork. A can of beer sat by his elbow. From time to time he took a slug, maintaining a constant pace.

I stood at the end of the bench, trying to catch his eye. He wore leather work gloves, a frayed Collingwood beanie and a grot-marinated gabardine raincoat. When he'd finished the brass elbow-joints, he pushed back the armature, fitted a grinding wheel and started on a rusted pair of hedge clippers, sending out a spray of sparks. The bench was strewn with similar detritus. Corroded shears, rusted machetes, the heads of mattocks and axes. At this rate, I'd be waiting all day.

A lead ran from the grinder to a power board at my feet. I reached down and pulled out the plug. The motor shuddered to a halt, its bearings screaming. The bent figure straightened up and turned.

It was Gilpin all right, although it took me a moment to be certain. He must have been about sixty, but he looked at least ten years older. Time had not dealt well with Sid and little of the spivvy cockerel remained. Patchy stubble covered his cheeks and his eyes were half-buried in sagging pillows of flesh.

He tore off his ratty gloves and glowered at me.

'This is fucken harassment,' he exploded, spit flying from his lips. 'You lot, you think you can just barge in here any time you like. I've got until 5 p.m. Friday. Until then, I'm legally entitled to quiet possession. Now fuck off or I'll have the dog on you.'

I looked around reflexively. The dog was nowhere in sight.

'You've got the wrong end of the stick,' I said. 'I'm not here to evict you.'

Gilpin peered at me and wiped his mouth with the back of a bloated hand. His arm swept the merchandise. 'You want something?'

'I'm not a customer, Sid. I was at the Municipals when you worked there.'

He narrowed his gaze, trying to place me. Eventually, a tiny spark flickered.

'Talbot's bum boy? Whadda *you* want?'

'I've just come from Barry Quinlan's office,' I said. 'Senator Quinlan. He's heard you've been talking shit about him. Charlie Talbot, too.'

'Quinlan.' He spat out the name. 'Arsehole.'

'You'd be making a mistake to aggravate him.'

'He's the one made the mistake.' Gilpin raised his chin and widened his stance, the old Sid coming back. 'Sending some goon down here to intimidate me.'

Nobody had ever called me a goon before. Perhaps my new exercise regime was bearing fruit already.

'I'm not here to intimidate you, Sid. I'm here to deliver some free advice. You shouldn't go round telling porkies, trying to flog something you haven't got.'

Gilpin's breath was a laboured wheeze. For a long moment, we stared at each other. He hadn't just aged badly. He was not a well man. His eyes were filmy and jaundiced. He was mixing his medication with alcohol.

'Fucken Quinlan,' he said. 'And that weasel Charlie Talbot, you'd think he was Christ almighty, the stuff they've been printing about him in the papers. They'll be singing a different tune when they see what I've got.'

'And what's that, Sid?' I said. 'Water on the brain?'

He took a gulp from the can on the bench. In the sullen silence that followed, I could hear the slosh and stew of some half-formed idea slithering into life.

'You go back to Quinlan,' he said. 'Tell him I've got evidence he's a thief and a liar. Maybe worse, even. Talbot, too.'

'What sort of evidence?'

'Doc-u-mentary evidence,' he said. The can tilted high, almost empty. It wasn't much past noon.

'Doc-u-mentary evidence?' I said. 'Like what?'

'The sort I can stick in an envelope and send to the coppers. Really give them something to think about.' He licked his lips with relish. 'Maybe they'll begin to wonder if those two didn't have good reason to want Merv Cutlett dead. And who knows, maybe I'll get my memory back? Tell the coppers a few things that slipped my mind last time I talked to them.'

I felt sorry for him, the wretch. Flat broke. Sick as a dog.

High as the Goodyear blimp on a cocktail of ill health, pills, booze and malice.

'Let me get you to a doctor, have someone take a quick look. Maybe some income support.'

His face hardened into a snarl. 'Don't you fucken patronise me.'

Abruptly, he scooted backwards, coat-tails flapping, through the gate in the Cyclone partition. He swung it closed and shot the bolt, securing it with a twisted coat hanger.

'I'll show youse all,' he sneered through the wire. 'Just you wait and see.'

Prancing around and rubbing his hands like he was auditioning for the role of Fagin in a Julius Streicher production of *Oliver!*, he reached into the ice-cream chiller, pulled out a fresh can and disappeared into the roofless room, shutting the door behind him.

He didn't just need a doctor. He needed the burly chaps in white with the butterfly net.

The door flew open and he emerged with something in his hands. Small items bundled together with a rubber band. He stripped off the band and advanced towards the fence.

'Know what these are?'

I hooked my fingers on the links and peered through the chain mesh. He held two thin booklets, one in each hand.

'Passports?' I ventured.

'Bankbooks.' He stuffed one in his pocket and opened the other, extending it towards me at eye level.

I hadn't seen a savings passbook for years. They were obsolete, gone the way of the whalebone corset and the Betamax VCR. Gilpin shoved it at my face, close enough to read. Commonwealth Bank, 341 Victoria Street, Melbourne.

I remembered the branch. It occupied the building on the corner of Lygon Street, an august two-storey structure from the 1880s. It was something else now. Luxury apartments, probably. The side entrance of the Trades Hall was straight across the street.

The account holder's name was typed in a punch-card font. Barry Quinlan, it said. The columns showed a sequence of deposits over a six-month period, the first in February 1978. The amounts varied, averaging between one and two thousand dollars. The total balance was $18,022.07. It was withdrawn in a lump sum, all but the small change.

He held up the second passbook. The name at the top was Charles Talbot. The sum withdrawn was $14,225, leaving a balance of $2.04.

'More than thirty grand all up,' he said. 'Big bikkies in those days.'

I nodded. A year's wage, pre-tax, for a specialist tradesman or a mid-level manager. My own income that year would've been lucky to reach fifteen grand. He wrapped the rubber band around the passbooks and stowed them inside his coat, swapping them for his fresh can of beer. He popped the tab and foam oozed out. He licked it off his hand and waited for my reaction.

'They had bank accounts,' I said. 'So what?'

'And they cleaned them out on 27 July,' he said. 'Recognise the date, do you?'

I shrugged. 'Should I?'

'It's the Monday after Merv Cutlett went down,' he sneered. 'Interesting, eh?'

It was. Unfortunately.

'You've lost me, Sid,' I said. 'I've got no idea what you're talking about.'

'Quinlan will, though.' He took a long swig. 'So you get on your bike, sport. Go tell the senator that unless he sees me right, I'll make sure these little babies come to the attention of the coppers.'

I stayed where I was, fingers threaded through the wire. 'If these bankbooks are such hot property, how come Quinlan and Talbot let you get your mitts on them? It all sounds like crap to me, Sid.'

He flicked his wrist forward, shooing me away. I was merely the messenger, and a dumb one at that. 'Off you go, then. Scoot.'

'What do you want, Sid?'

He sneered. 'What do you reckon I want?'

'Money won't help if you're too crook to spend it. Let me get you to a doctor, eh?'

He sucked his breath inwards sharply and his eyes went hard. 'Fuck your doctor and fuck you and fuck Quinlan.' He pounded the front of his coat with the flat of his hand. 'These are going straight to the coppers.'

There was real menace in his voice. The guy was barking mad. Maybe the kennel and the chalk-stick turds were his.

'The senator's in Canberra for the next few days,' I said. 'Is this something I should talk about on the phone? Calls to federal parliament are recorded, you know.'

Gilpin's paranoid cunning was racing ahead of itself. Whatever his plan, he hadn't thought it all the way through. 'When's he coming back?'

'Later in the week.' I had to say something. 'Thursday.'

'Tell him he's got until Wednesday, close of business.'

'You have a figure in mind?'

'Tell him to make me an offer.' He fixed me in his yellow, puffer-fish gaze, an idea crossing his eyes like a fast-burning fuse. 'And while you're at it, take the same message to whatsername. That stuck-up bint from the office. The one Talbot had his tongue out for. Married her, didn't he? She must be worth quite a few bob now. Careful bloke like him would've been insured to the hilt. And the super. Politicians have always got a shitload of that.' He chugged on his can. 'Oh, yeah. She'd pay almost anything, I bet, to preserve Charlie-boy's good name.'

He stayed in his cage as I walked up the aisle of worthless trash. As I neared the door, he called out.

'Don't get any smart ideas. They're well stashed. And if I see you or anyone else around the place, the deal's off.'

When I looked back at the shed from the kerb, he was standing at the back corner, his coat drawn around him, watching me go.

Fliteplan Travel operated from a low-rise art deco apartment block in St Kilda Road, the vestige of a bygone era on an avenue of glass-clad office buildings. The elms were shedding their foliage and eddies of brittle brown chaff swirled around the angular metal sculptures in the granite forecourt of the advertising agency next door.

I climbed the stairs to the second floor, found the flat with the sign on the door, gave a light rap and went straight in.

Fliteplan did most of its business over the phone, so Margot hadn't wasted any money on décor. The living room doubled as her office, and I could hear muted female voices and computer tapping noises from the direction of main bedroom. A big window overlooked Fawkner Park, level with the treetops, and the wall of the kitchenette had been replaced with a laminex bench.

Margot was sitting at her table, working her way through the mail. She'd painted up and fluffed her hair, but her face was still drawn and a bit emptied-out. She looked up and gave me a convalescent smile.

'Murray, love,' she said. 'What a pleasant surprise.'

'A surprise,' I agreed sombrely, 'but not too pleasant, I'm afraid.' I shut the door leading towards the rooms where the staff were working. 'I've just been to see Sid Gilpin.'

Margot cocked her head sideways and stared at me, mystified.

I sat down at the table. The neat piles of envelopes were the same sort as I'd seen at the house. Condolence cards. Margot had been slicing them open with a letter opener and making a list.

'He's all hopped up,' I said. 'Mad as a cut snake. He showed me his so-called evidence of corruption at the Municipals. It's a couple of old bankbooks. One in Charlie's name, the other in Barry Quinlan's. Substantial sums were deposited in the months before Merv Cutlett's death, then withdrawn immediately afterwards.'

Margot gave me a blank look and shrugged.

'You don't know anything about this?'

She shook her head. 'You told me nobody was taking Gilpin seriously.'

'That might change.' There was no point in pussy-footing. 'A journalist, Vic Valentine, has taken an interest.'

The thin wash of colour drained out of Margot's face. 'The crime reporter?'

'He's not a bad bloke, as journalists go,' I said. 'Gilpin tried to flog him the corruption story but Valentine gave him the bum's rush. Since then, unfortunately, another angle has come up. Valentine's got inside information on the state of the remains. The forensics suggest that Cutlett was shot, then dumped in the lake.'

Margot furrowed her brow. 'Shot?'

'There's a hole in the skull, apparently.'

'A bullet hole?'

'It's absurd, I know.'

Margot reached into her handbag, its strap slung over the back of her seat, and fished out a pack of cigarettes. 'Open the window, will you, Murray?' she said. 'Can't smoke in here. Hell to pay.'

I slid open the glass. A concrete windowbox was built into the ledge. Red geraniums. Margot held a cigarette to bloodless lips. I found my lighter and summoned up a flame. Margot inhaled sharply, her hand trembling.

'The police think Charlie shot Merv Cutlett?'

I shrugged my shoulders. 'Far as I know, they still haven't got a positive ID on the remains. They're waving around photos of a wristwatch found at the recovery scene, trying to establish if it belonged to Merv. I'm pretty sure it didn't. But even without a confirmed identification, it seems a fair bet they're proceeding on the assumption it's him. The hole in the skull can't be ignored and there's some inconsistencies in Charlie and Barry Quinlan's original testimony. Exact location of the accident and so forth. So they've got a potential victim and possible perpetrators. Right now, I imagine they're casting about for a possible motive.'

'And you think these bankbooks might give them one?'

'Gilpin certainly does,' I said. 'He's threatening to send them to the cops anonymously. Set the cat among the pigeons. He's prepared to back off, he says, but it'll cost.'

She drew back hard and exhaled. 'The little shit.'

I went into the kitchenette, found a saucer and put it on the table between us. Margot tapped her gasper hard against the rim. It didn't need ashing.

'How much does he want?'

'Money won't fix it,' I said. 'Sid's off with the goblins.'

She tapped a couple more times, her thoughts turned inward. 'What about Barry Quinlan? Have you talked to him?'

'I came straight to you,' I said.

A draft came through the window, ruffling the pages of Margot's notepad. She used the saucer as a paperweight and stood, staring out over the windowbox, one hand on her throat. She suddenly looked about a million years old.

'"Don't worry",' she said. 'That's what Charlie told me. "It's over and done with". And I believed him because that's what I wanted to believe. But of course it's not over, is it?'

She left her cigarette burning in the saucer, sending up a thin curl of smoke. I picked it up and took a drag. It tasted of nothing. 'I'll do whatever I can to help,' I said. 'These bankbooks…'

'I don't know anything about them.' Her tone was sharp. She turned her back and stared out into the park. 'But I do know that Charlie didn't kill Merv Cutlett. And neither did Barry Quinlan.'

'Of course not,' I started. 'I'm not…'

'It was me,' she said. 'I'm the one who put a bullet in his brain.'

A woman, late twenties, with funky specs and a hedgehog haircut bounded out of the work area, a coffee mug in each hand.

'Oops,' she blurted. 'Didn't realise we had a visitor.'

I hastily grubbed the cigarette out in the saucer. Margot didn't miss a beat.

'Jodie, this is Murray,' she said. 'A friend.'

Jodie had registered the tension in the air. She gave me a cagey nod. Friend or not, I was obviously the bearer of bad news. A smoker in other people's workplace, come to heap even more sorry business on her boss's shoulders.

She clanked her mugs down on the metal sink top and began to run a stream of water into an electric jug. 'Can I get you a cup of something?'

Margot slid the window shut. 'That new lunch place next door,' she said. 'Today might be a good time for you and Michele to give it a try.'

Jodie took the hint. Shooting daggers at me through her Jenny Kee eyewear, she collected her workmate Michele and the two of them scuttled through the pregnant silence and disappeared out the front door.

'I want a full report,' Margot called after them, reassuringly.

Then she turned and stared through the window, her elbow cupped in one hand. An elegantly turned-out businesswoman in her fifties, shoulders square, her hair just a shade lighter than the overcast sky. Down in the park, the spindly fingers of the treetops clawed uselessly at the air.

The silence stretched out, taut as a piano string. The bell had been rung. There was no unringing it. I extended a fresh cigarette. She smiled bleakly and let me light it for her, steady now. When she sat down, I reached across the table and gave her hand a reassuring squeeze. It was ice.

She took a deep breath and began to talk.

'Charlie would never tell me what happened up there at Nillahcootie,' she said. 'He'd only ever say that it wasn't my fault, none of it, Cutlett's death included, and that nobody else knew. About me, I mean. But whatever happened at the lake, it gave Barry Quinlan some sort of a hold over him, at least for a while. If this comes out, Quinlan will blame Charlie for everything. I won't let that happen. I'll go to the police myself.'

The words were gushing out, tumbling over each other, dissolving her hard-maintained self-control. A fearful and frightening look had entered her eyes. I held up the palm of my hand.

'Stop,' I said. 'Wait.'

I went into the kitchenette, switched on the jug and opened the top door of the refrigerator. On the shelf beside the ice-cubes was a bottle of Stolichnaya. I poured a tot, put the glass on the table in front of her, sat down and lit myself a cigarette. Margot blew her nose on a tissue, downed the vodka and shuddered.

'There's no hurry,' I said. 'Take your time.'

She breathed deep, nodded and started again.

'It happened the Friday night,' she began. 'We'd been flat out all day at the office. Prue was home sick with the Hong Kong flu, the temp was out of her depth and the photo-copier was on the blink. There were the phones, the fortnightly pay figures. Organisers in and out. Heaps of typing and copying. To cap it off, Charlie landed Mavis with a last-minute job, typing up some documents for a meeting up at the Shack that weekend.'

She scratched her ash on the rim of the saucer. 'Remember how we all felt sorry for him, the way Merv dragged him up there whenever they had something important to settle?'

She was circling, trying to find a way to tell it.

'Anyway,' she continued. 'Five o'clock came and Mavis still hadn't finished. It was her wedding anniversary, one of the big ones. Her family was throwing a turn and there was no question of her working late. Charlie was getting anxious, so I offered to stay back and finish the job. Kind of hoping, I suppose.'

I'd been too dense to notice it at the time, but for months there'd been an unvoiced attraction between Charlie and Margot. Lingering looks and hungry glances, never acted upon. Her offer, and Charlie's acceptance of it, must have been loaded with implicit possibilities.

'Mum was minding Katie, so I rang and told her I'd be a bit late. Charlie went home to Elsternwick to have tea with Shirley and the kids. He said he'd be back at seven-thirty to pick up the papers. After that, he'd collect Merv for the drive up to the Shack.'

Margot went back to the window and stood staring out into the park. I leaned into the fragile silence, letting her take her time.

It was past seven when Charlie phoned to say he was running late. 'He said he'd swing past in half an hour, to wait with the stuff at the side door of the Trades Hall, outside Cutlett's office. I could hear his kids in the background and I knew there was no hope of anything happening between us that night.'

Disappointed, dutiful, Margot did as she was asked. As she hurried along the footpath, Merv Cutlett and Sid Gilpin staggered out of the John Curtin.

'Pissed, of course,' she said. 'I walked faster, tried to shake them off, but we were all going in the same direction and they started trying to crack on to me. Nothing heavy, just a bit of drunken teasing. They were in a pretty good mood, and I didn't want to get them offside, so I slowed down and walked across the street with them.'

I could picture it clearly. Margot, hugging the buff envelope of papers to herself against the evening chill. Two blokes rolling out of the pub, full of beer, full of themselves. The three of them waiting at the traffic light, the suggestive joviality, Margot's resigned acquiescence.

'I was hoping that Charlie had already arrived, that he'd be waiting when we got to Merv's office. But he wasn't. Merv and Gilpin were both a lot drunker than I first thought. Merv wanted to get something from his office, something he had to take up to the Shack with him. The side door was locked and he kept dropping his keys. When Gilpin tried to help him, he told him to fuck off, there were still some things he was capable of doing himself. He told him to make himself useful, go get some fish'n'chips for the drive. Gilpin was rabbiting on about whether he should get flake or couta and did Merv want a bloody potato cake, and Merv was fumbling with the door. I was just wishing that Charlie would hurry up and arrive so I could go and pick up Katie.'

Margot absently fingered her wedding ring, a plain band with a row of small diamonds, twisting it round and round. I took the vodka glass into the kitchen and threw the switch on the electric jug.

'As soon as Gilpin was gone, Merv got the door open. He went down the steps and unlocked his office. A few seconds later, he called up to me. "Hey, girlie. Come and give me a hand."' She rolled her eyes. 'Like an idiot, I went down.'

A phone started to ring in the work area. Margot ignored it, butted out her half-smoked cigarette and lit another.

'He was standing behind the door. As soon as I stepped inside, he jumped me. Put his arms around me and tried to kiss me. He was always a bit of a letch, but this was the first time he'd ever got physical. I didn't really take it seriously, just pushed him way. But he stumbled backwards and dragged me down with him. And when I tried to stand up, he shoved his knee between my legs and pinned me underneath him. He was slobbering all over my face and telling me I was beautiful.'

She spoke in a flat, drained monotone, paying out the words one at a time. It was as if she was making an accounting to herself, as well as to me.

'I told him not to be stupid, that he was hurting me, but he wouldn't listen. He held his hand over my mouth and started tearing at my clothes. I was kicking and struggling, trying to get up, but he had my hair pinned to the carpet.

That awful brown shagpile. I couldn't breathe. He ripped my pantyhose and started to undo his pants. He was only a skinny bloke but he was strong, a lot stronger than me. I was really, really scared.'

The jug boiled and switched itself off with a sharp click. I gingerly rinsed Jodie's mugs and spooned coffee into a plunger, my attention wavering no more than an inch from Margot's face.

'I was struggling, trying to get out from under him. I grabbed the lead to the desk lamp and pulled it. The lamp crashed onto the floor and I grabbed it by the stem and hit him with it,' her hand bludgeoned the air. 'Hit him as hard as I bloody could.' Abruptly, she stopped, her fist poised as if still closed around the stem of the lamp. 'You ever see Merv's desk lamp?'

I put two mugs of coffee on the table. 'Solid brass shell casing, right?' I said. 'One of Merv's very tasteful items of militaria.'

She nodded. 'The base was a kind of starburst of bullets.' She fanned out her fingers. 'Anyway, it did the trick. Knocked him out cold. I rolled him off me and managed to find my feet. At that exact moment, Charlie came through the door.'

I pictured what he saw. Cutlett, insensible on the floor, his pants undone. Margot, dishevelled and terror-stricken, standing over him with the lamp in her hand.

'Charlie immediately took charge of the situation. He was so calm, so gentle. He took the lamp away from me, put his arms around me, just held me until I stopped trembling. Then he sat me down in a chair and examined Merv. He was still out cold. I thought I'd killed him, but Charlie said there was no blood, he was just stunned, that he'd be okay.'

She went into the kitchenette and came back with a jar of sugar and the bottle of vodka. She poured a nip of Stoli into each of our coffees and sat back down.

'He was wonderful,' she said. 'He wanted to know if I was hurt, did I need a doctor. He was going to call the police, but I wouldn't let him. We all knew stories about girls who'd gone to the cops and wished they hadn't. I wasn't thinking straight. The main thing I was worried about was being late to pick up Katie. Charlie said he'd sort things out. He made sure I was okay, escorted me to the toilet to clean up, called a taxi and sent me home. He told me not to worry, that he'd take care of Merv.'

She started to light another cigarette. I took it from her and slipped it back in the packet. There were five butts in the saucer and only one of them was mine.

'And so he did,' I said.

'Yeah.' She laughed harshly. 'Splish, splash.'

She took a sip of her coffee and grimaced at the taste. But at least the tension was draining from her face.

'I did exactly what he said. I picked up Katie and went home. All that night and all the next day, I kept thinking he'd ring me. He didn't. I realised why when I saw the Saturday evening news.'

Charlie had taken care of Merv all right, successfully disposed of his body, evidently aided by Barry Quinlan. He'd taken care of Margot, too, made sure that she wasn't called to account for Cutlett's death, spared her the ordeal of the judicial process.

'I can't even begin to guess what he told Barry Quinlan and Col Bishop. All he'd ever tell me was that neither of them knew that I was responsible,' she said. 'I knew he couldn't possibly have told Shirley. Whatever he did, he'd done for me. I didn't need to know the details. Does that make sense?'

I nodded. The vodka gave a bitter aftertaste to the coffee. I added sugar, but it didn't help much.

'I couldn't bear the idea that he should have to explain himself. To me, or anyone else. The important thing was that he understood how grateful I felt. If he ever tried to raise it, I'd just put my fingers to his lips and turn away. And when he died…well there was nothing left to say.'

Nor was there anything I could say. I reached across and gave her hand another squeeze. It wasn't so cold anymore. That was something. Certain things were clearer now, but we were still only half-way there. We faced each other across the rims of our mugs, sipping the vile coffee. Margot waited for me to speak.

'Got any biscuits?' I said.

She laughed, and the tension in the room slackened a little. While she searched the kitchen cupboards, I digested the implications of her confession.

If Vic Valentine was right about the forensics, Merv's lamp accounted for the hole in his skull. The rope had probably been used to weigh the body down. Getting him into the car wouldn't have been a problem, not if Charlie was parked right outside the door. He was burlier than Merv and it would only have been a few seconds' work to get him across the footpath. Anybody who happened to notice would've just seen a bloke helping his pissed-legless mate, not an unusual occurrence in that neighbourhood at the time. By the time Sid Gilpin arrived with the flake and chips, they'd already left.

'So,' said Margot, putting an open packet of Tim Tams on the table. 'There you have it. I didn't mean to kill Merv

Cutlett, and I didn't ask Charlie to do what he did. But those bankbooks haven't got anything to do with it. And if Sid Gilpin or Barry Quinlan or anybody else tries to make out they do, that Charlie was some kind of a crook, I'll…' She was angry again now. 'I'll…' She broke one of the biscuits in half. 'Jesus, Murray, I don't know what I'll do.'

'Then don't do anything,' I said. 'As soon as you're okay to drive, go home. If the police get back in touch, which I doubt, just tell them you're not feeling well. You've done your fair share of confessing for the moment. Just leave things to me for a while, okay?'

'What are you going to do?'

'I'm not completely sure,' I said. 'I'll ring you later.'

She looked down at the half-opened pile of condolence letters. I gathered them up, along with a Tim Tam, and got to my feet. 'I'll take care of these. You go home.'

We embraced. The brittleness was still there, but there was something else as well. Something steely I hadn't registered last time. 'It'll be all right,' I said. 'I promise.'

I hoped to Christ I was right.

'Parliament House,' I told the cab driver.

Whatever else I'd got myself into, I still had a living to make. In twenty minutes the Health and Social Services Policy Committee would be looking at my empty chair and making tut-tutting noises.

'Permanent House?' said the chirpy sub-continental behind the wheel. 'Near airport.'

'No such luck,' I said. '*Parliament* House. Big joint, top end of Bourke Street. More columns than the *Weekend Australian*.'

We cruised towards the CBD, stopping to have a cup of tea and a chat with every red light on the way. I pulled out my phone and called Inky.

'Another record-breaking performance on Saturday,' I said, mouth full of chocolate biscuit.

'Leppitsch played well.'

'If you don't count getting reported for striking.' As we

reached the Shrine of Remembrance, it started to drizzle. 'I've spoken with Barry Quinlan. I've also had a word with Sid Gilpin.'

'And?'

'Well, Quinlan didn't let any cats out of any bags, if that's what you're asking. He seems pretty relaxed. Didn't give me any openings. Gilpin, on the other hand, is wound up tighter than a clockwork monkey. He's talking all sorts of crazy shit. Little wonder the media's giving him a wide berth. But it might be an idea to give Vic Valentine a buzz, see if there's any further activity on the walloper front.'

'Something in particular you're concerned about?'

'Just curious about progress on dem bones. No point in spinning our wheels if it isn't even Cutlett.'

'I'll see what I can find out.'

The cab driver had found the slowest tram in Melbourne to follow, peering at it through the slapping wipers as though intrigued by the sight. He bore not the slightest resemblance to the official driver ID photo on the dashboard. Perhaps it was the first tram he'd ever seen.

I checked my message bank, hoping that Lanie had called to accept my invitation to the Croupiers' Gala. No such luck. Ayisha was the only caller. I dialled the electorate office. Mike Kyriakis had phoned, she reported, wanting to know if I'd made up my mind.

'He's talked himself into running,' she said. 'What do you want me to tell him?'

'Tell him if he holds off announcing his bid until tonight, I'll take readings of the branch secretaries, see if I can't rustle him up some support. First round votes only. Nobody's going to die in a ditch for him.'

'By you, I presume you mean me.'

'You don't keep a dog and bark yourself.'

'Careful Murray,' Ayisha said. 'I know where you live.'

'But first, can you please call Phil Sebastian at Barry Quinlan's office,' I said. 'Tell him we're poised to assist and you're setting up some appointments with local movers and shakers on Wednesday. Turn on the charm.'

'Appointments with who?'

'Nobody,' I said. 'We're blowing smoke.'

'Does that mean…?'

'Anybody else call?' I said, cutting her off short. 'An Andrea Lane?'

While I was talking, I flipped through Margot's pile of condolence cards. A parchment-quality envelope with a heraldic device in the corner caught my eye. A lion rampant surmounting the words *Mildura Grand Hotel.*

'No Lanes,' said Ayisha. 'Just the usual. Nothing that can't wait.'

When I left the Grand, I hadn't thought to enquire about Charlie's bill. It suddenly occurred to me that he'd flagged out, but maybe he hadn't checked out. Surely the hotel hadn't forwarded his bill to his widow? I thumbed open the envelope. It contained a letter of condolence, signed from the management and staff, and a courtesy slip with Charlie's uncollected messages attached. Calls he'd missed while he was busy eating breakfast and dying of a heart attack. There were only two. One was taken at 7:45, the other at 9:15. Please call urgently. Two different numbers, but the same name on each slip.

'Before you do anything else, do me a favour, will you?' I said to Ayisha. 'Call the House and give my apologies for the Health and Social Services Committee meeting.'

I rang off and dialled the number on the second slip, the

one left at 9:15. Business hours. The phone was answered after three rings.

'Pro Vice-Chancellor's office,' said a plummy female voice.

'I have a message to ring Colin Bishop urgently.'

'The professor isn't here at the moment. He's at a conferring ceremony at our city campus.'

'The one in Flinders Street?'

'That's correct. If it's urgent, perhaps I can assist.'

I doubted it. I thanked her, hung up and tapped the cabby's elbow. 'Just here, thanks, mate.' We were at the lights outside Flinders Street station.

'Parmalat House?' He looked uncertainly towards the railway station, the finest example of Indo-Colonial architecture in the southern hemisphere.

'That's right, mate,' I said, scribbling a voucher and thrusting it into his hand. 'Good job.'

The city campus of the Maribyrnong University was a twelve-storey office building above a shopping arcade near the corner of Queen Street. Student types were dawdling around the lifts, toting folders and chatting in Cantonese. I scanned the directory and decided the top-floor Assembly Hall was the likeliest prospect for the diploma-bestowing solemnities.

The Assembly Hall owed less to the traditions of Oxbridge than the aesthetics of a hotel-basement ballroom. The seats were crammed with polyglot parents and well-wishers while graduands wearing rented academic gowns and their best trainers stood in a shuffling line waiting for their names to be called. One by one, they stepped forward to receive the rolled parchment in a cardboard tube that certified them to be fully credentialled Bachelors of Food

Handling and Spinsters of Tourism Marketing. The faculty, doing its best to add lustre to the occasion, was sitting solemnly on the dais in floppy velvet scholars' caps and colour-coded gowns. They looked like a high school production of *A Man for All Seasons*. Colin Bishop was standing centre stage, dishing out the diplomas.

There seemed still to be another fifty or so customers waiting their turn, so I sidled along the back wall and slipped outside onto a long balcony that overlooked the river and Southbank. The drizzle had lifted and a couple of rough-nut fathers were sneaking a quick fag at one end. I botted a light, took my smoke and my phone out of earshot and dialled Peter Thorsen's office. After a short wait, the deputy leader came on the line.

'That matter we discussed,' I said. 'Still in the market for a kamikaze pilot, or has your Turkish mate Durmaz already found one for you?'

'Durmaz couldn't find Anatolia in an atlas,' said Thorsen. 'Got a taker, have you?'

'Two conditions,' I said. 'First, if I get this bloke to run, I want a definite commitment that I'll be a member of any shadow cabinet you form if and when you're elected leader, and that I'll remain there until the next election.'

Across the river, work crews were erecting stages in the forecourt of the new casino building, getting everything chip-shape for the grand opening on Thursday evening. This gambling caper, I thought, it can really suck you in.

'Second,' I continued. 'This stalking horse, he's a mate. I don't want to see him completely humiliated. I need your assurance that you'll do your best to get him some central panel votes, at least for the first round.'

Thorsen thought for a moment. 'Done and done.'

'In writing.'

A written commitment to include me in his putative front-bench team would be a token of Thorsen's good faith, nothing more. If niggle came to nudge, it wasn't worth the paper it was written on. An undertaking to steal votes from Phil Sebastian, however, was documentary evidence that he was conspiring to white-ant his liege lord, Alan Metcalfe.

Thorsen didn't hesitate. 'Yes to the first, no to the second.'

'Done,' I said. Some you win, some you just try for size.

'So who's your candidate?'

'Mike Kyriakis, Mayor of Broadmeadows, hero of the rank and file, pillar of the influential Greek community, valued member of the Left.'

'Beautiful,' said Thorsen. 'Fits like a glove. I'm penning my promise as we speak.'

A sustained, concluding burst of applause came from the conferring ceremony. The Exalted Ones were processing down the central aisle, followed by the newly minted graduates. The audience was on its feet, clapping proudly. I went back inside and contributed to the goodwill. May Providence smile upon them and all who consume their portion-controlled comestibles.

The procession arrived at an area lined with tables laid out with teacups and self-serve urns. There, it broke into its constituent parts and began milling around, joined immediately by members of the audience. Cameras began to flash and a congratulatory din arose.

I waded into the crowd and found Colin Bishop being dragooned into a photo-op with a beaming, tube-brandishing young lady and her camera-wielding mother. He recognised me and projected a telepathic plea. If this wasn't nipped in the bud, he'd be fair game for the rest of them.

'Pro vice-chancellor,' I cried, charging into shot. 'Come quickly. You're needed in the symposium. The dean's had an aphorism. He's defalcated on the bursar again.'

Grabbing him by the vestments, I dragged him into the lift lobby, shouldered open the fire door and steered him into the stairwell.

'Thank you, Murray.' He shook himself free, pushed his glasses back up the bridge of his nose and checked that his beard was still attached. 'It's the clobber. They always want a picture with the robes. You've got someone graduating today? One of your kids? I'll just go and hang this up.'

I blocked his way. 'Before you do,' I said. 'A word in your Thomas Cranmer-like orifice, if you don't mind.'

He registered my stance and the edge in my voice. 'What's wrong? Are you upset about something?'

'I'm upset that you lied to me, Col. I'm upset that you think I'm an idiot.'

'Lied?' He furrowed his brow and blinked, owl-like behind his spectacles. 'Idiot?'

'Is there an echo in here?' I said. 'You heard me. Out at the cemetery at Charlie Talbot's funeral, you said you'd lost touch with him, hadn't spoken with him in years, that you'd been meaning to catch up but never seemed to get around to it. Turns out that you rang him at seven-thirty on the morning he died. At a country hotel. Funny time and place to call somebody out of the blue. Slip your mind, did it, Col?'

His mouth did the goldfish thing. 'I…'

'What was so urgent that morning, Col?' I brandished the message slips. 'That's what your messages said. "Urgent".'

He took a step backwards and stumbled. I grabbed him

and didn't let go, even after he had a steadying grip on the tubular steel banister. His eyes were wide with fear. But that didn't stop me. I wasn't going to hurt him, just ask a few questions.

'Something you read in the paper that morning, was it? Human remains found in Lake Nillahcootie, presumed to be a long-lost drowning victim. You thought it might be a good idea if you all got your heads together—you, Charlie and Barry—make sure you still had your stories straight when the cops came around checking the details again?'

He stared at me, open mouthed, like I was Mario the Magnificent, mind-reader extraordinaire. He made a blustery noise and started shaking his head.

'You didn't tell them anything you might regret, I hope.'

Bishop shook his head, then nodded, then shook it again. His floppy velvet hat bounced around, adding to the pathos. To think this man had once taught self-assertion to officials of the Nurses' Federation.

'I wouldn't…'

'You wouldn't what, Col? You wouldn't have a fit of the wobblies and decide to make a clean breast of it? Of course you wouldn't. Because that would mean dobbing in Barry Quinlan. And Barry wouldn't like that, would he? Told you to get a grip, did he? Told you when you rang him that morning and told you again at the funeral?'

I was winging it. Firing wildly and hoping for a reaction. Bishop's mouth was opening and closing, but nothing was coming out.

If nothing else, I'd managed to freak him out. He started sweating, actual beads of moisture forming on his forehead. He took off his extra-large chocolate beret and wiped himself. I'd pummelled him into submission. He was on the ropes. I paused for breath and he summoned up his indignation.

'Now listen…'

The door bumped against my back. Somebody wanted to use the stairs. I held the door shut.

'No, you listen, Professor,' I said. 'You're in deep shit right now, and I'm here to throw you a lifeline. Take me somewhere we can talk in private.'

He gulped, turned and trotted down the fire stairs. I followed him down three floors and along a corridor to a door with a name plate that read VISITING FELLOWS. That was us, all right.

The room contained two empty desks with cheap office chairs and a window that looked onto a blank wall. I herded him ahead of me into one of the chairs and loomed over him.

'Now tell me what happened when you got to the Shack and found Merv Cutlett dead.'

'Dead?' The pro vice-chancellor blinked. 'Where on earth did you get that idea? He was alive as you and me.'

I sank into the vacant chair. Its hydraulics were kaput and it deflated slowly beneath me, folding my knees into my chest.

Colin Bishop took off his silly hat and scratched at his thinning hair, staring at me like I'd lost my marbles. I suddenly realised I was his Sid Gilpin. A raving lunatic spinning wild fantasies out of random scraps of information.

'Are you okay, Murray?' he said soothingly. 'What's all this about?'

Now that I'd stopped raving, he was going all pastoral care on me. Next thing, he'd be suggesting a doctor. I had to find a different approach before he smothered me in solicitude. I elevated my posterior and fiddled with my piston. The seat rose beneath me.

'Those questions you asked at the cemetery about Charlie's final last words and so forth, they've been playing on my mind, Col. Truth is, he did say something. It didn't make sense to me at the time. I thought it was just heavy breathing. But now I think he was saying, "Merv, Merv".'

The rabbit-in-the-headlights look came back into Bishop's face.

'I didn't see the report in the *Herald Sun* about Lake Nillahcootie until after the funeral. And then, when I found those message slips from the hotel in Charlie Talbot's effects, I thought…well, the heart attack and everything. I thought maybe there are things I'm entitled to know. Especially now that the police have been to see me, asking questions about Charlie and his relationship with Merv Cutlett.'

My apologetic, wounded tone had the right effect. The voltage dropped and Bishop gave an understanding nod. He opened his mouth. Before he could apply the soft soap, I changed tack again.

'It's pretty clear the cops think something untoward happened to Merv Cutlett,' I said. 'And now that the press is taking an interest, there's some concern among, well, certain people as to the potential fall-out. Since I happened to have a background at the Municipals, albeit minor, I've been tasked on a very confidential basis to appraise myself of the essential facts of the situation and to minimise the prospect of an adverse outcome.'

Col was going cross-eyed trying to unravel this combination of obfuscation, misrepresentation and management-speak.

'There are a number of issues of concern here,' I said, counting them off on my fingers. 'First, Charlie Talbot's reputation. Second, Barry Quinlan's exposure to risk. Third, the overall standing of the party.'

Bishop nodded along with the beat.

'So far your name hasn't come up,' I said. 'But it's there in the Coroner's report and…well, suffice to say, I'll do my best to see that your interests are protected. Assuming, of course, you're frank with me.'

Bishop took off his glasses and massaged the bridge of his nose. There was no getting around the fact that I knew considerably more than I should about this matter. Also, I was clearly capable of going off like a Catherine wheel if he didn't at least go through the motions.

'What do you want, Murray?'

'The truth, Col,' I said. 'My objective is to keep the lid on this thing. I can't do that if I've only got half the picture.'

He didn't exactly look enthusiastic. Rain washed across the window, darkening the room.

'I've told you the truth,' he said. 'Cutlett was alive and well when Barry and I got to the Shack.'

'Have it your own way then, Col.' I stood up. 'But if anybody takes the fall over this, you can bet it won't be Barry Quinlan.'

Bishop gestured for me to sit back down. 'He was alive,' he said glumly. 'But he wasn't too well. He usually got blotto on the drive up from Melbourne, so we expected he'd be a bit the worse for wear, but we'd never seen him in such a bad way. He was sprawled on a couch, semi-conscious, groaning and grunting. Charlie said he'd slipped and hit the back of his head on the corner of the car door when they stopped for a roadside leak. His hair was matted with dried blood, but he wouldn't let Charlie near him to clean it up.'

So Charlie had told Margot the truth, I thought. Her blow with the lamp wasn't fatal. Merv must have come round at some point, probably while he was being bundled into the car. Charlie probably assumed that he'd recover on the way to the Shack. And when he got his wits back, he'd be both chastened and grateful that his behaviour with

Margot had been covered up. That would also account for Charlie's fabrication about his condition.

'The three of us got hold of him and tried to take a look, but that just stirred him up. Bastard kicked me in the shins.' Bishop rubbed his lower leg, demonstrating the precise location. 'We waited until he flaked again, then dragged him into a bedroom and dumped him on the bed. We took off his shoes, tossed the bedspread over him, turned on his electric blanket and left him to sleep it off.'

'But he didn't wake up?' I said.

Bishop took a handkerchief from his pocket and wiped his glasses, fully committed now. 'We had a drink, went to bed. Next morning, it wasn't even light, I got up for a pee. On the way back from the bathroom, I stuck my head in Merv's door. He was flat on his back, just like we'd left him. Something didn't look right. All this gunk had leaked out of the back of his head onto the pillow. It was…' he smiled weakly, 'very unpleasant. And he didn't seem to be breathing.'

'So you woke up Charlie and Barry.'

He nodded. 'We tried to revive him. CPR, mouth-to-mouth. It was useless. His body was warm but that was probably because of the electric blanket. It was set on high and it had been running all night.'

'Why didn't you call an ambulance?' I said.

'I wanted to,' Bishop said. 'So did Charlie. He was at his wits' end. I think he blamed himself for not being more forceful. He thought if he'd got Merv medical attention earlier, he'd still be alive. But Barry didn't agree. It was too late for an ambulance, he said. Cutlett was obviously dead. It wasn't like they could bring him back to life.'

'And Barry was concerned about the way it might look?' I said.

'You know what he's like,' Bishop nodded. 'Always one step ahead. Cutlett dying under those circumstances, at that time, alone with three of his known political adversaries. Years of patient work were at risk. Something like this could have made us pariahs in the union movement. Or laughing stocks. Or worse still, a bit of both.'

'He told you that it would be better to stage an accident. Drop Merv's body in the lake, make it look like a tragic boating mishap.'

'He was very persuasive.' Col Bishop stared down between his knees, studying the carpet. 'Play it right and the body might not be found for hours, days even, he said. The head injury could easily have been down to a knock from the boat.'

'What did Charlie say?'

'Not much.' He thought about it. 'Actually, he was a lot less resistant to the idea than you might expect.'

And so it was done. In the pre-dawn darkness, the boat was launched and the body loaded. Charlie and Barry pushed off onto the fog-shrouded lake while Bishop remained behind, lit the fire, burned the fluid-stained pillow and waited for the others to return.

'Barry said they'd be back in fifteen or twenty minutes at the most,' he said. 'But they were gone for much longer than that. A storm blew up and rain was bucketing down. I thought they'd capsized or hit a submerged tree or something.'

He wanted me, I could see, to understand what an ordeal this had been for him. That he, too, had shouldered his share of the terrible burden. The blank-faced window behind him was a tremulous, rain-streaked shimmer. A wintry pall suffused the small room.

'It was getting light and there was still no sign of them. Then Sid Gilpin turned up. He'd driven part of the way the previous night, been breathalysed going through Seymour and the cops had confiscated his car keys. He'd had to spend the night in a motel before he could get them back.'

'He was party to the planned discussions, was he?' I said.

Bishop shrugged. 'I told him the story we'd concocted, that Merv had insisted on taking the other two out fishing and they were still somewhere on the lake. Then the boat turned up. They'd had trouble with the motor. Charlie was soaked to the skin and turning blue. His teeth were chattering so hard he could hardly speak. But Gilpin being there was a plus. You know, a witness from the other side. Barry said that Merv had fallen overboard and Charlie had jumped in and tried to save him. Merv had gone under and they'd lost sight of him.'

'And Gilpin bought it?'

'Hook, line and sinker. He tore back into the house to call the police and get a search happening, but the phone was locked. That's the way Merv kept it when he wasn't in residence. In case somebody broke in and used it to make free long-distance calls. The key must still have been on the ring in his pocket. Gilpin jumped in his car and tore off to the Barjarg roadhouse to raise the alarm. Barry gave them directions to where the accident had happened, misleading I assume, and they started to search.'

Bishop turned out his hands and stared me square in the face with his baleful owl eyes. 'So there you have it. We kept it under wraps for twenty years. Stuck with our stories when the police interviewed us again last week. As far as I know, Charlie took it to the grave with him. You're the only other person who knows what really happened.'

He tugged back the flap of his academic gown, glanced at his watch and looked around the visiting fellows' office with an air of impatient captivity.

'Sid Gilpin seems to have a talent for turning up,' I said. 'He's done it again. The prospect of Merv's resurrection has got him all excited. He claims to have evidence of a scam at the Municipals.'

Bishop tilted his scarecrow neck sideways. 'Such as?'

'A pair of bankbooks,' I said.

'Jesus,' Bishop snorted. 'Not *them* again?'

'Again?' I said.

Bishop squirmed in his seat. 'I really should go back up and let myself be seen. My absence will have been noted.'

I'd overplayed my hand badly in the stairwell and getting this far had been sheer good luck. 'Yes, of course,' I said, reaching for the door handle. 'You've been very generous with your time.'

'No need to get unctuous, Murray,' he said. 'I've got more at stake here than you, or the Labor Party. Just let me get this academic rigmarole out of the way.'

We hurried along the deserted corridor, Bishop's gown swishing as we passed the empty tutorial rooms and silent offices of the Department of Outdoor Recreation. Evidently the staff and students were outdoors somewhere, recreating in the rain.

'You remember how the union dues were collected?' he said.

'The usual way, I assume. Payroll deductions.'

'In most workplaces, public utilities, big municipalities and so forth, that was the case. But with some of the smaller employers, shire councils, say, it was handled by a union representative. The rep got a ten percent commission and a bonus for each new member signed up or every arrears brought back into the fold. Small beer, but a nice top-up for somebody on a base-grade wage.'

We reached the lifts and I pushed the button. 'What's this got to do with the bankbooks?'

'Those training programs you and I ran, they were very educational,' he said. 'While you were back at base, filling ring binders with diagrams and photocopying course materials, I was doing more than raising industrial education standards among the toiling masses. I was doing a bit of digging.'

The lift arrived, empty, and we stepped in. Bishop firmed his university-monogrammed tie and donned his velvet sombrero. I hit the button for the top floor. The doors slid shut and the lift began its ascent.

'I'd picked up some whispers that Sid Gilpin was extorting kickbacks out of some of the collection agents, threatening to give the job to someone else if they didn't pay up. He created the impression he was acting on Merv's behalf. But that didn't ring true to me. For all his faults, dipping into the till wasn't Merv's style. Charlie agreed.'

The lift doors opened. We'd been gone for a good half-hour and the crowd was thinning. A blue-edged gown, one of the big chiefs, spotted Bishop. 'Ah, there you are!' he declared. 'We've been wondering where you got to.'

Bishop cocked his scraggly beard in the direction of the balcony, indicating I should await him there. 'I've been hiding from the paparazzi,' he declared jovially, allowing himself to be led away.

It was well past three and a hasty Tim Tam was the closest I'd come to lunch. I was hungry enough to fang the furry dice off a Ford Falcon. I fronted the buffet table, but the best I could scrape up were a couple of quarters of picked-over tuna and mayonnaise sandwich. I took the fishy cardboard and a styrofoam cup of tea onto the balcony. The rain was back down to a fine drizzle and I savoured my repast with my back against the wall, sheltered by the overhanging eaves.

A string of flat-topped boats chugged up the river and parked in front of the casino. Entertainment stages, I wondered? Fireworks launch platforms? Premier Geoffries' royal barge on a practice run? I thought about Lanie, wiped the fish oil off my fingers and got out my phone to check my messages.

No joy. But while I had the phone out, I rang Fliteplan. As instructed, Margot had gone home. I'd call her there later, see if she was okay. It had been a busy and relentlessly informative morning. I wondered what I'd got myself into.

After a while, the drizzle stopped and people came out onto the balcony to look at the view or smoke cigarettes. I had one myself, just to be sociable. The crowd had drifted away and the caterers had started to pack up when Colin Bishop appeared, now minus the bonnet and frock.

'Where were we?' he said, leaning on the balustrade beside me.

'Cutlett and Gilpin,' I reminded him. 'Corruption and bankbooks.'

'Ah, yes,' he nodded. 'Poor old Merv. Behind that gruff exterior he was a deeply lonely man, you know. His war service had cost him his youth and his long-term health. Politics alienated him from his family—hard-line Catholics, the Cutletts, rabidly right wing. His wife divorced him and he bullied his daughter into a life of domestic begrudgery as his housekeeper. He couldn't relate to women at all.'

You don't know the half of it, I thought.

'The union was his entire life, but men like Charlie Talbot were trying to steal it from under him. Technocratic types spouting jargon about rationalisation, consensus and the social wage. Gilpin was just a bottom-tier organiser, an ex-garbo, but he read Merv like a book. He got alongside him, pandered to him, drank with him, made all the right noises. Played Tonto to Merv's Lone Ranger. Gave him loyalty and got trust in return. Not to mention a meal ticket.'

Col had obviously become quite reflective since his pro vice-chancellorship, but while this psychologising was all very interesting, it wasn't exactly germane. And the cold wind blowing up the river was threatening to freeze my nuts off.

'The bankbooks,' I prompted.

'Yes, of course.' Bishop swerved back to the point. 'Charlie didn't believe that Merv was corrupt, but he knew a trump card when he was dealt one. He got me to put together a full dossier on Gilpin's little fiddle. Names, amounts, statutory declarations, the irrefutable works. Then, at the height of Merv's intransigence on the amalgamation issue, Charlie showed it to him. Quietly, in confidence, and out of deep concern for his reputation.'

In the past five minutes, I'd learned more about the Federated Union of Municipal Employees than I'd picked up in all the months I'd worked there.

'Merv realised that Charlie had him by the short and curlies. Not only was he unaware of what was happening in his own office, he was at risk of having his reputation trashed in the eyes of his members. At that point, he stopped stone-walling and began to seriously negotiate the terms of his departure. What he wanted, above all, was to retain his dignity and his historic connection with the union.'

'A seat on the board and an appropriate honorarium,' I said. There was one cigarette left in my pack. That made a total of six smoked so far that day, well over my limit. We're all dead men on furlough, I told myself. Turning my back on the breeze, I cupped my hands and lit up.

'Gilpin knew there'd be no golden parachute for him,' said Bishop. 'So he'd bought himself some insurance, just in case Merv ever got backed into a corner. He opened accounts in Charlie and Barry's names at the bank across the road from the Trades Hall. You remember how easy it was in those days. No ten-point checks or photo ID. A gas bill was enough for most banks. Gilpin channelled his kickback earnings through the accounts, making it look like Charlie and Barry were trousering regular pay-offs of some sort.'

'Pretty smart,' I said.

Bishop stroked his beard and nodded. On the street below us, I could see a busker in a kilt playing the bagpipes at the underpass entrance to Flinders Street station. Fortunately, he was too far away to be heard.

'Merv wasn't going to look a gift like that in the mouth. He showed the bankbooks to Charlie and Barry. Quietly, in confidence, and out of deep concern for their reputations.'

'Mexican stand-off.'

Bishop nodded again. 'That's what the meeting at the Shack was supposed to be about. Cutting a deal that accommodated all parties. They'd get the dossier, we'd get the bankbooks. Merv would sign off on the amalgamation, Gilpin would get some fuck-off money. But once Merv had the bankbooks in his hand, he didn't need Gilpin anymore. When Charlie picked him up at his office on the Friday night, he'd sent Gilpin off on some fool's errand. The two of them left without him. But Sid must have realised that Merv was cutting him out of the loop and barrelled after them in a blue streak. If the cops hadn't picked him up for driving over the limit, the whole thing would've played out very differently.'

I knew that wasn't the real reason Gilpin had been left behind. Charlie obviously wasn't going to stick around and put himself in the position of having to explain why Merv was prostrate on the shagpile with his dick hanging out and a hole in the back of his head.

'If Merv had the bankbooks,' I said. 'How did Gilpin get them back?'

'He pinched them.'

Jesus, if this got any more complex, I'd need a degree in nuclear physics to follow it. And if it got any longer, I'd catch pneumonia. I shivered and shook myself, hinting that we should move inside. Bishop continued, oblivious. Fucking fresh-air nut.

'Barry took the books off Merv when he was non-compos and tossed them in his briefcase. They were just sitting there in plain view when Gilpin made his dash into the Shack to use the phone. He was only inside a few seconds, but it was long enough to take a quick shufti and grab them. We discovered what he'd done almost immediately, of course. But there was a lot going on by then, and bigger matters at stake.'

'You didn't try to get them back later?' I said.

'That would only have complicated matters. Gilpin cleaned out the accounts and made himself scarce. We wrote off the money and let sleeping dogs lie.'

It started to drizzle. I flicked my cigarette butt in the general direction of the casino and we hurried inside. Staff were stacking the seating and dismantling the dais. We headed into a quiet corner, our voices hushed.

'The sleeping dog kept the passbooks,' I said. 'He's picked up that the police suspect things are a bit iffy in the manner of Merv's death. He's threatening to send the books their way, just to stir things up. Unless, of course, somebody makes him a better offer.'

'He's crazy,' said Bishop. 'Their threat value is twenty years past its use-by date.'

'He's crazy all right,' I said. 'Certifiable. But you and Barry illegally disposed of a body and perjured yourselves at an inquest. Not a good look for men in your current positions. And your story's already springing leaks, otherwise I wouldn't be here.'

Bishop stroked his fungus and gave it some thought. 'Does Quinlan know about this?'

'He will as soon as I tell him,' I said.

'Don't use the phone,' said Bishop. 'Barry was very clear on that point.'

'He's a very wise man,' I said. 'By the way, did the police show you a picture of a watch?'

'Yes,' he nodded. 'What's that all about?'

'Buggered if I know,' I said.

For want of a better idea, I decided to put in an appearance at my place of work.

As I was walking into the vestibule, Alan Metcalfe emerged from the direction of the Legislative Assembly at the pointy end of a flying wedge of frontbenchers. Daryl Keels of the Right, Ken Crouch of the Left, deputy Peter Thorsen and a small phalanx of spear-carriers.

Metcalfe gave me a curt, magisterial nod as they swept past. Without breaking stride, Thorsen reached into his jacket and handed me an envelope.

'Good timing, Murray,' he said, tipping me a jovial there-you-go wink. 'That letter you wanted, re the constituent matter.'

'Good on you, Peter,' I said, pocketing his treasonous pledge as we each continued on our way.

It was one of those moments that makes politics a sport worth playing.

After an hour or so of dutiful paperwork at my desk in the Henhouse, I adjourned to the carpark and thence to the Safeway in Smith Street, Collingwood, which lay exactly twixt House and home.

Out of respect for the street's heritage status, the Victorian-era façade of the supermarket building had been retained. Its windows empty, it stood attached to the front of the strip-lit modern grocery emporium like the plywood set from a Western movie. I drove up the ramp to the rooftop carpark, then walked though the cluster of buskers and ferals sheltering in the entranceway.

One of them stepped into my path, cold-sores on her lips and track marks on the backs of her bony hands. ''Scuse me, mate,' she started up. 'You couldn't help me could you, 'cause I've lost me train ticket to Frankston and…'

'Forget Frankston,' I poured my loose change into her palm, all three dollars of it. 'Get yourself a hit.'

The supermarket was busy with home-bound shoppers and desperate singles cruising for a pick-up. Toilet paper, breakfast cereal, tea-bags. I browsed the condoms.

Lanie still hadn't called. Don't get your boxers in a knot, I told myself. It's only Monday. Give it time.

The classic plain ones, I decided. Ribbed might look a bit kinky.

In the meat section, I phoned Red to check on his whereabouts and discuss ongoing menu issues. He was home hitting the books. Did I have any thoughts on the consequences of the French Revolution?

'Too early to tell,' I said. 'How does spaghetti bolognese sound?'

He made a slurping noise. I took it for a yes, loaded up on mince and joined the line at the register. All the check-out chicks were Vietnamese students and all the bag-boys were Ethiopian. While I waited in line, I tried to imagine the results if they ever had children together. Long distance runners with doctorates in chemical engineering? Very tall restaurant owners?

'Proice check on gwuckermoley?' bellowed the Oriental pearl at the register, unequivocally true-blue.

I humped the groceries to the car, shuffled home through the drizzly rush-hour and conscripted Red into the unpacking. 'Mothballs?' he said, emptying the cleaners and chemicals bag.

'No thanks. They give me heartburn. Let's stick with the spag bog.'

Spaghetti bolognese was the bedrock of Red's culinary repertoire. He browned some mince, added a jumbo jar of tomato puree and phoned a friend while he stirred. I took the mothballs into my den of antiquity and hauled my archive boxes down off the top shelf.

I'd got there just in time. As I levered the lid off the first cardboard carton, a startled silverfish slithered back into the haphazard pile of documents that filled the box. I reached in and removed the contents. A fine powder of insect-droppings had accumulated in the crevices at the bottom. Not a whiff remained of the naphthalene flakes I'd scattered there only three or four years earlier.

Dropping a handful of mothballs into the box, I began replacing the pages, scanning them as I went. This was the archaeological record of my life and times, the hieroglyphs of a vanished civilisation, intelligible only to the expert eye. Why I'd saved this stuff in the first place, and why I continued to store it, was a mystery to baffle the Sphinx. Here were my initials, scratched with a stick in the sands of time. Or, in the instance to hand, scribbled in biro on the menu of the 1972 Young Labor Conference dinner.

In total, the evidence of my passage filled two and three-quarter pop-up Ikea storage boxes. A Politics 201 essay on Checks and Balances in the Australian Constitution. A diatribe addressed to the editor of *Rabelais*, the student newspaper at La Trobe University. The notification letter of my acceptance as a graduate trainee in the Commonwealth public service.

The papers were stored in no particular order. Cataloguing them could wait, something to occupy my sunset years at the Old Apparatchiks Home. Only occasionally did I pause between mothballs to peruse a memory. A staff photo from the Labour Resource Centre, Wendy beside me, her belly big with the imminent Red. A well-received position paper I'd written in 1980 on the untapped potential of co-operative credit agencies. All the vanished dreams of social democracy were mouldering in my boxes, snacks for the weevils. Sic transit Jack Mundey.

Half-way through the second box I found what I was looking for. The cheap newsprint had faded to a parchment yellow and the creases were permanent, but the silverfish hadn't yet done their worst. The eight issues of the *Federated Union of Municipal Employees News* that I had edited, probably the only copies still in existence. I knelt on the floor and carefully turned the pages.

Charlie's photograph appeared at the top of his monthly reports as Victorian State Secretary. The same photo every time, a simple passport-sized head-shot. He was somewhere in his early forties at the time, slightly younger than I was now. His face had aged over the years, but it hadn't really changed.

There was a magnifying glass among the oddments in my top drawer. I switched on the desk lamp and took a closer look. The eyes, crescents of old ink in a genial teddy-bear visage, contradicted nothing I thought I knew about the man.

Something about the story of that morning at Lake Nillahcootie was nagging at me. Something didn't quite gel. I could accept the fact that Charlie had hauled Merv Cutlett's limp form into his car and driven him, semi-comatose, to the Shack. His judgment was clouded by his concern for Margot and he had obviously misread the seriousness of Merv's injury. The disposal of the body, too, had its desperate logic.

But Charlie jumping into the water? It was an unnecessary embellishment. The man-overboard story didn't need it. Not only that, it smacked of self-aggrandisement. Not Charlie's style. Something else had happened out there in the boat, I was sure of it. A piece of the jigsaw was missing.

I leafed through the pages, scanning the other photographs. Most were of Merv Cutlett. Merv the Great Leader and Merv at Work, stern-faced defender of the working class behind his redoubt of logs-of-claim and keys-of-access. I found Charlie again, one of the figures in the background of Merv Shares a Laugh. *Annual Picnic December 1977*, read the caption.

The crowd basking in the great one's presence included Sid Gilpin. He was wearing a wide-collared short-sleeved sports shirt, the top buttons open to better display the medallion around his neck. His left arm was draped around one of the skylarking crew. On his left wrist was a chunky metal band.

My heart skipped a beat. Could it be a watch, I

wondered? A Seiko Sports Chronometer, as seen in the Polaroids that Detective Constable Robbie Stromboli had shown me at my electorate office? I put my nose to the lens and squinted at the blurry monochromatic image. Sid's jewellery was a name bracelet. I couldn't read the engraving, but I knew what it said. *Wanker*.

'Grub's up!'

Red banged a spoon on a saucepan lid. The dinner gong had sounded.

We tucked into our pasta with gusto, washing it down with orange cordial. Beer and wine were only for shelf-stacking nights. Not that Red's day hadn't been busy. Monday was his heaviest timetable and there'd been post-school toil over a hot assignment, due within the week. Unusually, Theatre Studies was giving him the pip.

'Motherfucking Courage,' he complained through a forkful of saucy tagliatelle. 'Brecht.'

His school had a reputation for liberality, giving it a roomy niche among the progressive element in Melbourne's middle class. To offset parental qualms about elitism, its curriculum offered Marxist agitprop along with interschool rowing and the international baccalaureate. But Red found Bertolt far too preachy, especially when he was expected to turn in a six-hundred-word essay on the cigar-chomping old Stalinist's dramaturgical critique of bourgeois ethics.

'Give me Lorca any day,' he said, mopping his plate with a crust.

'They didn't have any,' I said. 'You'll have to settle for Yoplait.'

'Not Jean-Louis Yoplait, founder of the Comédie Française?'

'Apricot Yoplait, his temptingly luscious mistress.'

After we'd eaten, Red returned to his homework. I took a half bottle of sav blanc into my den and hit the phone. First I called Margot and made reassuring noises. She sounded washed out, but she didn't put up a fight.

Next I rang Mike Kyriakis. Both his home and mobile numbers were engaged. I had a few sips and tried again. And again.

He was working the phones too. So far, so good.

I put everything but the *FUME News* back in the archive boxes, added the last of the moths' knackers and stowed them away again. Then I reclined on the couch, wine in hand, and contemplated the situation.

The proper, responsible course of action was obvious. Wait until the remains were officially identified. If the police continued to regard the death as a possible homicide, try to persuade Margot and the others to appraise them of the true circumstances.

It would be the best thing for all concerned. Given the passage of time, the police might well decide not to pursue the matter further. Even if they did, they'd probably have a hard time convincing the Director of Public Prosecutions they could make the charges stick. The physical evidence was questionable and sworn admissions were unlikely to be forthcoming. In the meantime, I should butt out and stop making promises I had no idea how to keep.

But I wasn't going to do that, was I? Not while mad, bad Sid still had those fucking bankbooks.

The phone rang. It was Helen Wright.

'We've just sent out a press release for Mike Kyriakis, alerting the media to his intention to run for Coolaroo,' she said. 'And you remember that kid there on Sunday, the young tyro sitting on the floor? Well, he spent the whole day tooling around the electorate with the membership lists. Seems there's a lot more party members on the books than on the ground. Unless some of them are living six to a room, the Right has been padding the books. Heavily. We're running up a hit list for the returning officer. If the central panel wasn't stitched up so tight, we'd actually have a real chance.'

'We?' I said. 'You sound like Mike's campaign manager.'

'It's just a hobby,' she said. 'During the day, I work for Phil Sebastian.'

'You're a very wicked woman, Helen Wright,' I said. 'To think that until last week, you worked for the straightest man in Australian politics.'

'Ah, Charlie was such a square,' she said, a smile in her voice. 'I haven't had this much fun in years.'

When Red stuck his head around the door at bed time to say goodnight, I told him there was a chance I'd be late for dinner tomorrow.

'I'm going out of town,' I said. 'When I get back there's something I'd like to talk to you about.'

That something was our respective putative careers.

For years I'd been telling myself that I was standing aloof from the petty squabbles. Truth was, I'd been sitting on the fence for so long I had a crease in my arse the size of the Mariana Trench.

Suddenly, and to my surprise, Thorsen's offer of a shadow ministry had fanned the few slumbering embers of my ambition into life. But state Labor was a dead end. I'd be in a twilight home before we got back into power. Federal politics at least offered the prospect of a shot at office.

It was shit or get off the pot, I'd decided. And Canberra was the only place worth shitting.

I caught the eleven-thirty shuttle from Tullamarine, the first flight available at short notice, after a brief but comprehensive meeting with Ayisha at the electorate office on my way to the airport. The cab dropped me at the Senate-side entrance to the federal parliament building just before one o'clock.

Say what you like about Australian politicians, we make no effort to conceal our delusions of grandeur. And there is no better evidence of our robust self-image than the seat of national government.

Part-boomerang, part-bunker, all modern conveniences, it tunnels into the heart of the nation like a glorified rabbit burrow. A pharaonic tumulus crowned with a metallic flagstaff of such monumental banality as to make a rotary clothesline look like the Eiffel Tower.

Before I left home, I contacted Barry Quinlan's office and was told he might be able to find a few minutes before Question Time. So after I'd been scanned for hidden weapons and issued with my visitor's pass, I shook off my escort and headed to Ozzie's for a snippet of lunch before our little chin-wag.

It was a typical, glorious early-May day in the Australian Capital Territory. The sky was Delft-ware blue, streaked with the white vapour trail of a high-flying jet and the maples in the parliamentary courtyards were a claret blaze amid the ornamental pools.

Ozzie's, the in-house coffee shop, occupied a wide, glass-walled intersection at the apex of the bicameral boomerang. Its tables were deployed to catch the traffic, offering its customers an excellent view of the passing political wildlife. Politicians and media hacks converged there to graze on light refreshments and freshly made gossip.

As I stood in line for a salad roll, I cast an eye over the faces and configurations. Given the hour, there was considerable coming and going. I spied the federal Treasurer, a moon-faced ponce, quipping with a table of journalists, pretending to have a sense of humour. A notoriously eccentric National Party backbencher from Queensland was treating a couple of his ruminant constituents to a cup of tea and a scone.

And there, amid a group of men so badly dressed that they could only have been ABC journalists, was Kelly Cusack. She was wearing a delectably snug navy-blue skirt-suit and a cream silk blouse. As she saw me see her, she smiled to herself as if struck by a slightly amusing idea.

'Uh-oh,' I thought.

She walked straight towards me, then reached through the queue to tug a paper napkin from the dispenser on the counter, contriving to brush against me in the process.

'Oh hello, Murray,' she said, like she'd just noticed me. I heard the faint rustle of her blouse and there was a lilt in her voice that needed no clarification.

Taking her napkin, she departed along the window-lined corridor, twitching her tail behind her. I put my salad roll on the back burner, waited twenty seconds and nonchalantly followed. The corridor turned and I found her standing alone at the open door of an empty elevator.

'You're kidding?' I said.

'You game?'

This wasn't on the schedule, but I was prepared to be flexible. I followed her into the lift and the doors whooshed shut.

'I've got a meeting in twenty minutes,' I said.

'So let's skip the foreplay.'

There were three buttons. She pushed the one marked M.

Five seconds later, the doors slid open and we stepped out. We were facing a blank wall with a sign that read 'This room is not intended for eating, drinking, smoking or any other purpose.'

'Mezzanine?' I said.

'Meditation.'

The meditation room was a long and narrow curve with light grey carpet and a series of alcoves set behind low blond-wood screens. Slit windows, one per alcove, offered views of the encircling Brindabellas. A selection of devotional texts sat on a lacquer table. *The Book of Mormon. The Tibetan Book of the Dead. Steps to Christ.* The space radiated a calming, vaguely Japanese feel. We had it to ourselves.

Kelly led me down a step into the furthermost of the alcoves. Unless there'd been some recent changes in church policy, it was not one of the steps to Christ. Behind the privacy screen was a cushioned bench. Kelly pushed me backwards onto it and unsnapped her suspenders.

Suspenders! My hesitation vanished. I heard the sound of one fly unzipping and my little bald monk emerged from his place of seclusion. Kelly turned her back and lowered herself onto my lap, assuming the position known to the sages as Reverse Cowgirl. I sought the four-fold path to nirvana.

'God,' I exhaled, my jewel within the lotus.

'*Om,*' came a nasal hum. '*Om mane padme hum.*'

'*Om,*' answered a second, different voice.

'Shit!' hissed Kelly, clenching her kundalini. 'It's the WA Greens!'

Through some unprecedented quirk in the electoral system, Western Australia, the most racist, development-worshipping state in the nation, had returned two Green Party senators at the previous national poll.

Derided by the major parties as fruit-bats in the political canopy, the Greens had risen to the occasion. In a country where politics is mostly the province of besuited men apparently cloned from the same suburban solicitor, the WA Greens were neither men nor besuited. Nor did they dwell within sight of any known constellation. They were a matching pair of bona-fide superannuated hippy Earth Mothers. In the straitlaced environs of the Senate, they were truly a breath of fresh incense.

'Ting,' said a brass finger bell.

'*Om mane padme hum*,' chanted the two voices.

We had failed to notice their presence when we arrived. And the image of two middle-aged tie-dyed tree-huggers communing with the tantric ineffable in the next alcove, so close I could smell their patchouli oil, instantly neutralised the effect of Kelly's nylon-clad thighs.

Her yoni bore down, enclosing my lingam. But the bald bonze was already backing out of the temple, retreating to his lonely sanctuary, renouncing all desire. Kelly squirmed irritably.

'Sorry,' I whispered. 'I just don't have it in me today.'

She gave a sharp, irritated click of her tongue, and dismounted. 'You're not the only one.'

We refastened our clips and zips, summoned the lift and stepped inside.

I was contrite. 'It was just too freaky, man.'

Kelly pouted. 'I've always wanted to do it in there.'

'And I'm sure you will one day, my dear.'

She laughed. 'I'm sure I will, too.'

We stepped out into the real world and walked back towards Ozzie's together. We both knew, I suspected, that it was our moment of parting. But it couldn't end without words.

'I can't do it anymore,' I said. 'I don't have the nerve.'

What I wanted was a woman I could make love to, lie

beside all night, wake up with, then do it all over again, then go out for breakfast for all the world to see. I missed kissing, too. Those were things Kelly could never give me. Not that it hadn't been fun.

'Our relationship…' I started.

'Relationship?' she raised an amused eyebrow. 'I thought I was fucking you against a tree in a public park, you thought we were having a relationship?'

'Our serial shagathon, then…'

'That's more like it.'

A Liberal minister hurried past, bound for the Reps, nodding to Kelly as he passed. We paused at a Fred Williams, one of the many primo-quality artworks that hung along the corridors, and pretended to discuss it.

'You're a sexual Maserati, Kelly,' I said. 'Zero to a hundred in twenty seconds flat. It's a brilliant ride but I just can't take the pace. I keep expecting us to flip over and burst into flames. It's a sad admission, I know, but I think I'd be more comfortable with a Subaru. Last Friday in the Legislative Council, I've been sweating about it ever since. And this bareback stuff, it makes me feel guilty.'

She patted my cheek and smiled kindly. 'You want out, eh?'

I gave a wan nod and gazed contemplatively at Fred's daubs.

'You're just an old softie, aren't you?' said Kelly. 'No offence intended.'

'None taken.'

'Then out you get, sport. No root, no ride. You were only ever a pit-stop anyway.'

'No hard feelings?'

'No hard anything, unfortunately.'

'Come on. That was just today.'

Already we were joking about it, veterans of many a hairy scrape. We continued along the corridor, our fork in the road just ahead. 'Moving right along,' I said. 'Can I ask what you meant last Friday about Peter Thorsen getting up the numbers for a spill?'

Kelly twitched her coiffure dismissively. 'Old news,' she said. 'That's why I rarely talk politics with you, Murray. You're always two steps behind the play. Haven't you heard?'

'Heard what?'

'About an hour ago, Alan Metcalfe announced that he's commissioned an independent review of internal party procedures in Victoria. He's found a top legal eagle from Labor Lawyers to chair it and given him an open brief. Says he wants to encourage participation, end branch stacking, make the party more accountable to its members, all the usual piffle. A thorough, broad-ranging review, conducted without fear or favour. He's given it until the end of the year to hand down its recommendations.'

I gave a low whistle of admiration. 'During which time nobody can challenge him without looking like they're trying to forestall a democratic overhaul of the party. Six months for the submissions and recommendations, add another six for discussion of implementation and he's bought himself another year.'

'If Peter Thorsen was planning on doing a Fletcher Christian, he's left it too late. Captain Metcalfe still holds the helm.'

We were almost back at Ozzie's. I was expected in Barry Quinlan's office in five minutes.

'By the way,' said Kelly. 'Since our relationship is now strictly professional, mind if I ask what brings you to Canberra?'

'A meeting with Barry Quinlan,' I said. No reason to conceal it. She'd know soon enough anyway. Somebody was sure to notice me and Quinlan together and this place leaked like a surplus Soviet submarine.

'Don't tell me,' said Kelly knowingly. 'The Coolaroo connection. It overlaps your electorate, doesn't it? Poor Senator Quinlan, he's really got himself in deep shit buying into that exercise.'

'I wouldn't call Mike Kyriakis deep shit,' I said. 'A piece of poo on the footpath, perhaps. Something Barry won't have any trouble wiping off his ballerina-size shoe.'

'Mike Kyriakis?' She furrowed her brow. 'That guy in the *Herald Sun* this morning, the local mayor throwing his hat in the ring? That's not what I mean, Murray. Wake up and smell the coffee.'

We'd got to Ozzie's and there was plenty of coffee to be smelled, most of it congealing in the bottom of cups left on the tables by the departing lunch-hour crowd.

'Please explain,' I said. It was the phrase of the moment.

'The local plebiscite is just a side-show, Murray, you know that. The central panel delegates will have the final say. Quinlan thought he had them sewn up, but the unions don't like his choice of candidate. They want one of their own. Word is, they're going to drop somebody into the ballot at the last minute. It'll be the unions versus the parliamentary party. If there was a way for Quinlan to dump Sebastian and find another candidate, someone with both a union and a parliamentary background, he'd jump at it. If he loses this one, his days as power-broker are over. Or so I've been led to believe.'

'It's all above my head,' I said. 'See you round, Kelly.'

'But not quite as much of me, eh, Murray?'

Away she went, heels clacking, and I went to meet the man I'd come to Canberra to see. I could only hope that my next conversation would end as amicably.

In accordance with the Westminster tradition, the House of Representatives and the Senate are demarcated by the tint of their floor coverings and soft furnishings. Green for lower, red for upper. Apart from anything else, this helps the less acute members of the federal parliament find their way back to their seats.

Although both the Reps and the Senate were sitting, and thus a fair fraction of the 226 federal legislators employed by the Australian taxpayer must have been taking advantage of the colour-coded décor, I encountered nobody as I hurried along the rhubarb-toned carpet leading to Barry Quinlan's suite.

Barry was coming out the door just as I hove into sight. Judging by his pace, he was keen to take his seat before Question Time kicked off.

Not so fast, Barry, I thought. I've got a few questions of my own.

'Thought you'd dipped out,' he said amiably. 'We'd better make it quick.' He tilted his head, inviting me back inside his office.

This time, I wanted him alone. Somewhere beyond the reach of watch-tappers and file-handers, the providers of pretexts if he started looking for an easy out. I turned back the way I'd come, back towards the central nub of the vast building, the direction of the Senate chamber.

'We can do this on foot,' I said.

He fell into step with me, brushing a fleck of invisible dandruff off the lapel of his beautifully cut jacket. 'So, what can I do for you in person that I can't do on the phone?'

'You can talk to me about that day at Lake Nillahcootie,' I said.

He gave a sidelong glance and registered that I was serious. 'You seem to be taking a great deal of interest in this matter, Murray.'

The corridor was hung with botanical illustrations by Joseph Banks, priceless originals every one. Quinlan was still looking at me, his shrewd eyes narrow.

'Frankly Barry, I'd rather not know about it. But that's not the way events have transpired.'

We reached an internal courtyard, an expanse of black marble surrounding a low, shallow fountain. The ceiling was open to the floor above and a party of schoolchildren were standing at the railing, looking down at the tops of our heads. Shoulder to shoulder, our voices muffled by burbling water, we slowly began to circumnavigate the ornamental pool. Looking, I imagined, as if we were discussing weighty matters of state.

'I know what really happened,' I said. 'Not that cock-and-bull story about Cutlett getting pissed and falling overboard.'

Quinlan's jaw tightened. 'Murray, mate,' he said. 'I've got no idea what the fuck you're talking about.'

'How about you cut the crap, Barry? I'm trying to do you a favour.'

'What makes you think I need any favours?'

Muted giggles descended from above. The schoolkids were dropping coins into the water.

'Suit yourself,' I said. 'It's not my problem if the genie gets out of the bottle. I'll tell Sid Gilpin to go ahead, do his worst, Barry Quinlan has nothing to hide.'

'Gilpin?' he snorted. 'What's Gilpin got to do with anything?'

'He asked me to give you a message. That's why I'm here. He showed me a couple of bankbooks.'

'Bankbooks? What bankbooks?'

'Cast your mind back, Barry,' I said. 'The bogus accounts Gilpin opened to make it look like you and Charlie Talbot were scamming the Municipals. The ones he nicked from your briefcase.'

Quinlan put his hand on his forehead and moved it back over his wavy black hair. 'You've been talking to Colin Bishop, haven't you? The silly fucking goose.'

'Don't worry,' I said. 'The cone of silence is still intact. Your problem's not Bishop. It's Gilpin. He's back for a second bite of the cherry. He kept the bankbooks. He's threatening to send them to the police anonymously. Stir things up. Then he'll start making allegations.'

Quinlan narrowed his eyes. 'What sort of allegations?'

'Think about it, Barry. Why do you think the Homicide Squad is asking questions about relations in the union? They obviously suspect there's more to Cutlett's death than originally reported. Right now I'll lay you odds they're looking for a motive. And Sid Gilpin is offering to supply them with one.'

Quinlan made a dismissive gesture, like flicking water off his wrist. 'Old bankbooks,' he said. 'Not exactly a smoking gun.'

'But intriguing enough to keep the cops on the boil, poking around, asking questions. You're a big target, Barry. You don't want something like this hanging over your head.'

Quinlan's well-polished toe was tapping a tattoo on the black marble floor. His eyebrows had moved so close they were almost touching.

'Gilpin wants money, I assume.'

I reached down, dipped my fingertips in the fountain and stirred the water slightly. 'Gilpin's stony broke and woofing bonkers, Barry, and he thinks you're the cut-and-come-again pudding. You'll have to find a more effective way of dealing with him.'

'Like?'

I let the drips fall from my fingers. 'It seems to me that you need someone willing to apply himself to the problem. Somebody who can see that your good name remains untarnished. The way things sit right now, Barry, you need a friend.'

'A friend?' He gave a derisive snort. 'Are you trying to horsetrade with me?

'Not at all,' I said.

'But you want something?'

'Of course.'

'Let's hear it then.'

'Just your assurance that if any of this comes out, for any reason whatsoever, you won't try to shift the blame to Charlie Talbot, hang his reputation out to dry.'

'Why would I do that?'

'Because you're a realist, Barry,' I said. 'Because you're alive and Charlie's dead, and the dead don't care.'

Quinlan stared me hard in the face, taking my measure. 'You think I'm a cunt, don't you?'

'I don't really have an opinion, Barry. I'm just the messenger boy. But I do know that even if Charlie no longer cares what happens to his good name, Margot does. And his three daughters and all the other people who looked up to him.'

Quinlan broke eye contact and turned his head away. I should have left it there. But I had to sink in the boot. I couldn't stop myself.

'You thought of everything that morning, didn't you? Even having Charlie jump overboard. Nice detail, that. Lent a real touch of verisimilitude to the lie. Easy to convince, was he? Take all your powers of persuasion? Or did he need a helping hand? Bit of a shove?'

Quinlan's face remained averted. I'd gone too far. He was going to walk away. My stomach was churning.

'Well?' I said. 'If the shit hits the fan, Charlie doesn't feature. You cop it all. Deal or no deal?'

He turned, slowly, and I was facing a naked man. The carapace of his tailoring had cracked open. All front had dissolved. He took a deep breath.

'I'm going to tell you something that nobody else knows, not even Col Bishop. Something I've lived with for nearly twenty years. Something Charlie Talbot lived with until the day he died.'

I waited. Water trickled over the edge of the fountain.

'Merv Cutlett,' he said at last. 'He wasn't dead when we threw him into the lake.'

And they reckon Rasputin was hard to kill. By comparison, Merv Cutlett was Lazarus on a trampoline.

My jaw almost hit the black marble floor. Barry Quinlan registered my shock.

'Oh, we thought he was,' he said. 'We were convinced of it. He wasn't breathing and he didn't have a pulse. Not that we could detect, at least. He was limp as a rag doll when we rolled him out of the boat. But the moment he hit the water, he came alive. The shock must have kick-started him.'

Quinlan shuffled uncomfortably, a man unaccustomed to candid admissions.

'He went under, then bobbed straight back up. He took this great gasp of air…' Quinlan inhaled demonstratively, the inrushing breath resonating against the back of his throat like a plaintive moan, '…then he sank back under the water.'

He paused, conjuring the image into the space between us.

'And, no,' he said. 'For your information, Charlie Talbot

didn't need a lot of persuading. Truth be told, I was surprised how easy it was to convince him that dumping Merv was something that had to be done. But disposing of a dead body was one thing, letting an injured man drown was another. It was a different matter entirely. For both of us.'

He looked me briefly in the eye, then dropped his gaze.

'Charlie drew the line, Murray. He drew it without a moment's thought or hesitation. He was in the water like a shot. Bang, straight over the side. He got hold of Merv and dragged him back up to the surface and tried to keep his head above the water. But the rain came plummeting down like some fucking judgment from above, and the wind started blowing the boat away. And I was bloody useless.'

Quinlan's hands were moving, moulding and shaping the empty air. 'I grabbed the wheel and slammed the lever into reverse but the motor stalled. The rain's absolutely sheeting down and churning up the surface. I'm looking back over my shoulder and trying to get the thing started and the rain's running down my face and getting in my eyes.'

He wasn't talking to me anymore. He was telling himself what happened, trying to put it into words.

'I push the starter and push it and finally it kicks over. The rain is almost horizontal, pelting down and I see this arm sticking up and I steer towards it.' His arm carved a wide, sweeping arc though the air, the trajectory of the boat. 'And I slam the lever into neutral and rush to the side and grab hold of the sleeve as I go past and I almost get dragged overboard and it's Charlie and I'm pulling him back into the boat and…'

Abruptly, the torrent of words stopped.

The schoolchildren had moved away, bored. The faces looking down at us were Asian now. Flat, incurious. Korean?

They started taking photos and dropping coins. Plop, plop, plop. What were they wishing for, I wondered? A job for life at Daewoo? A year's supply of kimchi?

'He was spluttering and shaking. He said he'd lost hold of him, that he'd gone back under. I circled around again, but there was no sign of him. Charlie was shivering so much I thought he was going into shock. We weren't going to find Cutlett without help, but I had no idea where we were by that stage. You could just make out the shoreline and some of the dead trees sticking up looked familiar. I tried to get my bearings but the only way back was to head for the shore and follow it. The whole way, I'm thinking "Maybe it's not too late, maybe we can get help soon enough to save him," and I'm wondering how we're going to explain things if that happens and Charlie, he's just a devastated shuddering wreck.'

He cleared his throat, raised his chin and inhaled deeply through his nose. There was a long moment of silence.

'So now you know.'

He squared his shoulders and began to fix his cuffs, making sure the amount showing was just right, marshalling his composure. I looked at my shoes. Compared with Quinlan's they looked cheap and shabby.

'I don't need your absolution,' he said. 'And I don't give a rat's arse about your opinion of me. But if you think Charlie Talbot's good name is something I'd treat lightly, you're a very poor fucking judge of character. Now tell me what you really want and I'll do my best to see that you get it.'

Ayisha was hunched over the conference table in the general work area when I let myself into the electorate office just after five o'clock. Her hair was pinned up, she had a phone glued to her ear and her much-chewed pencil was cross-hatching an asterisk against a name on a list. Other lists were laid out in a line on the table in front of her, all heavily marked and annotated. I recognised them as the ones we'd roughed out at our meeting before I left for Canberra.

Empty take-away coffee cups littered one of the bench-desks, along with copies of that morning's *Herald Sun* and *Age*. The newspapers were open at their coverage of Mike Kyriakis's announcement of his intention to contest the Coolaroo preselection. *ALP Bid Clash* headed the *Herald Sun* report, its most prominent page three story. The *Age* had gone with *Labor Mayor in By-election Contest*. Page eleven, below the fold, six pars.

Beneath the *Age* piece was a pointer to a 2000-word

Michelle Grattan eye-glazer on the op-ed page. *Labor Needs to Regain Trust of Core Supporters*. I'd read it on the flight to Canberra between the safety aerobics and the artisan-crafted macadamia-chip cookie. The cookie was easier to digest and the crash procedure lecture contained more useful information.

Ayisha's pencil inscribed a question mark against one of the names on her list, over-wrote it several times, drew a circle around it and underlined it. 'Just a tick,' she said, then covered the mouthpiece with her hand and turned towards me. 'Well?' she said. 'Yes or no?'

'Yes.'

She gave me a sceptical look. 'Are you sure you're not having a mid-life crisis?'

'Call it a mid-life epiphany,' I said. 'Mike?'

'He'll be here at six. Helen, too.'

'Peter Thorsen?'

'In his office until five-thirty. And the whip wants you to ring him.'

'Any other messages?' My mobile was still drawing a blank, Lanie-wise. Please God, I prayed, I've been a good boy. Let her have called.

Ayisha shook her head. 'Nothing pressing.'

'No Andrea Lane?'

Ayisha gave me a cunning look. I ignored it and went into my office. I hung up my jacket, loosened my tie and rolled up my sleeves. Whenever the temperature dropped below twenty, Ayisha turned the heating on full bore. My African violet must have thought it was back in Angola. I gave it a drink and hit the dog.

'Yes, what now?' barked Inky, answering his phone after one ring.

'It's Murray.'

'Sorry, mate. Thought it was my ex.'

'Which one?'

At last count, Dennis Donnelly had been married three times and begotten offspring on two other women. He was rumoured to have paid maintenance on seven children over a thirty-year period. Little wonder the poor bastard had an ulcer.

'Mind your own beeswax,' he said. 'I suppose you want to know the latest from Vic Valentine? I'm still waiting on his call. But in the meantime, I gave the police media liaison mob a bell. A very obliging young lady constable told me they're still working on identifying what she coyly described as the material remains. To that end, they've located the burial site of Cutlett *mater* and *pater*, to wit the Mooroopna cemetery, and they're awaiting an exhumation order for DNA purposes.'

There was a pause followed by the muffled crunch of an antacid meeting its match. 'I also had a call from an old mate in Adelaide, a former assistant secretary of the South Australian branch of the Municipals. He's had a visit from the local rozzers, acting on behalf. They showed him a photo of a watch, said it was found with the aforementioned material remains, and wanted to know if it was Merv's.'

'And was it?'

'Not unless he was moonlighting as a *Cleo* centrefold. Quite a flashy piece of tick-tockery apparently.'

'So it's not Merv,' I said.

'We live in hope.'

I left Inky to his domestic altercations and rang Peter Thorsen's office. Del was just finishing up for the day. She said Peter was on a call and put me on hold with instructions to ring back if he didn't answer within five minutes. Chopin's concerto for solo telephone kept me riveted for four and a half. Then Thorsen picked up.

'A wide-ranging, open-ended and time-consuming review,' I said. 'That should keep you out of mischief for the foreseeable future.'

'Some you win, mate, some you lose. Some you don't even get to fight.'

'Too true,' I agreed. 'But before you fold your tents and steal off into the night, I'm calling to remind you that we had a two-part agreement.'

'Meaning you still expect me to go into bat for kamikaze Kyriakis.'

'Is that a problem?'

'I told you I'd do my best and I will.' He sighed wearily. 'But the market in central panel votes has gone through the ceiling in the past twenty-four hours. I can't do more than try.'

'That's all I've ever asked,' I said. 'Care to put a number on your best possible projection? No names, no pack drill.'

'Phew,' he exhaled. 'Hard to say. How long's a piece of string? Four, tops.'

'Love that Motown sound,' I said.

'I'll be there.'

'Standing in the shadows of love?' I warbled as I hung up.

Darkness was falling fast and the strident beep of a reversing fork-lift was coming from the direction of Vinnie Amato's Fresh Fruit and Veg, crates of produce being shunted inside for the night. The rain had dried up while I was in Canberra and long pink-grey mares' tails streaked the skyline above the Green Fingers garden centre like a flock of attenuated galahs.

I dialled Margot's number.

'Murray,' she said. Her voice was an equal mix of fatigue and anxiety.

'How're you doing, sweetheart?'

'I'm okay,' she said.

'I can't chat,' I said. 'I'm at the office. But I'll drop round to the house tomorrow night and we can talk face-to-face. Things aren't as bad as you thought, Margot. It wasn't your fault. None of it. Not here, not there. You've got no cause to beat yourself up.'

'You mean…'

'Gotta go,' I said. 'You know what it's like, a politician's lot and all of that. See you soon, eh?'

I hung up, trusting she'd understand my briskness. Then I rang Red and told him to go ahead and eat without me, but leave me some of the spag sauce.

Ayisha rapped on the glass wall. Mike Kyriakis and Helen Wright had arrived. I joined them at the conference table, where they'd pulled up seats and started comparing their lists with ours.

'Evening all,' I said, assuming the chair position at the head of the table. 'As you know, Ayisha's been complaining for some time that her job doesn't give her enough opportunities for travel.'

My electorate officer gave a derisory, mocking hoot. 'My fault is it?'

'Politics is all about self-sacrifice,' I said.

Ayisha made a jerk-off gesture. The other two were looking mystified, Helen in a round, dimply way, Mike in a solemn, arms-crossed way.

'He means that he's decided to take a leaf out of your book, Mike,' said Ayisha.

233

Comprehension began to dawn. Mike looked at Helen, Helen looked at Mike, they both looked at me.

'That's right,' said Ayisha. 'This fool is putting his hand up for Coolaroo, too.'

Mike and Helen were looking at me like I'd mislaid my marbles.

'Bullshit,' said Helen. 'You can't be serious.'

'No, he's fair dinkum,' said Ayisha. 'And before you ask, it's not a mid-life crisis. It's a mid-life epiphany.'

The time had come to put my cards on the table. 'It's true,' I said.

Mike's disbelief was turning dark. He began gathering up his lists. 'You'll split the vote,' he said. 'By myself I had a pretty good chance of drawing blood. With two of us, it'll be a joke. Why are you doing this Murray? You're already sitting pretty. Why cruel my pitch?'

His sense of betrayal was palpable. Helen and Ayisha watched us in breathless silence.

'Hear me out, Mike,' I said. 'I think I've found a way to make this a win-win situation, or rather a win-lose-win-draw-lose-win-win situation. And I haven't come to the table empty-handed. I've got some cards up my sleeve.'

Mike looked dubious, but he put down his lists and leaned back in his chair. 'Well, since I'm here.'

'You remember on Sunday at Charlie's wake,' I started. 'That hypothetical scenario that Sivan cooked up, the one where a split opened up in the central panel?'

They leaned forward, all three of them, and I reached for a blank sheet of paper.

'Just hand me that abacus,' I said.

The President's gavel descended with a brisk, resounding clap and we lowered ourselves onto our red velvet cushions. It was ten-thirty on Wednesday morning and the Legislative Council of the Parliament of Victoria was now officially in session.

Beside and below me on the opposition benches sat my ten fellow Labor members. Facing us from the government benches were twice as many Liberal and National members. Between us was the Clerk's table where Kelly Cusack and I had conferred the previous Friday.

In six hours I was due to meet Sid Gilpin to relieve him of the bankbooks. In the meantime, however, there was work to be done.

Of a sort. In this particular instance, it consisted of listening to my colleague, Judy Mathering, the Manager of Opposition Business in the upper house and strong proponent of well-fitted foundation garments and sensible footwear, move and speak to a motion.

I settled my backside on the upholstery, and watched as Judy turned her stocky frame towards the President's podium, cleared her throat and begged leave to introduce a Condolence Motion on behalf of the people of Victoria to the family of the recently deceased Mr Charles Talbot, MHR.

My gaze moved up to the well-stocked public gallery where Charlie's three daughters were seated with various of his grandchildren, sons-in-law, nieces and nephews. They sat sombrely, as though in chapel. After almost two weeks of formal farewells, this was the last of the official elegies and I sensed that they would be relieved when it was all over.

Margot was there, too, at the other end of the pew, flanked by Charlie's older sister Jeanette and his younger brother Ray. This gesture of solidarity, I hoped, signalled an eventual thaw in overall familial relations.

The President granted leave and Judy began to read her speech. Her theme was Charlie's service as a parliamentarian and his contribution as a minister in the various portfolios he held during Labor's tenure in Canberra. Judy was no spellbinder and her reedy voice carried an unintentionally hectoring undertone, but this was not an occasion for politicking.

For once, members on the government benches made an effort to uphold the dignity of their office. Most refrained from their usual crotch scratching, nose picking and gum chewing. Several lowered their multiple chins reverently.

I, too, bowed my head and consulted my thoughts. They concerned my plan to deal with Gilpin. There was nothing sophisticated about it. Cunning would be wasted on the mercurial Sid. A blunt instrument was called for. Success depended on wielding it effectively.

Judy Mathering's voice was a steady, hypnotic cadence, rising and falling in the echoing space of the chamber.

> …*the loss of a man whose contribution to public life in the country, and to the welfare of so many people, sprang from a deep-seated commitment to the principles of social justice and…*

I lifted my eyes and studied Margot. It was hard to tell at that distance, but she seemed a lot more tranquil this morning. As tranquil as is proper, at least, for a grieving widow on public display.

She'd met me at the door when I arrived at the Diggers Rest house just after nine the previous night. Katie was tucked up in bed and Sarah the Carer was off duty for the evening, living it up at some student soiree. Margot had a glass in her hand and several under her belt, making me glad I'd come in person. She could sound misleadingly sober on the phone when she tried.

'I'm missing him hard,' she slurred, falling into my reassuring embrace. 'Charlie, oh Charlie, come back.'

For an hour I sat with her on the couch, recounting most of what I'd learned since our talk in the Fliteplan office.

> …*which demonstrated his capacity for creative solutions to the problems of the day…*

Not all of it, of course. But enough of the essentials to convince her that she'd been mistaken in assuming that she'd left Merv Cutlett dead on the floor of his Trades Hall office. Both Quinlan and Bishop had credibly attested to Merv's grouchiness when they arrived at the Shack, painting him more like a bear with a sore head than a man on his last legs.

Neither of them knew about her involvement, I assured her. By the time I left, she was prepared to accept that he had indeed accidentally drowned and Charlie had truly done his best to save the old prick's life.

> *...before going on to play an important role as one of the architects of Labor's return to power in 1983 and its subsequent long and eventful period in government...*

I lowered my eyes and nodded along with Judy's words. I'd helped her polish them that morning after I clocked on at the Henhouse, so I knew them almost by heart.

Apart from lending Judy a hand, I'd spent the morning sequestered in my cubicle, catching up on neglected paperwork and performing acts of administrative contrition for the Whip, whose calls I'd failed to answer in the five days since Inky Donnelly ambushed me with his copy of the *Herald Sun* and his questions about the Municipals.

In between pushing my pen, I'd spent a fair bit of time on the phone, conferring with Mike Kyriakis and Helen Wright.

Their reaction when I hit them with the news that I intended to enter the Coolaroo Derby was understandable. It had taken some heavy paddling, but eventually Mike had copped my proposition. Our interests, I'd argued, were congruent and with luck and good management we might both get what we wanted. He wanted to make a name for himself as a player. I wanted a reason to stay in politics.

> *...where his talents could be best used to safeguard and advance the interests of those who had elected him...*

Like working to defend universal health insurance, say. Reconciliation, and a regulated labour market and multiculturalism and a fair suck of the sausage. All the good stuff the Labor Party was supposed to stand for. And like Mike

Kyriakis, I really didn't have anything to lose by giving it a shot.

The plan I'd pitched in the electorate office was a leap-frogging preference-swap that called upon every iota of the knowledge I'd accumulated in my thirty-year membership of the ALP. It involved a hitherto-untested combination of the five basic moves in Labor decision making—the stack and whack, the roll and fold, the shift and shaft, the Brereton variation and the whoops-a-daisy.

A volatile brew indeed. But ultimately, it came down to Mike Kyriakis' spadework plus delivery on the pledges I'd exacted from Peter Thorsen and Senator Quinlan. And they were far from certainties. Particularly Quinlan's.

> *...a minister in a wide range of senior portfolios, all of them demanding an ability to reconcile widely divergent pressures...*

By the time I got home from Margot's place, Red had hit the hay. I checked the answering machine in the vain hope that Lanie had called, shovelled down some spoonfuls of cold spaghetti sauce, threw myself on the sofa, and thought about my next move.

The police were obviously not slacking off on the identification of the remains. Nor, presumably, had any suspicions aroused by the bullet-shaped hole in the skull been allayed. I'd promised both Margot and Quinlan, each for different reasons, that I'd make sure that Gilpin did not succeed in fanning those suspicions. The mad bastard had given me until Wednesday afternoon to respond to his threats. Problem was, I didn't have the foggiest inkling of what to do.

I lay there for a long time, my feet on the armrest, staring between my socks, before I came up with an idea.

It was a feeble idea, but it was the only one I had.

I took down the archive box and found the issue of the *FUME News* with the picnic photo. Then I went into the loo and collected the pile of newspaper supplements off the floor. I worked my way through the fashion pages until I found what I wanted. I tore out the page, put it in a large manila envelope with the newspaper and drove to the service station in Heidelberg Road. I spent half an hour and five dollars using the photocopier in the convenience store section, then went home to bed.

> *…in the hope that this gesture will offer some consolation to his family and those many others who share the loss of his passing…*

Judy was nearing the end of her speech. I again tilted my head upwards, this time looking directly at Charlie's daughters.

Having a politician for a parent can be hard on a child. For most of their early lives, Charlie was an absentee father. Shirley raised the kids while Dad, like a shearer, followed the work. And now that he was gone, all that remained was his reputation. If I could, I'd see they weren't robbed of that too.

Abruptly, Judy stopped speaking. The President called for a seconder and I raised my hand. The motion was put, a unanimous chorus of ayes rose to the gilded ceiling and Charlie Talbot's name was officially consigned to the history books.

My job was to make sure it stayed on the right page.

What I needed now was a short length of chain and a padlock.

The city skyline was a palisade of glistening steel as the mirrored walls of the office towers caught the last rays of the afternoon sun. Down on the ground, darkness was expanding to fill the space available. The commuters converging on Spencer Street station were already hunched against the imminent chill.

I drove around to approach the Tin Shed from the west, skirting the worst of the traffic, dipping beneath the railway bridge at Festival Hall and turning into what used to be Footscray Road. It had a new name now, but nobody knew what. It was a government secret, commercial and confidential. In the torn-up space between the docks and the future, the only points of reference were the words on the cranes. Transurban. Balderstone-Hornibrook. Nudge-Nudge. Wink-Wink.

I cruised past the shed's corrugated hump and spotted Gilpin feeding a fire in a 44-gallon drum at the back door.

Doubling back, I parked among the doorless refrigerators and wheel-less wheelbarrows and went around the back.

The drum was the one I'd taken for a kennel. Oily flames were flickering from the top, fuelled by Sid from a heap of broken furniture, old garden stakes, ink cartridges and stuffed toys. I wondered if he was cremating the dog. Turds aside, there was still no sign of it.

He watched my approach through a veil of dancing fumes, his puffed-up face giving him the look of a pestilential toad risen from some witch's cauldron.

'Evening, Sid,' I said. 'Glowing with health, as usual.'

'Knew you'd be back,' he sneered malevolently. 'Quinlan's shitting himself, is he? Mr High and Mighty in Canberra. Or did he pass the parcel to that Marjory, whatever her name is? Called himself a bloody unionist, wouldn't know one end of a shovel from the other.'

I gave him the wind-up. 'You want to deal or flap your gums?'

He sniffed and tossed a tattered *Readers' Digest* into the flaming drum. 'Whad've you got?'

I took an envelope from my pocket, lifted the flap and fanned the contents. The top bill was a real fifty. The rest were colour photocopies, cut to size. It looked like a lot of money. 'Where are the bankbooks?' I said.

He licked his lips avariciously and jerked his chin at the open door. I took a step towards it.

'Not so fast,' he snapped. 'Go round.'

I shrugged and started back the way I'd come. Gilpin scuttled though the door, swung it shut behind him and shot the bolt. I scooted over and closed the outside bolt. The door was now locked from both sides. I pocketed the real fifty and tossed the envelope of fakes into the fire. Then I walked around the rusting hulk of the building and sidled through the gap between the front doors.

The interior was even gloomier than before, lit now by low-wattage globes in the dangling row of Chinaman's hats. Gilpin was in his wire-mesh enclosure, twisting a coat hanger through the gate latch. The bench with the electric grinder had been cleared of its rusty blades. They were inside the cage, freshly sharpened and stacked on the floor.

'Ready to do business?' I said, walking down the aisle between the rows of merchandise. Tip-top stuff.

Tip-ready, more like it.

Sid fished in his gabardine and pulled out the bankbooks, fastened together with a rubber band. 'Depends,' he sniffed, giving them a waggle. 'How much you offering?'

So far, so good. The books were out in the open.

I reached into my side pocket and pulled out a cable lock I'd bought at a bike shop in Bourke Street near Parliament House. Looping it through the gate latch in the cyclone fence, I snapped the locking mechanism shut and thumbed the combination tumbler closed.

Gilpin jumped backwards and stuffed the bankbooks back into his folds.

'Fair trade requires a level playing field,' I said. 'The back door's locked, too. I can't get in, you can't get out. What could be fairer than that?'

Gilpin grunted, dragged a can of beer from his raincoat pocket and picked off the scab. Foam spurted out and dribbled over his hand. He licked it off and took a chug.

'You want to know what those bankbooks are worth to Quinlan and Mrs Talbot?' I took an envelope, identical to the other, out of my inside pocket. 'Same as what this is worth to you.'

The envelope contained a photocopy of the picnic page of the union news. The original image had been slightly modified. Gilpin was now sporting a watch. A chunky sports chronometer clipped from the wrist of a rather fetching male model. Some doctoring with a fine-point pen and White-out had been required, but the overall result was passably convincing.

I unfolded it and held it to the wire mesh. 'Recognise this, Sid? It's from the Municipals' rag. See it clearly, can you?'

Sid moved close and squinted through the wire.

'You were a real picture that day, Sid. The vibrant patterned shirt, the wide collar, the medallion. A very snappy combination. And the watch set it off a treat. A Seiko Sports Chronometer, if I'm not mistaken. Just like the one found with Merv Cutlett at the bottom of Lake Nillahcootie.'

Gilpin's eyes were narrow slits in puddings of flesh. His nose was touching the wire. He was obviously having trouble seeing.

'Take a closer look.' I rolled the sheet into a tube and slid it through the mesh. Gilpin unfurled it, grunting and snuffling, and tilted it to the light.

'This is bullshit. I never owned a watch like that.'

'Really?' I said. 'That's not the way Senator Quinlan remembers it. Me neither. Now that we've had a chance to think about it, we distinctly remember you flashing it around. Powerful man like the senator, I'm sure he won't have any trouble finding lots of other people who remember it, too.'

Gilpin crumpled the paper, dropped it to the floor and sneered at me contemptuously.

'Plenty more where that came from,' I said. 'I've got one in an envelope addressed to the police, matter of fact.'

He kicked the paper ball with the toe of his dirty trainer. 'This doesn't prove anything.'

'Who said it did, Sidney?' I asked sweetly. 'You seem to be missing the point. That thing,' I pointed to the paper at his feet, 'is just an example. An illustration, if you like. You send your piece of cir-cum-stantial evidence to the coppers, we send ours. You point the finger, we point the finger. This stir-the-possum game, two can play at it.'

'Evidence of what?' He sucked at his can and wiped his mouth on his sleeve. 'Smartarse.'

I gave an exasperated sigh. 'Jeeze, Sid, do I have to spell it out for you? You reckon the bankbooks will make the cops think Charlie Talbot and Barry Quinlan were on the fiddle, giving them a reason to knock off honest Merv Cutlett. By the same token, this photo of you and your watch will make them wonder why you lied to them. Maybe even wonder if you mightn't have given Merv a helping hand on his way to the bottom of the lake. You had a chance. You were out on the lake looking for him. You had a motive. He was selling you out. Just your bad luck that he grabbed your watch while you were pushing him under.'

Gilpin laughed, spraying spit and beer at me. 'What a load of crap,' he said. 'Give me the money or fuck off.'

He crumpled the can and tossed it aside. Then he shuffled over to the ice-cream cooler and got himself a fresh one. There were cans all over the floor. Christ, the bloke was a bottomless vat.

The last of the daylight was fading from the dirty windows. I'd been too optimistic, I realised, thinking I could bluff Bozo Brainiac with a bit of cut-and-paste and a tangle of half-baked logic.

'You've had your money already, Sid.' I said. 'There's no second helpings. Do yourself a favour, just give me the bankbooks.' I extended my open palm and waited patiently.

Gilpin stared at me sullenly. 'Fuck off,' he said.

I gave a disappointed shrug, took out my mobile and pushed a couple of buttons. While I pretended to wait for an answer, I gave Sid a you-asked-for-it look.

'Senator,' I said, turning my expression serious. 'No go, unfortunately.'

Gilpin moved closer to the mesh, head tilted. He pulled off his beanie, the better to hear me. I listened again, nodding into the phone. 'Understood. You're the boss.' I thumbed the phone off and put it back in my pocket.

Casting a saddened glance at Gilpin, I grabbed a couple of old paint cans and tossed them at the base of the mesh fence. I added another pair, then another. I prowled through the array of old junk spread across the floor, selecting items and flinging them towards the partition. Speaker cases, rotary phones, a wooden stool, a milk crate of old textbooks. Anything flingable, all of it flammable.

'You're a greedy bastard,' I said, shaking my head dolefully. 'And this time you've bitten off more than you can chew.'

Gilpin stood rooted to the spot, comprehension dawning across his puffy, booze-ravaged dial as I poured a bottle of sump oil over the pile. I wiped my hands on a rag, tossed it aside, and looked around.

'This joint's a hazard, mate. One spark from that grinder and *whoompf*.'

Gilpin scratched his stubble and spat on the floor. 'You're bluffing,' he said. 'You'd never get away with it.'

I took out my cigarette lighter. 'If the senator can't have them, nobody can. And let's face it, Sid, you won't be missed.'

Once again, I extended my palm to the latch and waited.

My other hand held the lighter, thumb on the striker. If this didn't work, I was fucked.

It worked. He fumbled in his coat, pulled out the bankbooks and poked them through the gap. I snatched them from his grasp. Sweat was trickling down my back.

Gilpin hooked his fingers through the mesh and rattled the cage. 'Let me out, you prick.' He looked pathetic. Sad, sick, trapped, abandoned.

'You need help,' I said. 'You shouldn't be mixing your medications. I'm going to call a doctor, get somebody down here to see to you.'

'Fuck you,' he said.

Yeah, I thought, and fuck my doctor. We'd been through this before. I turned and walked up the aisle to the front door, the chain mesh rattling behind me.

'I'll fucking kill you,' Gilpin shouted. 'That prick Quinlan, too.'

I consigned the bankbook in Charlie Talbot's name to the toxic inferno of the petrol-drum incinerator, slid open the bolt on the back door and drove away without a backward glance.

The bogus Quinlan I tucked snugly into my back pocket.

When Inky Donnelly stuck his leprechaun phiz around my door in the Henhouse at nine-thirty the next morning, it had hot dispatch plastered all over it.

'I've just been chatting with your mate Vic Valentine,' he said, rubbing his hands together with satisfaction. 'Looks like we're off the hook with the Merv Cutlett rigmarole.'

I was unaware that Inky had ever been anywhere near the hook, but I let it pass. His usual dishevelled self, Inky plopped himself down in my visitors' chair, eager to explain the nature of our un-hooking.

As part of my penance to the Whip, I'd agreed to put in a couple of extra sessions of bum-time in the Council chamber. Inky had caught me trying to get on top of the morning's agenda before kick-off time at ten. I leaned back and gave him my undivided.

'Seems that our intrepid chrome-domed ace reporter was present during a long and well-lubricated session at the

Wallopers' Arms last night. In the course of which he picked up the latest mail on the bones-in-the-lake saga. Apparently forensic science has run into a dead-end, so to speak. DNA has met its match, you might say.'

Inky was clearly enjoying himself, so I simply sat and enjoyed the show.

'You'll recall in the last nail-biting episode, the coppers were gearing up to exhume Cutlett's parents' grave in the Mooroopna cemetery, where they have been enjoying their eternal rest for some several decades? Well, it seems that the passage of time has taken its toll on the headstones in that forgotten corner of a Mooroopna field that will be forever Cutlett. The exact location of their graves cannot be determined with sufficient precision to meet the requirement of modern science. So, no parental DNA.'

'What about the daughter?' I said.

'Killed in a car accident in New Zealand in 1990 and cremated,' he beamed. 'And what with the watch drawing a blank at all corners of the compass, the remains have now been relegated to the Unsolved Mysteries file.'

'The hole in the head?'

He shrugged. 'Borers?'

'So there was never anything to worry about all along?'

'Who was worried?' He massaged his stomach. 'Cautious, that's all.'

'Well that's certainly good news, Inky,' I said.

'I knew you'd be pleased.' He slapped his knees and heaved himself into the vertical. 'And good news about Leppitsch being cleared by the tribunal. He should be worth four or five goals against the Eagles on Sunday.'

'And we'll need every one of them,' I said, returning to my reading material. 'But do me a favour, Ink. Next time you're curious about something, just look it up in the fucking encyclopaedia, will you?'

He tossed me a parting cheerio as he went out the door. 'Looking sharp today, Muzza.'

I had to agree, for Inky's was not the only welcome news I'd received that morning. While he was waiting his turn at the toaster during the breakfast rush, Red had got around to mentioning there'd been a phone call on Tuesday evening.

'Didn't you see the note?' he said, hovering impatiently as my post-run slices of multigrain took their own good time to turn brown.

I most certainly hadn't. 'What note?'

'It's round here somewhere.' He said, elbowing me aside and prematurely ejaculating my toast. 'Her name was Anthea Lean or something like that. From your Greek class, she said. Wanted you to ring her. I wrote down the number.'

He simultaneously fed bread into the toaster, stuffed his homework into his backpack, did up his shoelaces and gestured vaguely towards the midden of scrawled notes surrounding the telephone.

He'd been out the door for ten minutes before I managed to find and decode his hieroglyphics. The deplorable penmanship of the younger generation was a matter that had long concerned me in a general sense. Now it had come home to roost. Was that a three or a five? A nine or a seven? Dammit, I'd try all of them if necessary.

But seven-fifteen in the morning was a tad too early to call on a matter like this, however impatient I was. So, hoping for the best, I dusted off my Hugo Boss dress-to-impress suit, drove to Parliament House and bided my time until nine-twenty.

A chirpy young voice answered. 'You've called the Lanes,

Sarah and Andrea. Please leave a message and we'll return your call when we can.' There followed an encouraging tinkle of classical piano music. Mozart, or one of those guys.

'Er, this is Murray Whelan, returning your call, Andrea,' I said. 'Sorry I missed you. Um, please call me back on my mobile. The number's on the card.' To be on the safe side, I recited the numbers. My fingers were still crossed when Inky arrived.

What with speed-reading the agenda papers and chatting with Inky, I barely made it to the chamber in time for the kick-off. Not that the legislative pace was exactly cracking that morning. The condolence motion had drawn a near-full house, but that was just good form. The second reading of the brucellosis clauses of the Livestock Disease Control (Amendment) Bill had pulled only eight members. Five of theirs, three of ours.

We were the short-straw corps. Kingers of Geelong, Butcher of Dandenong and Whelan of Melbourne Upper. Personing the post was our sole role. Kingers and Butcher took the far extremities of the front bench and I sat in the middle up the back. The expression 'thin on the ground' came to mind as I subsided into the plush.

Across the floor of the chamber, the enemy ranks joshed among themselves until the siren sounded and the President bounced the ball. The Minister for Agriculture, an old-style National with a military moustache and enviable silver hair assumed the position and began to read from a bulldog-clipped sheaf of papers.

'Pursuant to the matters covered in section five, subsection nine…'

The public gallery was deserted. Kingers was doing a crossword puzzle, his newspaper buried in a departmental file. Butcher was checking the government benches, scouting for a possible interjection. Ambitious fellow, Butcher.

The preselection vote was Saturday afternoon, less than forty-eight hours away.

Unless Barry Quinlan already knew that the police investigation into the Lake Nillahcootie remains had been shelved, he still had very good reasons for wanting the bankbook out of circulation. By early next week, however, he'd probably be better informed, and its threat value would be nil.

A personal savings account, decades old. That's all it was. A name. Some dates. Money in, money out. Like the man said, not exactly a smoking gun. Its sole significance lay in the construction that might be placed upon it at a certain time under certain circumstances. Sid Gilpin had opened and operated it with exactly that point in mind. Two decades later, he thought he'd found a different purpose for it. Now it was my turn.

Blackmail is an ugly word. Perhaps that's why it appears only twenty-seven times in the official ALP rule-book. If Senator Quinlan was doing what he promised me beside the wishing well in Canberra, it would never need to be uttered. In the meantime, it wouldn't hurt to mouth it silently in his direction.

Ayisha had already let me know he was back in Melbourne, shoring up his authority. When we adjourned for lunch, I scuttled down to the Henhouse and gave him a call.

As we talked, noises leaked through the thin partition wall from the staffroom next door. Staffers and MPs were tucking into cut lunches, opening take-away containers, microwaving Cup-a-Soup and nattering among themselves. Outside, the sky was overcast. The temperature had risen overnight and an almost-pleasant humidity had superseded the previous day's damp chill.

'That thing we discussed,' I said, when Quinlan came on the line. 'It took quite a bit of doing, but I've got it in my possession. I thought you might like it as a souvenir.'

'That's very thoughtful of you, Murray.'

'My pleasure,' I said. 'You haven't forgotten your promise, I hope?'

'I said I'd do my best and that's exactly what I'm doing. But the situation is very fluid at the moment.'

Fluid? From what I'd heard, it was forming an oil-slick under his hand-stitched size sevens.

'So I understand,' I said. 'You wouldn't care to hazard some numbers?'

'Later in the day perhaps.'

'I look forward to it,' I said. 'You don't happen to be going to this casino shindig, I suppose.'

As well as every state parliamentarian and city councillor, the casino bosses had invited all Victorian members of federal parliament to partake of their hospitality. Barry was a big man for the gee-gees and a keen plier of the knife and fork, so it was odds-on that he'd taken up their offer.

'Excellent suggestion,' he said. 'We'll get our heads together over a post-prandial snifter. They'll be laying it on in spades, I daresay.'

I called Ayisha. She was out of the office, escorting Phil Sebastian to lunch with a Frank Abruzzo, a salami manufacturer with an over-inflated sense of his influence with the Italo-Australian small business wing of the Melbourne Upper component of the Coolaroo rank and file.

My mobile had been switched off while I was sitting in the chamber. I'd turned it on the moment I got out, but it still hadn't rung. I checked the message bank. Lanie had called.

'It's about tonight,' said her recorded voice. 'I'm not really contactable at the moment. I'll call you back, okay?'

There was a questioning tone in her voice. I'd been too late getting back to her. She wasn't sure we were still on for it. Damn, shit, bugger.

I hung up and rang Mike Kyriakis. He'd been sussing out the likely disposition of the union votes on the central panel through his wife's brother-in-law, an assistant state secretary of the Construction Workers Federation.

'Len Whitmore's considering a last minute jump into the ring,' Mike reported.

Whitmore, National Secretary of the CWF, had long been touted as a parliamentary contender. He ponced around the country in a bomber jacket, getting his photo in the paper at every non-industrial opportunity. A blatantly obvious attempt to position himself as a common-sense, good-bloke candidate should the parliamentary seat allocators ever have the wit to utilise his talents.

'Here's hoping,' I said. The CWF was militant. If Whitmore nominated, the moderate unions would be backed into Quinlan's corner.

We talked for a while, then I rang Helen Wright to touch base. She was out and about, so I grabbed a slice of quiche in Strangers Corridor and hit the benches for the afternoon session.

With the sick cows out of the way, our numbers had been beefed up to five for Question Time. I slung the Health Minister a curly one about the negative impact of hospital waiting times on senior citizens in the northern suburbs, then proceedings moved to final passage of the Gas Industry

Privatisation (Further Amendments) Bill. Carriage was a fait accompli, but the least we could do was put our objections on the record. Con Caramalides had supplied me with a magazine of bullets, which I fired at the required moments, working from Con's crib-sheet.

Thereafter, when I wasn't contributing to the general spear-rattling and name-calling, I ducked outside to the portico, switched on my mobile and checked the messages.

And a fat lot of good it did. Still no Andrea Lane.

The session adjourned at six, giving me a comfortable thirty minutes to drop my bundle in the Henhouse, try Lanie's home number again, stick a collapsible umbrella under my arm and trudge the five despondent blocks to the Adult Education Centre.

As usual, the stairs and corridors were congested with self-improving mature-age students of Introduction to Computers and Resume Writing for Success. I got to Greek for Beginners with five minutes to spare. Lanie hadn't yet turned up. Exchanging *yasous* with my arriving classmates, I lingered in the hallway.

And lingered and lingered and lingered. By the time everybody else was seated and Agapi, our teacher, was making starting noises, Lanie still hadn't shown.

When Agapi gave me the coming-or-not, I took a seat at the back next to the children's book illustrator and we proceeded immediately to Στη μπισινα.

Lanie arrived just as we were ετοιμοι να βουτηξουμε στο νερο. She broadcast an apologetic look to the room in general and grabbed the only spare seat, two rows in front of me. She was wearing a pair of jeans and a sweatshirt and carrying a sports bag. She'd just come from the gym or she was bound there immediately afterwards; either way the casino clearly didn't feature in her plans for the evening.

'*Malaka fungula*,' I muttered silently.

The rest of the lesson passed in a self-pitying funk. I'd been stood up in favour of a Stairmaster. But then maybe the gym wasn't such a bad idea in Lanie's case. Those jeans did nothing for the woman's bum.

At seven-thirty, Agapi collected our worksheets, handed out fresh ones and closed the lesson. In the general mill of departure, Lanie made straight for me. 'I'm really, really sorry,' she gushed. 'You must think I'm hopeless.'

'No, no.' I shrugged and laughed. *Aha-ha-ha*.

'I've been on tenterhooks all week,' she said. 'We've had the state netball finals and we didn't know if Sarah's team would be playing tonight or not. That's why I couldn't be sure on Sunday. Depended if they got through the semis, and in the end they didn't. Got knocked out last night. Still, she played well and there's a good chance she'll be selected for the national under sixteens.' She beamed proudly. 'And I've been up to here with new students.' Her finger drew a line across her redoubtable poitrine. 'And on top of everything else, bloody Telstra cut the phone off on Wednesday because of some mix-up with the bill. You were probably getting the no-longer-connected message when you called. How embarrassing. So, when you finally got through…' She paused abruptly. 'You must have asked someone else by now.'

I'd been drinking her in with rapt attention. 'No, no.' I shook my head furiously. 'It's my fault. My son's a half-wit. Chip off the old block. He only gave me your message this morning. I'd've called earlier but I didn't have your number. I haven't, um…' I glanced at her casual outfit. 'We could, er, go somewhere else instead, if you like.'

Not really. Not tonight, anyway. I couldn't jeopardise my chance for a discreet tête-à-tête with Barry Quinlan during the post-banquet mix-n-mingle.

'And miss the fun and games?' said Lanie brightly. 'No way.' She hoisted her gym bag. 'Do you know the Duxton Hotel?'

'Used to be the Commercial Travellers'?'

The Duxton's place in Melbourne hostelry history wasn't the point. She reached over and firmed the knot of my tie, an eighty-dollar silk Armani I'd bought myself for Christmas.

'328 Flinders Street. Meet me in the lobby in half an hour.' She spun on her heels and took off at a rapid clip.

Her bum wasn't big at all, not really.

I re-inflated my male ego, edged through the Understanding Modern Art crowd milling at the classroom door and went down to street level. The Duxton was less than two blocks away. I sauntered towards it, rehearsing some studly moves in the shop windows and whistling under my breath.

People were coming from all directions, heading towards the river. Some carried rolled-up banners, protesters bound for the anti-casino rally. Others were evidently angling for good vantage points to watch the fireworks or do some star-spotting. Kylie and Kerry would be representing the A-list and a who's-that cast of B and C celebrities would soon be debouching from hired limos for exclusive private dinners, before the doors were flung open to the punting public.

The Duxton was one of Melbourne's first skyscrapers. A fine example of Belle Époque Moderne, its twelve storeys had spent most of the twentieth century descending into shabby gentility as a home away from home for suitcase-and-sample men. Recently, it had been refurbished for the Asian package-tour trade. I found the lobby full of heaped suitcases and gregarious gents in comfortable trousers with faces like Genghis Khan. Not the trousers, the Chinamen.

I bought a Jamesons and water at the bar, sat in a new-smelling club armchair and re-read my entrée card to the blackjack dealers' beanfeast. Ribbon cutting and banquet, Crown Towers, eight for eight-thirty. Hotel entrance.

The evening was still mild but there was a promise of drizzle in the air. With luck, it would hold off until we'd walked across the Queen Street bridge to the designated entry-point.

At ten past eight, Lanie descended the wide staircase from the first floor, displaying herself for my appraisal.

Her chestnut hair was twisted up, a few strands left artfully free to draw the eye to the sculptural curve of her neck. Her torso was tightly wrapped in a bolt-width of titian-red brocade that accentuated her full figure and left her shoulders bare except for a rain-fleck of freckles. The skirt was black and multi-layered and flared out slightly as it dropped over her hips, falling just past her knees. She was wearing Medea mascara and loose-fitting silver bangles, giving her the sultry look of a wilful slave-girl. Her shoes, thank you Jesus, were flat.

She was like a store of plundered treasure. Truly here was a woman who made you want to rush out and steal a horse, lead a raid, sack a city. It was all I could do not to jump up on my chair and let out a howl to rouse the Duxton's vener-able Mongol horde.

For the moment, however, I'd be satisfied just to take her to the fun-fair. We'd share a sarsaparilla and I'd win her a kewpie-doll. On the way home, we'd sneak a quick pash in the back of the cab and I'd find out what sort of a kisser she was. Important, that. The *sine qua non* of all that might follow.

'Ready?' she said.

I presented the crook of my arm and strolled her towards the door, the man who broke the bank at Monte Carlo. As we passed reception, she took a key from her small black clutch and handed it to the girl behind the desk.

'Thanks, Amie.'

The girl beamed helpfully and returned the key to its slot. 'Anytime, Miss Lane.'

'Amie's one of my ex-students,' Lanie explained. 'She's just got her diploma in Hospitality Studies at Maribyrnong University.'

We crossed the road to Banana Alley, pulled along by the throng. When we reached the Queen Street bridge, we were confronted by a scene part Dante, part Cecil B. DeMille, part situationalist manifestation.

On the southern bank of the Yarra squatted the long, low lump of the casino. Here was the Temple of Mammon, intermittently lit by huge balls of flame belching from square, chimney-like pillars on the riverside promenade.

Facing it across the shimmering ribbon of water was the Multitude of the Righteous. This polyglot host of protesters had assembled in a featureless strip of urban park to display their opposition to the plutocratic–autocratic conspiracy behind the sucker-fleecing works on the opposite bank.

On the next bridge, King Street, the suckers were queued, bumper-to-bumper, scarcely able to contain their impatience to be fleeced. And on our bridge, Queen Street, milled those who had come for the show. Or, in our case, a free feed and party favours.

We stepped up our pace, mindful of the time and the density of the crowd. Every few metres, flyers were thrust at us by baby-faced Trotskyists, Gamblers' Helpline volunteers and touts for the Santa Fe titty bar.

'When do the fireworks start?' said Lanie, rubbing her bare arms against the faint chill rising from the river.

'They seem to have started already.'

I pointed from the bridge railing to the speaker's platform at the centre of the protest crowd. The clergyman at the microphone had just been upstaged by an actress who was baring her breasts in a statement of objection to media superficiality. That'll show 'em, I thought. The poor pastor didn't know whether to cheer, go blind or head for the Santa Fe.

As we reached the far side of the bridge, we hit a thick cluster of gawkers who were backed up behind a low wall of crash barriers. Across the street, cars were pulling up at a red carpet, disembarking their cargo of league footballers, former lead singers of former one-hit bands and various other VIPs. I spotted Vic Valentine's speed-pushing informant Jason as he stepped from a stretch limo with a soap opera starlet. Or was she a current affairs host? Hard to tell.

'That's where we need to get,' I told Lanie.

Putting my arm around her, I steered her through the fringes of the crowd. This gave me a pretext to press my face against her hair and inhale her slightly-musky, slightly-spicy fragrance. I was strongly tempted to nibble her neck, but decided that munching her jugular at this formative juncture in our relationship might send the wrong message.

We got to where the crowd petered out to a thin line with a lousy view. I let go of Lanie and squeezed through a narrow gap in the crash barriers. A constable detached himself from a strung-out line of bored cops. He advanced, arm extended, palm vertical, in a creditable impersonation of a real security guard.

Socialise the costs, I thought, privatise the profits.

'Sir,' he said. *Sir* as in get your arse back behind the barrier pronto, pal, Hugo Boss or no Hugo Boss.

I held up my entrée card. 'Sorry officer, I'm afraid I've come the wrong way.' Silly-billy me. 'My companion and I are invited guests.' I twisted my head back helplessly towards the well-dressed woman I'd left stranded behind me. 'I'm a member of parliament.'

The cop gave me a look of censure just short of outright contempt, inspected my ticket and beckoned Lanie through the gap. He pointed across the road. 'That way, *sir.*'

I took Lanie's hand and we walked towards the kerb where the red carpet started.

'Pity the Rolls is being washed tonight,' I said. 'Still, it's nice to see how the little people live.'

Lanie was lapping it up, already having fun. A cheeky minx, laughing at it all with her eyes. A white Fairlane with Commonwealth plates drew up at the roll-out Axminster and a compact, dapper, mid-sixtyish man in a dinner suit stepped from the back seat. The senator extended his hand and drew a woman of the same vintage from the interior, dark-haired in a tight perm and ankle-length evening gown.

'Do you know who that is?' I asked Lanie.

She shook her head. 'He looks vaguely familiar. Have I seen him on TV?'

'He's one of the world's greatest living actors,' I said.

'Two days ago he gave me a private performance that would've made Al Pacino weep tears of envy.'

I was half-turning to half-explain my little joke when a shout came from behind us. At the section of the crowd with the best view, a figure in a raincoat had climbed over the barrier. He was heading towards the red carpet.

A cop was moving to intercept him, and he increased his pace to a jog, then began to sprint. It was Sid Gilpin. He was heading straight for Barry Quinlan, pulling something from beneath the flaps of his coat. *Christ*, a machete. The blade was wide and dark and its edge was honed to a silver strip.

Security toughs in bomber jackets appeared out of nowhere. Cops were shouting and uniforms were converging on Gilpin. They were closing fast, but not fast enough.

Quinlan, oblivious to the ruckus, was advancing up the carpet, Mrs Quinlan beside him. Gilpin was ten paces away, fifteen, ten. For a sick man, he was moving astonishingly fast. I let go of Lanie's hand and raced forward.

I got to Quinlan a step ahead of Gilpin, slamming into his back with my lowered shoulder. Definitely a reportable offence. Quinlan bounced off me and flew forward. I hit the ground, maximum impact, just as the fireworks went off. They were really good. Worth every cent of the five million.

I could see them even with my eyes closed.

'Dad?'

Red's voice pulsated out of the void.

'How are you feeling?'

How did the damn fool boy think I felt? And why wasn't he doing something about the crazed monkey that was trying to break my head open with a sledgehammer?

'Dad?

He was close, a moving shape on the other side of my eyelids. If I tried, maybe I could see him. I commanded my eyelids to open. No, they said. Yes, I insisted. Red's worried face filled my vision, then drew back. I was lying in a bed. A green curtain surrounded us. We were in a hospital.

'Okay,' I said. 'Feel okay.'

'That's good.' He still looked worried.

I leaned forward and he propped me up with a pillow. The throbbing rushed back, then subsided. My mind was clearing, remembering what had happened.

First came the jarring impact, then the sensation of flying as my limp body was grabbed and rushed inside the building by a thicket of security men. In a vertiginous rush, they propelled me though a series of doors, my head reeling. I must have gone nighty-nights for a moment. Next thing I knew, I was lying in a moving ambulance. And then on a gurney in a corridor with somebody shining a light in my eye and asking me if I could remember my name. I must have got the answer wrong because the next time I surfaced I was being fed into a giant white plastic doughnut.

'You sure you're okay?' said Red.

A motherly, vaguely familiar woman in scrubs came through the curtain. 'Feeling better, Mr Whelan?' she said. 'How's the head?'

'Not too bad.' Apart from the white-hot harpoons that shot through my brain whenever I spoke.

'Doctor will be round to see you soon.' She checked my vitals, gave Red a reassuring smile and floated away.

Soon, in hospital parlance, meant three hours. Not that I could do much but wait anyway. Whenever I tried to get vertical, it was spin-out city.

Red told me that a woman called Andrea Lake had rung the house to say that I'd been clobbered by a protestor at the casino and been taken to Prince Henry's. He'd come straight over in a taxi. She was outside in the waiting area, dressed up like a bon-bon. There were a couple of guys, too, but he didn't know who they were.

I had a pretty fair idea.

Not being in any position to entertain a lady, I sent the lad out to tell Lanie that I was all right, and please not to wait. I'd call her as soon as I could. I was feeling a bit groggy, so I closed my eyes and wondered where my clothes had gone. Next thing I knew, the registrar was waking me. I was suffering from concussion, he told me, but the scan indicated no serious damage. To be on the safe side, they were keeping me overnight. By then it was two o'clock and I didn't see any point in objecting.

Red spent the night in the chair beside my bed, bless his sweaty socks.

Just after six, I went to the loo. Borneo dayaks had done something to my head, but my legs were back on duty and the giddiness was gone. Red found my suit in a plastic box under the bed. While I was putting it on, he went to find whoever needed telling that I was ready to go home. The bankbook had vanished.

Red came back with two men, plain-clothes cops from headquarters in St Kilda Road. They were there to drive me home, they said. And if I felt up to it, perhaps I might answer some questions.

Fine by me, I had a few of my own.

We drove through the empty streets with Red in the front seat while I talked to the more senior officer in the back. By the time we got to Clifton Hill, Red's ears were as pointy as Spock's and I had a reasonably clear picture of the situation.

Twinkle-toes Quinlan had taken it on the fly. He was a bit scuffed around the edges, but he'd responded well to a touch of five-star valet service and a steadying drink in the Bugsy Siegel Suite. The casino appreciated my self-sacrifice and trusted that I was prepared to overlook the rougher-than-usual handling meted out by its security staff in the confusion of the moment. Their representative would speak with me personally in the very near future.

The attempted assailant was a man named Gilpin. He was currently in custody. He claimed that Senator Quinlan had been persecuting him. Could I shed any light on the subject?

My lights, I reminded the officers, had recently been punched out. When I'd had a chance to recover, I'd be happy to provide a full statement and answer any further questions. In the meantime, I'd had a bitch of a night and thanks for the lift.

The honcho cop, a likeable fellow, escorted us to the door. 'A man in your position,' he said. 'I don't need to remind you that since charges have been laid this matter is now *sub judice*.'

'Ah jeez,' said Red. 'That means I can't tell anyone.'

As the cops drove away, young Tyson from the newsagent's rode past and threw the papers over the fence. The *Age* described the casino event as 'a hoop-la the likes of which Melbourne had never seen'. The knock-'em-downs didn't get a mention. The *Herald Sun* was similarly mum, and so was radio news.

The lid was on and that's where I hoped it stayed. Reports of a machete-wielding maniac taking swipes at its patrons were not something the casino was likely to welcome, and I had some valid reasons of my own for concurring.

Red begged off school and retired to catch a kip. I changed out of my silly galoot into trackie daks and a sloppy joe. Under the circumstances, seven-fifteen didn't seem too early to ring Lanie. I tried to sound hale. 'Great first date, eh?'

'You've got some interesting moves, I'll say that for you.'

She wanted to come straight over, but I fended her off. Domestic squalor and a walking-wounded shuffle were not the ideal follow up to my display of heroics. What I wanted most of all was a cup of tea and a good cry.

I'd barely got those out of the way before the phone

started ringing and the rest of the day kicked in. It didn't take Nostradamus to predict it was going to be busy.

Mike Kyriakis called first.

'We're fucked, mate,' he said. Overnight, *inter alia*, the wheels had started to fall off our Coolaroo strategy. The last-minute surprise candidate wasn't to be Len Whitmore of the concrete gang. That was a furphy. The contender now being touted was Andrew McIntyre, Vice President of the ACTU. And with McIntyre's name on the ballot, it was *arrivederci* Canberra.

'You sure?' I said.

Mike was pretty sure. If the unions were looking for a way to take Quinlan down a peg, McIntyre was custom made. On the other hand, there were a lot of rumours flying around. We decided to keep a weather eye on developments and get together around lunchtime.

I went out onto the deck. The sky was overcast and the weather was still trying to make up its mind which way to jump. I downed a couple of Panadol and answered the phone.

'You sound ratshit, Murray.' It was Ayisha. 'Hit the turps at the big event, did you?'

'Hit something else,' I said. 'I'll tell you about it later. But I'm not feeling too sprightly, so I'll be working from home today.'

'Nominations close at four,' she said. 'I'll lodge the form at quarter to, okay?'

Hiding my hand until the death knell was integral to the plan. The way things were turning out, it might just save me falling flat on my face. I told her about the McIntyre rumour and lined her up for the confab with Mike. Then Peter Thorsen rang.

'Didn't spot you at the opening last night,' he said. 'I heard you were attacked by one of the anti-casino lot.'

'It was a non-violent protest,' I said. 'You can't believe everything you hear. Or can you?'

'McIntyre?' he said. 'Looks like it. But your mate Kyriakis will still get the first-round votes I promised. Just wanted you to know.'

'If McIntyre runs, Mike will probably withdraw,' I said. 'And that nice letter you wrote me, I've already shredded it.'

'You're a gent, Murray. If I can ever do anything for you…'

'Don't make promises you might regret,' I said. 'And I know whereof I speak.'

The next caller was offering free quotations on cladding. I told her we were happy with our current clad, but thanks for ringing. I finished the papers and emptied the dishwasher, then Helen Wright rang.

'I've heard the McIntyre rumour,' I said. 'Tell me something I don't know.'

'Phil Sebastian's on the run,' she said. 'He cancelled the meetings I set up this morning with various of the branch secretaries. He's locked down with Barry Quinlan. They're putting the blowtorch to Quinlan's people on the central panel, trying to extract written guarantees of support.'

My mobile started to ring. I asked Helen to hold.

'Cop this.' Ayisha again. 'Alan Metcalfe's office rang. Apparently there's a story doing the rounds that you joined the protest rally last night and rugby-tackled one of the silvertails as he was getting out of his limo. People have been ringing them to say it's a good thing at least some Labor members have got a bit of fight in them. Seems you're becoming the emblem of rank-and-file dissent.'

Oh deary dear. This was all getting out of hand.

'The leader wants a word, of course. I think he'd like to run you out of town on a rail. I said you were down with the lurgie.'

No doubt about it. I had no choice but to pull the plug.

'When you come around, bring my nomination form,' I said. 'And a box of matches.'

I went back to Helen, included her into the midday get-together and took the phone off the hook. The least I could do was tell them all to their faces. Until then, what I needed most in the world was a little lie down in a darkened room with a cold compress.

The damp face cloth was just beginning to work its magic when somebody banged on the door. Two somebodies. Senator Quinlan and Alan Metcalfe. Barry had brought a bunch of flowers and Alan had a box of chocolates.

Not really. But they might as well have.

'I hope you're feeling better, Murray' said Metcalfe. 'Fair to say I know all about last night's incident. Both your actions at the time and your subsequent...'

'Cut the cackle, Alan.' Quinlan elbowed him aside. 'Thing is, Murray, Phil Sebastian's had a fit of the colly-wobbles. He's only prepared to run if it's a lay-down misere. Which, as of Andrew McIntyre's nomination an hour ago, it isn't. If Phil pulls out, we'll both have the credibility chocks kicked out from under us. Unless, of course, we put our pooled resources behind another candidate.'

I stepped back, waved them inside and padded down the hall ahead of them in my extra-thick, extra-comfy socks.

'We're looking for somebody with parliamentary experience and good local credibility. Somebody capable of mobilising rank-and-file support at short notice. Somebody who's not averse to taking a risk.' Quinlan tapped me on the shoulder. 'Oh, and by the way, thanks for saving my life.'

'You're welcome,' I said, and took them into the den.

The Coolaroo by-election was held in September.

Diana, Princess of Wales, hit a post in a Paris underpass the same week, so it didn't rate much coverage. Labor's overall vote dropped three percent, but nobody blamed me. It fitted the national trend.

I made my maiden speech in the House of Representatives in November. My theme was the need to maintain a bi-partisan commitment to multiculturalism. Ayisha, acting in her capacity as my federal staff advisor, suggested the topic. My Coolaroo electorate officer, Helen Wright, came up for the day to watch from the gallery. Overall, they rated me nine out of ten for content, seven out of ten for presentation.

As promised, I backed Mike Kyriakis as my replacement in Melbourne Upper, but he was pipped at the post by one of Metcalfe's people. He was disappointed, naturally. Still, as I reminded him afterwards, a Labor victory in Victoria is about as imminent as the second coming, so it wasn't exactly the end of the world. He doesn't see it that way, of course, and I suspect I'll need to keep a sharp eye on him when it's time to re-nominate.

In the meantime, I've got more than enough to keep me busy. As well as the regular commute to Canberra, where I'm sharing a pied-a-terre in Campbell with dull old Phil Sebastian, there's plenty of running around in my capacity as assistant to the Shadow Parliamentary Secretary for Quarantine and Customs. It's just the first step on a very long ladder, but you've got to start somewhere.

And it gives me an excuse to drop in on Red from time to time. He's in Sydney now. At NIDA, if you please. All that extra-curricular youth theatre stuff paid off big-time. It was probably his performance in Rosencrantz *v* Guildenstern that did the trick. Lucky break, really, that Whatsisname Bell, the Shakespeare bloke, happened to catch a perform-ance. The bit where Red stabbed Polonius in the arras was a real ball-tearer. Brought the house down, and not long after he received an invitation from NIDA to audition. An invitation!

Anyway, he's saving money by living with Wendy and Richard in their palatial spread. And Wendy's so chuffed about the status value of a son at NIDA that's she's turned into a regular stage-door mother. Poor bugger. Every now and then I swing through for a briefing on parrot-trafficking or Y2K readiness in passport-control and we have a meal together. If the Swans are playing a home game against the Lions, we catch the match.

They finished fifth at the end of the season, by the way, and their form is gradually improving. Margot's in good form, too. Quite a story to it, matter of fact.

She put the Diggers Rest place on the market and one of

the prospective buyers happened to be Terry Barraclough, the boyfriend who'd fathered Katie. He didn't know about Katie, or her condition. That was something else Margot had concealed.

He was mortified at the thought of the situation he'd left her in. Turned out he's been living overseas for the past two decades and has a very successful international career as a marketing consultant in the wine industry. He's divorced with grown-up children, and Margot and Katie have gone to stay with him at his place in the Napa Valley for three months. What Margot calls her trial re-marriage. If Katie settles in, she'll consider staying.

On the other side of the ledger, Sid Gilpin is currently enjoying confinement and treatment in a medium-security psychiatric institution, pending a review of his suitability to stand trial.

That eventuality appears to be something of receding horizon. By all-round implicit agreement, attempted assassinations of Australian politicians are considered a matter best swept under the carpet.

As for Kelly Cusack, our encounter at Parliament House was the last I saw of her. In the flesh, that is. Shortly after, she was promoted to doing the prime-time news for the national broadcaster's Queensland network. Doing very well, too. They like her up there because she looks so, well, *nice*.

And although it was fun while it lasted, I'm glad she and I went our separate ways before the thing with Lanie started. It made things so much simpler.

Coy as it sounds, Lanie and I came at it slowly after the excitement of our first, aborted get-together. We gave Greek conversation a miss that Sunday and she asked me around for a late lunch instead. Sarah was off at her father's, and we had the place to ourselves. Nice little split-level with a view over the peppercorn trees to Dights Falls. She fed me a chicken couscous and we drank a bottle of wine. There was talk of going for a walk by the river, but it started to rain.

So she opened another bottle and played me a lovely bit of Satie and we ended up flaked out on a pile of cushions on the floor with a tub of Norgen-Vaaz melting beside us.

We had the hots, all right, but both of us had been around the agora enough times to know that jumping into the sack can just as easily end things as start them.

We got there eventually and we're still there, almost a year later. Two sacks, actually, turn and turn about. Neither of us are quite ready for the full meld. And there's Sarah to consider.

As well as the freelance teaching racket, Lanie's picked up a regular gig tickling the ivories in the atrium bar at the Regent. Show tunes and jazz standards. And oh boy, does she look the goods, mood-lit behind a Steinway.

I drop by sometimes, just to bask. Then I take her home and roger her brainless.

We still haven't made it to the casino. The restaurants are pretty good, from all accounts, and the management is offering full comps, but it's just not our scene. When we do eat out, it's at Pireaus Blues, a great little Greek place in Brunswick Street that does a sensational rabbit *stifado*.

Haven't been there lately, unfortunately. As well as my parliamentary duties and whatnot, I've had my shoulder to the wheel of the republic referendum. The minimum-change model may not be very imaginative, but it's obviously the only way to go at this stage. I admit that the Resident for President slogan is a bit cheesy. Still, you can see the appeal in certain quarters. As I reminded Red over half-time pies at the SCG, an actor–president is not without precedent.

If things go according to plan, we'll have a republic by the new millennium. And a Labor government to inaugurate it.

I could be wrong, I suppose. What do I know?

Nobody ever tells me anything.